TRAPPED IN A WHIRLWIND

BY

SUZANNE FLOYD

COPYRIGHT

This is a work of fiction. All characters in this book have no existence outside the imagination of the author. The town of Greenbrier is a composite of many small towns found anywhere.

Cover by Bella Media Management

DECICATION

I dedicate this book to my husband Paul and our daughters, Camala and Shannon, and all my family. Thanks for all your support and encouragement.

Once Lost, now found. Eternally thankful! *Our Daily Bread*

PART ONE
CHAPTER ONE

"Where are you, Daniel? You were supposed to be home an hour ago. Happy Anniversary." Sarcasm dripped in Quinn's voice, but she didn't care, no one was listening. She slammed down the phone. His cell phone had been going straight to voice mail for the last hour. There was no answer at his office either. So where was he? Listening to the traffic reports, there hadn't been any accidents on his regular route home. Not even on the surface streets. He couldn't use the weather as an excuse either. This year the September weather in and around Denver was perfect, snow was at least another two weeks away. The roads leading to the foothills and their home were clear. There was nothing to keep him from coming home on time.

An hour later she gave up her vigil at the front window. If he was coming straight home from work like he promised, he would have been here hours ago. The evening was a bust! She ran her fingers through her auburn hair in frustration and anger; it didn't matter if it got mussed up. Their dinner reservation was long past. She might as well get out of her dress, the little black dress she'd bought especially for their anniversary.

Worry warred with anger, and anger was winning. This wasn't Daniel's first rodeo, but it would be his last at her expense, she vowed. After all his promises, his pleading to take him back, he pulls a stunt like this. On their anniversary, no less!

Upstairs, she stripped out of the dress, carefully hanging it up, working hard not to allow her emotions whirl out of control. "I've cried my last tear for you, Daniel Reed," she spoke to the empty room even as tears slid down her cheeks. She wasn't sure if the tears were from anger or the hurt she was trying to deny.

Dawn was turning the September sky pink, and she still prowled around the house. In the past he had used snowy conditions and bad roads to avoid coming home so he could stay with this or that girlfriend. She wondered what his excuse would be this time. He was getting more inventive. She needed to get ready for work, but how could she face a room full of rambunctious six-year-olds when her heart was breaking, and she was mad enough to spit nails all at the same time?

His cell phone was still going to voice mail at eight a.m., but he should be at his office in Denver by now.

"Daniel Reed's office. This is Barbara. May I help you?" Daniel's administrative assistant answered his private line. He probably saw it was her on caller ID, and didn't want to face her wrath. The coward, she thought.

"Hi, Barb, let me speak to Daniel. Please," she added belatedly. Her voice was curt, but she wasn't in the mood for small talk.

"Oh, hi, Quinn. He isn't in yet. He was so excited about your big night when he left here yesterday; I figured he wouldn't be in until late. Ah, are you okay?" She finally picked up on Quinn's distress.

"He isn't there?" A niggling of doubt and worry prickled at her mind. Barbara was a loyal administrative assistant, extremely loyal. Would she lie for him? "What time did he leave yesterday?" Quinn rubbed her stomach where nerves were suddenly eating at her.

Barbara gave a nervous little laugh. "He had a lunch meeting with a prospective client. He said he was going to go home when he finished. He didn't want to get caught in traffic leaving the city, and be late for your anniversary date. Is something wrong?"

Quinn ignored the question, asking one of her own. "Who was the client?"

"I can't give out any client information, Quinn. You know that. What's going on?"

"Um, I'm not sure. Call me if he comes in, okay? I'm not going to work. Thanks." She hung up before Barb could ask any more questions. Once again anger and worry warred inside her. This time, worry was winning. If he left extra early, what had happened? Why hadn't he made it home? All night.

For the third time in less than twenty-four hours, she began calling all the hospitals between Denver and Greenbrier, the small bedroom community where they lived. If he'd been in an accident, wouldn't the police contact her? He had his wallet with several items of identification. He even carried an emergency card with all sorts of numbers. Hanging up after talking to the last hospital, tears of fear and worry prickled behind her eyes. There hadn't been any accidents in the time frame when Daniel would have been driving home. No unidentified victims of any crime had been admitted. "So where is he?" Her words echoed in the empty house.

Even when he'd been fooling around, he came home to her, usually smelling of sex and another woman's perfume. Each time, he would promise it would never happen again, only to slip off the wagon within a month or two. When she finally gave up on their marriage and filed for divorce, he'd promised her that was all in the past. He'd never cheat on her again. She wanted to believe him, but his actions in the past made it hard now. If he was up to his old tricks, why would he do this on the one night he knew she'd be expecting him home on time?

The loud peal of the doorbell caused her heart to jump into her throat. Daniel wouldn't ring the bell. He'd come in through the garage, not use the front door. It could only be bad news. Quinn hesitantly opened the front door little more than a crack.

"Mrs. Reed, I'm Detective Doug Aguilar with the County Sheriff's Office." The name of the small town was more pretentious than reality. Sitting in an unincorporated section of the county, the sheriff's department had jurisdiction since there was no police department. He held out a badge and identification for her to see.

"Where's Daniel? Is he all right?" Her voice was barely

a whisper. It couldn't be good if a detective was on her doorstep before nine in the morning.

"May I come in? I need to speak with you." The man was in his fifties, with greying sideburns and mustache. His grave expression told her what words hadn't yet conveyed.

She wanted to say no, he couldn't come in. She didn't want to hear what she knew in her heart he was going to tell her. Reluctantly, she pushed the door open farther, unlocking the decorative screen door, and stepping aside to allow him in.

This wasn't the time for manners. She forgot them anyway. "What happened to Daniel? Where is he?" They were still standing in the foyer. "He didn't come home last night." She whispered the last words.

"I'm sorry to have to tell you this, Mrs. Reed. Your husband was killed last night." He confirmed her worst fears.

"No, that can't be. I called all the hospitals last night, and this morning. There weren't any accidents. Why wouldn't they tell me?" She was beginning to shake.

Detective Aguilar took her arm, gently leading her to the couch in the living room. He hated doing next-of-kin notifications. Especially this kind. "Your husband's car was found early this morning at the bottom of a steep ravine. The car was burned. I'm sorry, Ma'am."

"How did the accident happen? Why wouldn't the hospitals tell me?"

"No, ma'am, it wasn't an accident. Before the car went over, he'd been shot. The car had been deliberately set on fire."

"Shot?" Her head spun at the word. She couldn't take in everything he was saying. "Who…who would do that?" she stammered. "Why would someone shoot him? Are you sure it was Daniel?"

"Yes, ma'am, we're sure. I'm sorry." He didn't want to tell her that there was very little to identify the body, but there was enough other evidence to prove it was Daniel

Reed. "What can you tell me about his work?"

"He's an investment adviser. He never talks about his work. It's always confidential."

"Did he always take the same route home?" Quinn shook her head, unable to take in what he was saying. "I…I guess. I don't know. I work here in town. Daniel worked in downtown Denver. He never said what roads he took, but there aren't that many to choose from. I talked to Barbara this morning." Was that just an hour ago, she wondered? "She said he left early yesterday for a meeting. He was coming straight home from there." A sob tore from her throat. "It was our anniversary." Unable to contain the tears, she turned away from the detective.

"How long were you married?"

"Three years," she whispered.

"Again, I'm sorry for your loss, Mrs. Reed." His stomach twisted. Telling someone their loved one had been murdered was never easy. The young ones were the hardest. "I know this isn't a good time, but I have to ask some questions." He waited for a sign from her to continue. "Who is Barbara?" As yet they had very little information on the victim.

"His admin assistant. I called this morning to see if Daniel had come in to work. He didn't come home all night." Her voice broke again.

"Why would you think he'd be at work if he didn't come home last night?"

"Because." For a long moment she didn't elaborate. "I was so angry." She eventually whispered. "I'm sorry for doubting you, Daniel." Tears streamed down her pale cheeks again.

Detective Aguilar waited for this current round of tears to pass. There would be a lot more before they were finished with the investigation. "Doubting him, ma'am?" he prompted. "About what?"

She shook her head. He was dead; she couldn't heap coals on him now.

"Ma'am, anything you tell me will help to find who did this. Were you having trouble in your marriage?"

"We did for a while," she whispered. "Things have been better lately." You aren't supposed to speak ill of the dead, she thought. How can I tell about all the girlfriends over the past years without sounding bitter?

"But things haven't always been good?" he prompted again. Getting this kind of information out of the victim's family is never easy, for them or him.

"Not always," Quinn whispered again, but didn't expand on her answer.

"I know this is hard, but please tell me about it. It might lead us to the reason behind this."

"He hasn't always been faithful to our marriage," she whispered. "He…he had been cheating on me almost from the beginning. I finally had my fill and filed for divorce, but he promised if I would stay we could work things out. He'd never do it again. I thought everything was fine."

"Do you have any reason to think he was up to his old tricks?"

"No." She paused for a longer time. When she spoke again; he had to lean forward to hear her tortured words. "When we moved to Greenbrier instead of staying in Denver, he bought a studio apartment in downtown. He said it was for those nights when the roads were too bad to drive. Only I discovered that wasn't what he was really using it for." Her voice grew softer. "It was where he took his girlfriends on the nights he stayed in town. That way there were no hotel charges to give him away."

"Where is the apartment? Do you have a key?"

Quinn shook her head. "When I confronted him with his latest affair, and presented him with divorce papers, he begged me to forgive him. He sold the condo in an effort to prove he was going to change."

"And you believed him?"

She lifted one shoulder in a shrug. "I wanted to, but it was hard. In the last six months, he'd been working to win

7

back my trust. We were supposed to go out to dinner last night. It was our third anniversary." Tears rolled unchecked down her pale cheeks again.

"Can you give me the name of the woman he was seeing? Maybe she has a boyfriend or husband who took exception to the affair."

"You mean names." Quinn whispered again. It was hard to witness her humiliation.

Detective Aguilar never understood the need some men had to cheat on their wives. Quinn Reed was a pretty woman. She didn't appear to be a shrew, or mean spirited. Why would her husband go looking elsewhere? He'd been fooled before; maybe that was the case here.

"He always had an excuse why he had to stay in town; the roads were bad, he had a late meeting with clients, or an early one. When I would eventually find out the truth, he would beg my forgiveness, promising it would never happen again."

"But it always did?" The detective cocked his head, watching her.

She nodded, keeping her eyes trained on her lap. "His latest affair was with a young cocktail waitress. Her name is Tiffany Sanchez. I only know that because she called here asking when I was going to divorce him so they could get married. That was the final straw. I filed for divorce, but he promised it was over, and it would never happen again.

"Can you tell me where this Tiffany Sanchez worked?" Quinn shook her head, and he continued with his questions. "Was she married, or have a boyfriend?"

Quinn shrugged. "I didn't ask, but I assume she wasn't married since she was hoping to marry Daniel." Tears clogged her voice again.

"You don't know who the other affairs were with? It wasn't the same woman??"

She was quiet for a long moment. "I never wanted to know who he was sleeping with. He always had an explanation, or an excuse; a weak moment, something. He always said it was just a one night stand, it meant nothing. Lately he said he was working long hours to pay off our bills." They had been in debt up to their eyeballs. He said he was working hard to rectify that problem.

"This last time, you filed for divorce, yet you stayed with him. Why?"

Tears formed in her eyes again. "He promised me he would change. I wanted to believe him. We were working to make something of our marriage. Why did this happen? Who would do this?" Her tears spilled over again, streaking down her pretty face.

"Did your husband have any enemies? Anyone at work who might want him out of the way?" She might not want to answer these questions, but they were necessary.

She shrugged again. "I'm sorry, Detective. I knew very little about his work. He claimed it was confidential, and he couldn't talk about it. Barbara would know more about that than I do."

He stood up. For now he was finished questioning her. But there would be more questions later. "If you think of anything or anyone who might want to do him harm, please give me a call." He placed his card on the table beside the couch. In cases where the victim is married, the spouse is always a suspect. Quinn Reed had plenty of motives for wanting to be rid of her cheating husband. He couldn't see it though.

Still in a daze, Quinn followed him to the door. How could this be happening? Before the door closed, she asked tentatively, "Has anyone called his parents yet? His mother will need to be told." She shuddered at the thought. That wasn't going to be a pretty scene.

CHAPTER TWO

After leaving Quinn Reed, Detective Aguilar went to notify Daniel Reed's parents, or at least his mother. He wasn't sure where Reed's father was. The only description he could think of for the older Mrs. Reed was "shrew."

"You need to arrest her. She did this to my son," the older woman had announced with haughty certainty after being told of her son's murder. "She never loved him. She was just interested in his money." She didn't shed a tear over her dead son.

"Your son was wealthy?" As yet they didn't have any financials on the victim, and very little other information. But the impression he got from Reed's widow was that they were having some financial troubles, along with the other problems.

"Of course!" she stated with self-righteous indignation. "Don't you know who I am, who my husband is?"

"Um, no, ma'am."

"My husband is Barnard Reed of Baker, Reed, and White." She said it like that should be all the explanation he needed to know. It meant nothing to the detective. "He is senior partner at the prestigious investment firm."

He gave a slight nod, hoping she would accept that as recognition. "I just have a few questions about your son. Did he have any enemies? Can you think of anyone who would do this?"

"I already told you who killed him," the older woman snapped. "It's *that woman*! She never liked Daniel." The way she said 'that woman' made it sound like she meant 'that bitch.'

"Why do you say that, Mrs. Reed? If she didn't like him, why would she marry him?"

She gave a heavy sigh. "I already told you this. She was after his money. We made sure she signed a prenuptial agreement though. She would get nothing in a divorce, but in the case of my son's death, she would receive a tidy sum." What that tidy sum amounted to, she left unsaid.

"Were you aware they were having marital problems?"

She sat ramrod straight, her head held high. "I know everything about my son. He kept no secrets from me. About a year ago, my son realized his marriage was a mistake. He came to tell me he wanted a divorce, but that woman wouldn't give him one. She knew she would get nothing in a divorce, so she convinced him to give their marriage another try. That must be when she cooked up this scheme to murder my son."

"Wow," Detective Aguilar gave a soft whistle as he headed to his car a few minutes later. "If she isn't the mother-in-law from hell, she's second in line for the title." He sat in his car jotting down notes from the interview, giving his head another shake. She would be enough to make any woman want out of a marriage. She hadn't shed a tear when told her son was dead, or any other time during the interview. She just wanted Quinn Reed arrested. Her account of the almost divorce was far different from the one the widow had given him. He was inclined to believe Quinn Reed over Eunice. Apparently the woman only told the truth when it benefited her. But he doubted it had little to do with reality.

Suddenly the garage door rolled up, and an expensive Jaguar shot out, barely waiting for the door to open enough to exit. If the speedometer registered speed in reverse, it would be over thirty by the time she hit the street. She stopped long enough to throw the car into gear before peeling out, leaving a long line of rubber on the street.

Doug started his car, hitting the lights and siren at the same time. In the short distance she'd gone, the radar clocked her at fifty. When he walked up to her window, she was tapping the steering wheel impatiently. "What is it now, Officer? I'm in a hurry."

"It's Detective, and I could tell you were in a hurry. You went from zero to fifty in a matter of seconds."

11

"Yes?" She said it like it was no big deal. "May I go now? As I said, I'm in a hurry."

"No, you may not go. The speed limit on these winding streets is twenty-five. I'm giving you a ticket."

"A ticket?" she screeched. "I've just lost my only son. Where is your compassion?"

"Compassion wouldn't mean much if you caused an accident." He took his time writing the ticket. This woman didn't deserve compassion. "Drive safely, Mrs. Reed," he cautioned, handing her the ticket. "You don't want your family to have two funerals to plan." Without a backward glance, he went back to his car, a mischievous grin tilting his lips into his mustache. That gave him a great deal of satisfaction. Narrow winding streets led down the mountain from the house. All it would take was one misstep for her to go sailing off the side, and she would end up with her son in the morgue.

~~~

Quinn was still in shock when the doorbell rang for the second time that morning. "Go away," she whispered. She didn't want to talk to anyone. Whoever was at the door wasn't going to be ignored though. They kept pushing the bell, demanding entrance. It can only be one person, she thought. She slowly opened the door. "Hello, Eunice. I'm sorry about Daniel. I know how much he meant to you and Barnard." She didn't unlock the screen door to let the older woman come in.

"Are you going to keep me standing out here forever?" Eunice snapped, tapping her foot impatiently.

Only if I thought I could get away with it, Quinn thought as she obeyed the command and stepped aside to allow Eunice entrance.

The older woman marched into the living room like a general ready to review the troops. With a disdainful eye, she scanned the room looking for any little thing out of place. Taking a swipe at the seat of a chair to brush off any unseen dirt, she sat down on the edge. "Are you admitting you did this to Daniel?" She glared up at Quinn.

"What?! Of course not. I didn't do anything to him."

"Humph! I told that horrible detective that you're behind this awful thing." She wiped at a nonexistent tear. "You took my son away from me."

"I married your son! I didn't take him away from you. I believe we've had this conversation in the past. I loved Daniel."

"Oh, yes, you loved him so much you were going to divorce him. But of course, you changed your mind when I reminded you that you would get nothing in a divorce. Then you decided it was better to be a widow than a divorcee. That way you'd get his money." This was a far different story from the one she had told the detective. But truth was relative, and was only to be used when it benefited Eunice.

"The only money Daniel had he worked for. He had no money of his own," Quinn reminded her. "You held all the purse strings. You took great pleasure in reminding him of that." This argument was a long time in coming. But why did it have to be now?

"You broke my son's heart when you filed for divorce."

"And he broke mine by having multiple affairs!" Quinn retaliated. "I refused to put up with that any longer. When he realized I was serious, he decided he wanted our marriage more than he wanted other the women."

"That's ridiculous!" Eunice scoffed. "All men have affairs. It means nothing."

"Well, it meant something to me." Quinn glared at her mother-in-law. "Just because you're willing to put up with Barnard's dalliances, doesn't mean I have to…had to." She corrected herself on a whisper.

"I didn't come here to debate men and their needs. I came here to tell you that I'm not going to let you get away with this. I will prove that you had my son killed." She stood up, marching to the door where she turned, giving one last parting shot. "I will be taking care of the funeral.

You are *not* welcome." With that, she was out the door, slamming it behind her.

Quinn sagged down on the chair. Was it worth going to battle with the old bat to have a say in the funeral? Probably not, she decided. She had no money to pay for a funeral anyway. Daniel liked living large. Accustomed to his father's wealth and unwilling to give up the affluent lifestyle, he managed to live beyond both of their paychecks. He always believed his mother would bail him out of any squeeze he got himself into. See how well that worked, she thought, tears once again stinging her eyes. This was one squeeze Eunice couldn't fix.

"Damn you, Daniel. Why did you have to go and die just when we were getting things worked out? Who would do this to you?" She spoke in the otherwise empty house.

Not for the first time, Quinn wished she had someone to help fight her battles, no matter what they were. But that wasn't to be. Her parents had died in a small plane crash when she was a junior in college. Her older sister's husband was in the military, stationed in Germany. But Ginger couldn't come home right now. Her baby was due any day.

But she wasn't alone, she reminded herself. Her faith taught her that God was always just a prayer away. But with everything heaped on her now, she felt unable to pray. "Are you still there God?" she whispered, hoping He was listening.

After she and Daniel were married, he went to church with her a few times, but not for long. She continued going until she discovered his many affairs. She'd been too ashamed to go after that. One of the conditions for taking him back was that he would attend church with her. He'd been going, but she knew it was only at her insistence. His heart and his head weren't in it. Finally she'd stopped going as well, too embarrassed by Daniel's obvious dislike of being there.

Until right then, she hadn't realized just how isolated

she had become. Her friends were all in Denver where she had lived until she and Daniel were married. He had insisted they move to the posh mountain town of Greenbrier. Close enough to Denver to commute each day, but it made keeping even close friendships alive difficult. Most of her friends had moved on with their lives, resorting to the occasional phone call or email. How would she reconnect with them now? He had also discouraged her from making friends with her coworkers, insisting she only socialize with his friends. He even objected when she called Ginger once a month. That left her pretty much on her own.

Once Daniel's murder hit the news, the phone didn't stop ringing. The few friends she and Daniel had, called, offering condolences; reporters called with prying, personal questions. She wanted to turn off her phone, but was afraid the detective might call with more information. She didn't want to miss that.

Late in the afternoon Barbara called, tears choking her voice. "Oh, Quinn, I am so sorry this happened. Daniel was a good man. He was so excited about your anniversary." She didn't know about his many affairs.

"Thank you, Barbara," Quinn tried to keep her tears at bay without much success. "Have the police been there?"

"They're still here," she whispered. "They're going through all of Daniel's files."

"Did you tell them who his last appointment was with? Maybe he could tell them something."

"You don't think a client had something to do with his…" She couldn't bring herself to say murder.

"I don't know, Barb, but please tell them anything that might help. I want this person to pay." Her voice was full of vengeance now. She wasn't as heartbroken as she should be, but some of the blame for that could be laid at Daniel's feet. He had been cheating on her from the first week of their marriage. It was only in the last six months that their marriage could be called the real thing.

~~~

It was another week before the Medical Examiner released Daniel's body. Eunice and Barnard Reed planned the funeral for the following day. What would they do if I just showed up, Quinn wondered? Barnard was always more interested in his own pleasures to care what happened to his son. Eunice on the other hand would most likely pitch a real fit.

Finally, deciding she didn't care what kind of fit Eunice pitched, she was going to the funeral. Daniel was her husband. He hadn't always been the best, but he'd been working on it.

"What are you doing here?" Eunice hissed as Quinn stepped into the funeral home. "I told you not to come. You aren't welcome."

"Daniel was my husband," she stated firmly, holding her head up. "You can't keep me from being here." The entire time she and Daniel were married, Quinn had quaked every time she had to deal with her mother-in-law. She'd put up with anything Eunice dished out. She refused to do it any longer.

"Daniel is dead because of you!" Eunice continued her tirade. "I can't help it if the police are unwilling to see that." Her voice was growing louder with each word.

"Leave the girl alone, Eunice," Barnard walked up to the two women. "Come sit down." He tried to steer his wife away from Quinn, but she would have none of it.

"You never cared about Daniel," Eunice turned on her husband. "All you cared about was yourself. I'm not going to let this..." Before she could finish her sentence, Detective Aguilar stepped between the warring couple.

"I think you've given your friends enough of a show for now, Mrs. Reed. Go inside, sit down, and be quiet. Do it now!" It wasn't a request. His tone of voice allowed no room for argument. Eunice flounced off, muttering under her breath.

"You've made an enemy, Detective," Quinn gave him a

rueful smile. "Thank you for coming to my rescue."

"The only enemy I worry about is one holding a gun, and I doubt she would know what to do with one."

"I wouldn't be so sure about that."

"Does she own a gun?" he frowned at her. It wasn't unheard of for a parent to kill his or her child when said child didn't obey the rules set forth.

Quinn shook her head. "If she did, it would be me in that casket, not Daniel." She released a weary sigh. For three years, she had battled Daniel's mother alone. He had turned a blind eye to the way Eunice treated her. After today, I'll be free of the woman, she told herself.

It didn't take long to realize how wrong she was on that score.

CHAPTER THREE

Sitting in the last row instead of up front where the spouse should sit, Quinn watched the people. Would his killer show up? Is that why Detective Aguilar was there? Most of the people were strangers to her, probably friends and acquaintances of Barnard and Eunice. June Veracruz, along with several other teachers she worked with had come to show their support. She could only hope they hadn't been witness to the scene Eunice caused.

To her surprise, Cindy Brubaker, one of her college friends also showed up. Sitting down beside her, Cindy took her hand in support. No words were needed even though it had been three years since they had seen each other. She was there, that's all that mattered. At the moment Quinn desperately needed a friend.

A dark haired beauty caught her attention when she came through the door as the service began. She'd never seen the woman before. Did she work with Daniel? Was she a friend of the family? Was she Tiffany Sanchez? The questions whizzed through Quinn's mind. It would take a great deal of nerve to show up at the funeral of a married lover.

Quinn remained in her seat when the service ended, hoping to get a better look at the young woman. As she filed past Quinn, she paused for a split second, her pouty lips quirked up slightly. What was that about, Quinn asked herself? She didn't know who the woman was or how to find out. It was a sure bet Eunice wouldn't tell her anything.

She didn't stay for the reception Eunice planned. It was one battle she could forego. "Can I take you out for lunch?" Cindy asked as they left the building together before pulling Quinn in for a hug. "I'm sorry about Daniel." It wasn't the time or place to ask why they had lost contact. Maybe in the weeks ahead they could reconnect.

The day after the funeral Quinn went back to work, she

was out of time off, and she still had bills to pay. Everyone was full of sympathy, bringing on a fresh bout of tears. "If there's anything you need, don't hesitate to call me." Tom Barton, a fellow teacher, waited until just before the first bell rang catching her alone. In a matter of minutes twenty-five squealing six-year olds would descend on her.

"Thank you, Tom." She wanted him to go away. It would upset the kids to see their teacher was crying.

"I'll bet you're glad to be free of that witch of a mother-in-law."

She drew in a sharp breath. "What do you mean?" She'd never said anything about Eunice at work. His words dried up any tears that had threatened to fall.

"We saw that little drama she put on at the funeral." He stepped closer, his voice a conspiratorial whisper now.

Quinn cringed. How had she missed seeing him the day before? She had stayed after the service only long enough to see where the young woman went. But she had disappeared, and Quinn still didn't know who the woman was. The only one of her colleagues to speak to her at the funeral had been June Veracruz. If Tom was correct, they had all witnessed that scene between her and Eunice. Before she could comment, the first wave of first graders erupted into the room. "Mrs. Reed, we missed you. Were you sick?" Six year old Macey came to a screeching halt in front of her. "I missed you." With one front tooth missing, the words came out in a lisp.

"Thank you, Macey. That's very nice of you. I'm doing better." How do you explain murder to a six year old? That was definitely above her pay grade.

As the other students came in with happy squeals to see her again, she was grateful Tom didn't stick around. His parting whisper caused a shiver to move up her spine. "Anything you need, Quinn, anything at all, I'm here for you."

He couldn't mean that the way it sounded, could he? Daniel had only been gone two weeks. He certainly wouldn't be hitting on her. Deciding she had taken Tom's comment the wrong way, she tried to concentrate on the students clamoring for her attention. Just to be on the safe side, she planned on avoiding him.

At lunch, June Veracruz sat down with her in the teachers' lounge. "How are you holding up, honey?" In her fifties and pleasingly plump, June had a sweet mothering nature. She took all the teachers under her wing, especially the younger women.

Tears sparkled in Quinn's eyes again. "I'm working on it. The kids help. They're so sweet." June patted her hand, and Quinn gripped the older woman's like it was a lifeline. Daniel's refusal to socialize had made it difficult to make friends. The few times she had insisted he attend some function with her, he had been standoffish to put it mildly, further alienating her from her coworkers.

At last the day was over. It had been trying, but it was about to get worse. Eunice's Jaguar was sitting in the middle of the driveway when Quinn got home, preventing her from getting into her own garage. "I should just keep going," she muttered to herself. "It would serve her right to leave her sitting in her car for another hour."

But Eunice wasn't in her car. While Quinn debated whether to drive away, the older woman opened the front door staring out at her.

Seeing red, Quinn got out of her car, slamming the door. "What are you doing in my house? How did you get in?" She stormed up the steps to the door, ready for a fight.

"This is my son's house. He gave me a key after he bought it." She stepped outside, preventing Quinn from going in.

"Daniel and I bought this house together; it was ours, now it's mine. Your son is gone. You have no business being here." The words were harsh, but it was the only way to deal with the woman.

"Yes, I'm certain you're glad he's gone. Well, I'm here to tell you, I'm not going to let you get away with what you've done. You won't benefit from my son's death."

"Benefit?" Quinn almost laughed at that. "I'm left with a pile of bills and very little money to pay them."

A nasty smile curled Eunice's lips, pleased by Quinn's admission. "My attorney will be in touch with you." With that parting shot, Eunice pushed her way past Quinn, nearly knocking her over in the process. Quinn wasn't sure what an attorney would have to say to her, but that was Eunice's way of handling everything: threaten to sue.

Changing the locks on all the doors was the first order of business, Quinn decided as she stepped into her living room. "What the…" She stopped, staring at the empty room. Her heart sank further with each room she entered. That horrible woman had taken everything. Everything but Quinn's clothes, those she left scattered around the empty bedroom. "She even took the damn hangers," Quinn muttered. There were no dishes for her to eat off of or clean towels in the bathroom. Eunice must have arrived minutes after I left for school, she thought.

"What do I do now?" Detective Aguilar's card was in her purse. That morning she had picked it up off the counter. Now she was glad. Eunice would have taken that along with everything else if she'd left it behind.

"Detective Aguilar, may I help you?" His tone was impersonal at best, causing Quinn to doubt the wisdom of calling him.

"Um, yes, Detective, this is Quinn Reed. I need to report a…theft? A burglary?" She wasn't sure which it was, or if there was anything the police could do.

"All right, Mrs. Reed. I'll send a patrol car. Don't go in the house in case the burglars are still there." He started to hang up.

"Oh, she's already gone."

"She?" He put the phone back to his ear, thinking he'd heard wrong.

"Yes, Eunice Reed met me at the door when I got home from work. She'd cleaned out my house." A hysterical giggle threatened to escape. "She took everything but my bills." She had to laugh or she would erupt into a fit of tears. "I'm on my way." He slammed down the phone. "That bitch!"

The other detectives looked up, but he didn't explain. He was already out the door.

"How did she get in?" A short time later, he stood in the empty living room, shaking his head.

Quinn shrugged. "She said Daniel gave her a key when we moved in. He never told me."

"The house was in your name as well as his?" Quinn nodded. "But her name isn't on the deed?"

"No, I wouldn't have lived here if it had been. I wouldn't have stayed here one night alone if I'd known he had given her that key. I would have had the locks changed that first day."

"Have you checked with any of your neighbors? Why didn't anyone call the police when a moving van pulled up, or at least call you?" He realized how silly that sounded the minute the words left his lips. In the foothills, houses were far apart. Even if they were close together, a hill or twist in the road blocked the view of each neighbor.

"I don't really know any of my neighbors. Daniel hadn't been big on socializing," she admitted quietly. Unless they were buxom blondes, or could further his career. She didn't put those thoughts into words.

"Do you have family or friends you can stay with until we get this sorted out?"

Tom's offer came to mind, and she gave an involuntary shudder. He would be the last person she'd call. "Um, I guess." But who could she really call? Cindy and the few friends she had left in Denver were more than forty miles away. Even if they were closer, they were married with small children. She couldn't impose on them even for one night. There were several female teachers who were single, but she didn't know any of them well enough to intrude. She thought of calling June Veracruz, but decided against

22

imposing on the woman. "I can stay here," she decided. He started to object, but she cut him off. "She has everything she came for. She won't be back."

"Why did she stay here until you got home? Did she think she could get away with stealing everything you own?"

"She wanted to rub my nose in what she did." Quinn gave a fatalistic shrug. "She didn't consider what she did was wrong. Daniel was her son, and I was the usurper."

"Well, I've got news for her," he growled. "She can't take what doesn't belong to her. There are laws against it."

It was a long, barren night. Without pots, pans or dishes, she couldn't fix anything to eat. Of course, that suggested there was food to fix. Eunice had cleaned out everything in the kitchen as well as the rest of the house. Fast food would do for one night.

A locksmith met her at the house to change the locks while she ate her taco salad from the nearby take-out restaurant. Then she inflated the air mattress she bought for a bed. What a come-down, she thought. Thanks so much Daniel. If he'd had the backbone to stand up to his mother, she wouldn't be running roughshod over my life now.

~~~

"Oh, for heaven's sake, Eunice. What were you thinking?" Barnard glared at his wife.

"I was thinking of my son. That woman isn't going to benefit from what she did to him."

"He was my son, too," Barnard argued.

Detective Aguilar thought this was a common argument between them. "Mrs. Reed, your daughter-in-law didn't kill your son." He fought to keep his temper in check. He was tired after a long day, and wanted to go home to his own family. Instead he was here trying to reason with an unreasonable woman.

"Of course she didn't kill him herself," Eunice stated, looking at him like he was a dimwitted child. A lesser man would be made to feel small under that intimidating glare.

23

"She would have someone else do it for her." Barnard scoffed at that, receiving a glare and a slap on the shoulder for his effort.

"Do you have any proof of that?" Detective Aguilar lifted one eyebrow in question.

"My son is dead, isn't he?"

He gave a weary sigh. "Yes, he is, and I'm sorry for your loss. But I need evidence, and there is no evidence to back up what you're saying. I didn't come here to argue this point. You can't go into Mrs. Reed's house, the young...er other Mrs. Reed's house," he clarified, "taking everything she owns. What you took belongs to Quinn, not you."

"Quinn? I knew it," she spat at him. "She's woven her spell on you, too. The evidence you need could be staring you right in the face, and you wouldn't see it." He rolled his eyes. This was like arguing with a brick wall. She believed what she wanted, no matter what he said or what the evidence showed.

"You either return everything, and I mean everything you took out of that house today, or you will be arrested for grand theft."

"I only took what belonged to my son."

"And what belonged to your son also belonged to his wife. That means you had no right to take it. You *will* return everything by this time tomorrow, or I will be here with a warrant for your arrest. Do I make myself perfectly clear?" He was through arguing.

Eunice Reed remained stubbornly silent, her arms folded across her chest.

"I'll make the arrangements, Detective," Barnard sighed, turning a glaring look on his wife.

"It's just like you to take her side," Eunice hissed. "You've always been interested in everything wearing a skirt."

"Not everything," Barnard retorted. "You're wearing a skirt." Doug Aguilar couldn't suppress his chuckle as he walked out. Those two deserved each other. If Daniel Reed was anything like his mother, it's a wonder Quinn had stayed with him as long as she had. More likely though, he was like his father. It wasn't men's cologne he'd smelled on Barnard Reed. It was a very expensive woman's perfume. Like father, like son. They were both catting around. He wondered if Eunice was aware of what her husband was doing. Of course she was, he decided. Nothing got past her. She just didn't care as long as she could claim the title and the prestige of being married to a wealthy man. What her husband did in his spare time was his business.

~~~

Quinn spent a restless night. It had taken forever to inflate the stupid mattress, and she only managed that with the help of the locksmith. It wasn't as easy as the advertisement on the package claimed.

Finally managing to fall into an uneasy sleep, she sat up straight in bed at two in the morning. "The safe!" Daniel had insisted on having a safe installed in their closet when they had nothing to put in it. Had Eunice known about that? Had Daniel given her the combination as well as a key to the house?

She couldn't go back to sleep until she knew the answers to those questions. With dread, she turned on the light in the walk-in closet, grateful that Eunice had left her with light bulbs. She'd taken everything else.

Pressing on the secret compartment Daniel had installed to hide the safe, she examined the combination. It was still set on ten. Every time the safe was opened, he had insisted the combination was to be left on ten when it was relocked. It was his little paranoid trick that would tell him if someone had tampered with the safe. She wasn't sure who he thought would get in the safe since they were the only people living in the house. The only things she knew Daniel kept there weren't worth stealing.

Either Eunice didn't know about the safe or she knew

his trick. With shaking fingers, she entered the combination. Giving the handle a twist, she closed her eyes as she pulled open the heavy door. Did she want to know if Daniel had betrayed her again by telling his mother about the safe?

Peeking through her eye lashes, a relieved sigh escaped her parted lips. Nothing seemed to be missing. The few pieces of jewelry Daniel had given her, along with her mother's jewelry, were still in place. There was something else resting inside, something she hadn't expected. Three small bundles of cash sat on top of the documents he had kept locked in there.

"Fifty thousand dollars," she whispered. "Where did he get that much money? Why hadn't he told me about it?" The other documents held no surprises; their wills, the deed to the house; just the normal legal papers most people have. But where had he gotten so much money?

After that, sleep was impossible. Had he been doing something illegal? Is that where all that money came from? It wasn't illegal to keep cash, but if he had that much money, why didn't he pay off some of their bills?

Dark circles shadowed her green eyes looking like bruises on her fair skin when she looked in the mirror the next morning. Eunice had scattered her makeup bottles over the bathroom counter, but they were still intact. At least she hadn't taken it with her, Quinn thought. Maybe concealer would hide what couldn't be erased.

Almost too tired to function in the classroom, Quinn struggled to keep her mind on the lessons. She couldn't afford to take any more time off. Or could she? With fifty thousand dollars in cash now at her disposal, her bills would be covered for a couple of months. After that, she didn't know what she was going to do.

Finishing up the paperwork at the end of the day, she was looking forward to going home. Barnard had called first thing that morning to tell her the moving company would be at the house to return everything Eunice had taken the day before. Would the drama with her in-laws ever end? At least she'd have her own bed to sleep in tonight.

Lost in these thought, she was startled when Tom appeared behind her close enough that she could feel his breath on her neck. "Hi, Quinn, how'd your day go?"

She whirled around to face him, her heart pounding hard enough to jump out of her chest. She wasn't sure if it was because he had startled her, or she was afraid of the man. Placing her hand on his chest, she gave him a little shove. "Step back, Tom." She moved around him, putting her desk between them. His hungry eyes undressed her as they traveled down her body.

"What is it you want, Tom?" It was the wrong question to ask she decided when his eyes darkened leaving little doubt what he was thinking. "I'm in a hurry to get home." She continued before he could answer. It wasn't easy to control the shudder moving up her spine. The man was giving her the creeps.

"I thought you might like to go out to dinner. It isn't any fun eating alone."

"No, I have things I need to do." She wasn't going to say thank you for asking. It would only encourage him.

"I can help, then we can grab something to eat." He wiggled his eyebrows suggestively. He wasn't giving up easily.

"No, Tom. I'm not going out with you tonight or any other night. My husband was just killed." Hopefully he would get the hint. She should have known better. Men don't take hints.

"Well, I'm here to help with whatever you need. Women have needs the same as men."

Her mouth dropped open as he sauntered out of her room. Was he suggesting what it sounded like? Probably so. He had some nerve. He sounded like Eunice excusing Barnard's, then Daniel's, many affairs. She wanted no part of that, or him.

True to his word, Barnard and the movers were waiting

for her when she pulled into the driveway. How long would it take to put everything back where it came from? Hopefully they wouldn't just dump everything, leaving her with the mess to put away.

"I want to apologize for Eunice," Barnard began even before she was out of her car. "She had no right to do what she did."

"No, she didn't," Quinn agreed. "Why did she think she could get away with it?"

He shrugged. "That's Eunice. Now let's get this done. I have to be somewhere in an hour." He glanced at the expensive watch on his wrist.

To meet with a client or a mistress, she wondered? He had been the lead dog, when it came to affairs. She knew of three different mistresses he'd had just during the time she had been married to Daniel. There had probably been more she didn't know about. The man wasn't faithful to Eunice or any of the other women in his life. It was no wonder Daniel saw nothing wrong with it.

By ten o'clock, all of her furniture was back in place and she had the house in some semblance of order again. Dishes still needed to be unpacked and put away, but at least she had hangers for her clothes again. Food was another matter. Eunice had thrown the contents of her refrigerator in the dumpster.

Not everything had been returned though. Eunice kept all of Daniels personal belongings, including the desk in his home office. Well, at least I won't have to deal with disposing of his clothes; Quinn tried to look on the positive side. She was left with nothing of his, no keepsakes or mementos. She couldn't decide if that was a good thing or bad. For now she would let it go. Dealing with her former mother-in-law was more than she could handle.

Two days later, life had another surprise for her.

CHAPTER FOUR

"Hello Quinn."

She stared up at him, her feet frozen to the floor. Those two words still held a trace of the Italian accent that she had loved, sending shivers up her spine. Her mind transported her back to high school where Sergio DeCosta had been the most important person in her life until her junior year of high school. "Hello Sergio." She started to reach up to unlock the door, but thought better of it. "What are you doing here?"

"I heard about what happened to your husband. I came to offer my condolences."

His words sounded sincere, but how could she believe him? He'd disappeared from her life without a word. She hadn't heard from him again until that moment. "Where did you go? Why did you disappear? Why are you here now?" She had spent the remainder of high school, even her first years of college hoping he would come back. She had finally given up. Even after she met and married Daniel, thoughts of Sergio would creep into her mind unexpectedly. Maybe she had been as unfaithful to Daniel as he'd been to her, just in a different way.

"Would it be possible for me to come in so I could explain?" Again she started to reach for the lock, only to change her mind again.

"No, I don't think that would be a good idea. How did you hear about Daniel? Where do you live now?"

"I...ah...I live in Denver now. His murder was on all the news stations. I'm sorry for your loss, Quinn."

"You moved back here? How long have you been back?" Her voice was sharp. Her questions had nothing to do with Daniel, and everything to do with the feelings they had once shared.

"I moved back two years ago. I wanted to call you, but you were already married." Was there a note of censure in his voice? Had he expected her to wait for him when she had no idea where he went or if he'd ever return? "I'm sorry I left without telling you, Quinn. I had no choice."

"You always have a choice! You could have written, called, something, anything. I didn't even know if you were dead or alive." Tears pricked behind her eyes, but she refused to let them fall. She had shed her last tear for a man, she vowed.

"I couldn't, Quinn. I would like to have the chance to explain."

She hesitated for a long moment, undecided what she should do. Were there still feelings buried somewhere deep in her heart for this handsome man? The answer to that was easy. She just wasn't sure what those feelings were. Certainly anger, a sense of betrayal, but did she still love him? Until she could sort out those feelings, and find out who had killed Daniel, she needed to keep her distance from Sergio.

"You need to go. I don't want to hear your excuses." She'd had her fill of them from others in her life. She started to shut the door.

"If you ever need anything, Quinn, all you have to do is ask. I still love you." His words were soft, but she heard them before the door closed completely.

Leaning her head against the cool wood of the door, she couldn't stop the tears from flowing down her face. She had loved him so much. Why did he have to come back into her life now? If he had moved back to Denver two years ago, it would have been too late for them. She was already married to Daniel. Although that marriage had been falling apart, her marriage vows were binding, even though they hadn't been for her husband. He had pleaded with her to give him another chance. If he had lived, would he have remained faithful? That was something she would never know.

She couldn't let herself fall for Sergio again; she had to protect what was left of her heart. "It's too late for us." Her words echoed in the silent house, mocking her. She straightened away from the door, wiping the tears from her face. "I'm finished with all things relating to men." It was an empty vow, but it helped give her some strength.

~~~

Saturday was her day. She usually slept in, taking her time over coffee and the paper before getting dressed to start the day. Her night hadn't been very restful. Why had Sergio come to see her last night? What did he think it would accomplish? Was he hoping they could get back together? It was much too soon for that. Why had he said he still loved her? Her head was still spinning with all the questions. She needed to get some order back into her life.

At the loud peal of the doorbell, she groaned. She wasn't even dressed yet. Who would come by this early? Her heart skittered a little, thinking maybe Sergio decided to try again.

But it wasn't Sergio. Detective Aguilar was standing at her door, and if his expression was any indication of his mood, it was a foul one. Had they found the person who killed Daniel, she wondered? Pulling her robe closer around her, and finger combing her shoulder length auburn hair, she opened the door just far enough to speak to him. "Good morning, Detective. Can you give me a minute to get dressed?"

His gaze moved down her body through the slight opening. "You're covered up just fine. I need to talk to you. Now." Until this minute, he had always been polite, treating her with kid gloves. Those gloves were off now. What had happened to warrant the change? Unlocking the screen door and stepping back for him to enter, she wondered if Eunice had convinced him she was somehow involved in Daniel's murder.

"How do you know Dominic Marconi?" His question came out of left field. He paced across the room, too agitated to sit.

"I don't know anyone by that name. Is he the one who

killed Daniel?" Puzzled by his question, she shook her head, sinking down on the chair.

"Don't lie to me, Mrs. Reed. It will only make matters worse for you. Tell me about your relationship with Marconi." His voice was a low growl.

"I told you I don't know anyone by that name," she insisted. "Why do you think I do?"

He ran his long fingers through his thick, greying hair, frustrated enough to pull it out. He'd felt sorry for her. Her sweet, girl-next-door looks, and soft-spoken nature had thrown him off his game. Now he felt like a fool. It had been a long time since a suspect had pulled the wool over his eyes this badly.

"If you don't know him, why was he here last evening? Can you explain that?"

She stared at him, her mind reeling. "Are you having me followed?"

"No, but maybe I should be. For now, Marconi is the only one being following. That's how I know he was here yesterday, so you might as well tell me the truth."

She stood up now, her temper flaring at his accusations. "The only person to visit me last night was a friend from a long time ago." She faced him with her fists braced on her slim hips. "His name is Sergio DeCosta, not Dominic Marconi. We went to high school together. He stopped by to offer his condolences. If you were having him followed, you would know that he didn't even come in the house." Now she was glad she hadn't let Sergio come in.

He ignored her last comment, intent on catching her in a lie. "No Mrs. Reed, his name is Dominic Marconi, and his father is knee-deep in the Mafia in New York and Italy."

Her face went white, and she swayed on her feet. Taking her arm to keep her from falling over, Doug led her back to the chair she'd been sitting in. That reaction can't be faked. She didn't know his real name.

"Did he kill Daniel?" she whispered. "Why would he

Suzanne Floyd

do that?" Sergio's final words went through her mind. He still loved her. Would he kill Daniel if he thought she would be his then? Oh, God, how could I ever have loved someone in the Mafia?

"He wouldn't do the deed himself, but that doesn't mean he wasn't involved. The Mafia has long-reaching tentacles. When was the last time you saw him?"

She shook her head, choking back on a sob. "He left school in the middle of our junior year. I haven't seen him since. I didn't even know he was living in Denver again. Do you really think he had something to with Daniel's murder?" Her heart was breaking all over again. "Just because his father is Mafia, doesn't mean he is," she whispered. She didn't want it to be true.

"That's most unlikely. For your own safety, you need to stay away from him. You say you knew him in high school. What can you tell me about him back then?"

"He was quiet, polite, crazy-smart. He wanted to be an electrical engineer. He loved anything to do with computers." Even back then, he had a string of computers in his house that he could control from his laptop." She left out the most important part; they had been in love. They were going to go to college together and get married. Then he disappeared. She hadn't heard from him again until last night.

"He went by the name of Sergio DeCosta in school?" At her nod, he continued asking questions, each one was like a knife to her heart. "Did he live with his parents? Did you ever meet them?"

"He lived with his mother. I met her. She seemed nice. He said his father was dead."

Doug scoffed at that. "Why did he leave school?"

She shrugged. "I don't know. He was just gone one day. No one knew where he went." If she had listened to him last night, she would have the answer to that. But she'd let the hurt from all those years ago take over, refusing to listen to him. That was probably for the best, she decided.

She didn't want anything to do with the Mafia.

Asking a few more questions, he stood up to leave a few minutes later. "I'm sorry, Mrs. Reed." He wasn't sure what he was sorry for, he was just sorry. "As I said, stay away from him. It could be dangerous."

"But if he killed Daniel, I want to know. Maybe he'll let something slip to me."

"And if he did, what do you think he'd do about it? His kind doesn't leave witnesses behind." Before she could wrap her mind around that thought, he asked another question. "Has the older Mrs. Reed given you any more trouble?"

Chuckling for the first time since learning Daniel had been murdered, she looked up at him. "She would hate you for calling her that. She resented any mention of age. The fact that there were two Mrs. Reed's didn't sit well with her either. I'm sure she's as glad to be rid of me as I am to be rid of her."

For a long while after Doug Aguilar left, Quinn didn't move out of the chair. She wasn't sure she could stand on her own after the revelations he had just dropped on her. After Sergio's visit the night before, she had relived those high school years, those emotions. Her marriage hadn't been perfect, and she hadn't loved Daniel the way she had loved Sergio, but she never would have betrayed him. Now she would honor his memory, and what they were trying to rebuild together.

Sergio said he wanted to explain why he had left so suddenly. Should she give him that chance? If he had a hand in Daniel's death, she needed to know. Would he tell her? If he did, would he then kill her as Detective Aguilar suggested? At this point, did she even care? The two men she had loved in her life had both betrayed her. Not in the same way, but it was betrayal all the same. She needed to know why Daniel had died.

There was also the money that needed to be explained, but who could do that? The only one who knew the answer was gone. What would Detective Aguilar have thought about it? The accusation in his eyes when he first arrived this morning clearly said he suspected she had hired Sergio to kill Daniel. They had been in serious financial straits. Although it would only cover a small portion of what they owed, that much money could be considered a motive to do away with her husband.

There were even more surprises to come her way. Would it ever stop?

CHAPTER FIVE

Stepping out of the shower, she heard the doorbell yet again. Glancing at the clock, it was barely nine o'clock. Who it would be this time? Maybe she could just ignore it. Reporters had hounded her since this all started.

Ignoring the person at the door wasn't an option. The bell rang three more times before she could pull on clothes. Wrapping her hair in a towel, she headed for the living room. "Hold your horses," she shouted. Whoever was out there was certainly persistent. If Detective Aguilar was back, she just might give him a piece of her mind. She didn't know any more about Sergio than what she'd told him just an hour ago.

Yanking open the door with an angry jerk, she glared out through the screen. "Yes? What do you..." she stumbled to a halt. Rick Frost, Daniel's boss, stood on the other side looking as impatient as she felt. "I'm sorry it took me so long to answer the door. I was in the shower." She just barely reigned in her anger. She had never warmed up to the man.

"No, it's me who is sorry, Mrs. Reed, Quinn," he amended quickly. "I should have called before stopping by. I wanted to give you this." He held out an envelope. As yet she hadn't unlocked the screen. Now she would have to. Reluctantly opening the door, she hoped to take the envelope without inviting him in. Of course, he had other plans.

He stepped past her, going straight to the living room. How did he know where to go, she wondered? There were two doors leading off the foyer. How did he know which one led to the living room unless he'd been here before? The thought was an uncomfortable one. She had met Daniel's boss twice at office parties. To the best of her knowledge, he had never been in their house.

Sitting down on the couch, Rick made himself

comfortable, leaning back, and spreading his arms across the back. He waited until she was seated before holding out the envelope again making her stand up to retrieve it.

"What is this?" She held the envelope by the corner like it might explode in her hand.

He gave her a smile that didn't quite reach his eyes. "Open it and see. I think you'll be pleasantly surprised."

She'd had enough surprises to last a lifetime. Slipping her finger under the flap, she did as he suggested. Pulling out a check, she stared at it, then at Mr. Frost. "What is this? Where did it come from?" The dollar amount took her breath away.

"Our company insures all of its employees." He must have thought that explained the check. But it didn't.

"But why so much?" Most companies offered small policies, nothing like this.

He lifted one shoulder in a careless shrug. "We value our employees." He passed one hand along the side of his head, the gesture reminding Quinn of something out of the movie *Grease*. "I was wondering if you've had a chance to go through Daniel's papers."

"Um, no, why?" His question came out of left field.

"Daniel was working on something for a client. It's possible he took the papers home with him to work on. We need to have them back."

It was her turn to shrug. "I haven't seen anything pertaining to his work. If I come across it, I'll let you know." She stood up, indicating she was ready for him to leave. She still had a towel wrapped around her head. Any reasonable person would have taken the hint and left. Like most men, Rick Frost didn't take hints.

"If there is anything you need, anything at all, don't hesitate to call me." It sounded like he was suggesting the same thing Tom had earlier in the week. What was wrong with these men? Did they think she wouldn't be able to live without sex now that her husband was gone?

"I'll be just fine. I won't be needing help of *any* kind."

Maybe he'd get that hint. If not, she'd be a little more blunt next time.

For several minutes he didn't budge. She thought he might take root on her couch. "Thank you for bringing this by, Mr. Frost," Quinn finally broke the uncomfortable silence. "I don't mean to be impolite, but I'm rather busy today. You'll have to excuse me." No hint there, she thought. He couldn't mistake her meaning.

"Oh please, call me Rick." He stood up. "Well, I must be going, I'm rather busy myself. Remember, if there is anything I can do for you, don't hesitate to call." Again, he smoothed his hand over the side of his hair. Maybe he thought that was a flirty gesture. But Quinn thought she was going to need another shower.

In his early forties, Rick Frost would be considered by some women a good-looking man. He was certainly convinced of that fact. But he was a little too slick, too slimy, for her.

Locking the door behind him with a resounding click, she leaned against the solid wood waiting to hear his car leave. She wasn't going to take the chance that he would try something. When the powerful car roared off, a shudder passed through her. What was wrong with these men, she wondered again? Why did they think she would be interested in them?

~~~

After leaving Quinn, Doug Aguilar went to the fancy penthouse loft in downtown Denver belonging to Dominic Marconi. He might have called himself Sergio DeCosta in high school, maybe even now, but that didn't take away from the fact that his father was Antony Marconi, second-in-command of one of the most feared Mafia families in Italy. They had been working to get a toe hold in New York City for years.

"Dominic Marconi, I'm Detective Doug Aguilar with the Sheriff's Department." He held up his shield and identification for the other man to see. "I'd like to have a word with you." He wanted to push his way into the apartment, but held himself in check.

"The name is Sergio DeCosta, Detective. Please come in." He should be used to this treatment, but it never got easier. It was one more thing to place at that man's door. It mattered little that he hadn't seen the man but once in the last fifteen years. The authorities always believed the worst of him.

Doug brushed past the younger man. "Whatever," he muttered. Civility had gone out the window when he discovered Marconi had visited Quinn Reed.

Sergio showed the detective into a living room larger than the living room, dining room, and kitchen combined in the house he and his wife owned. Who said crime doesn't pay?

"What can I do for you this morning?" Sergio sat facing the older man.

"You can tell me about your relationship with Quinn Reed." He waited, letting the silence stretch out. If the younger man was nervous, it didn't show on his face.

"I have no relationship, as you call it, with Quinn. We knew each other in high school."

"Yet you went to see her last night." The statement was full of accusation.

"When I heard about the death of her husband, I wanted to offer my condolences. That is all." His Italian accent thickened whenever he was upset or nervous.

"Why are you using an assumed name?"

"Sergio DeCosta is my legal name. It has been since I was a small child. If you would like to see the papers, I can have my attorney bring them to you. I have done nothing illegal, now or ever in my life. If it becomes necessary for me to prove that, you will need to provide me with a search warrant."

"What do you have to hide, Marconi? Do I hear a little bit of a guilty conscience talking?"

"I have nothing to hide or to feel guilty over, and you

will call me by my name, or I will have to ask you to leave." Try as he might to hold it in check, he was beginning to lose his temper with this detective. He had spent all of his life running from the man who fathered him, from his reputation, and for what? To be harassed continually by the police, by anyone who discovered who his real father was.

"Can you tell me where you were on September tenth between noon and five in the evening?" He already knew some of this information, but he wanted to see what Marconi had to say for himself.

"I assume those are Denver times. I was in New York with a client."

"Can you prove that?" Doug kept his tone casual, but he was feeling anything but casual.

"Will my boarding pass suffice? I arrived at La Guardia Airport at ten-fifteen New York time. I met with my client in his office until noon when we went to lunch. We were at the restaurant until after two p.m. at which time I took a taxi to my hotel. I was there the remainder of the evening. You can check with my client if you like."

"I'll do that."

"I had nothing to do with Daniel Reed's death if that is what you are implying."

"The day he was murdered Daniel Reed had lunch with a prospective client. He kept his calendar on his cell phone. What do you know about that?"

Sergio frowned at him. "I know nothing about it. I have never met Daniel Reed, or spoken to him."

"The name of that client was Sergio DeCosta. I don't suppose you know anything about that either?" The name hadn't meant anything to him when he first saw it in Reed's calendar. Then the feds informed him of the name Marconi was currently using, and his visit to Quinn Reed. Why is local law enforcement the last to know when a mob figure moves into the area?

Sergio's stomach churned. He was always guilty until

proven innocent, not the other way around. "No, I have no information about that. Maybe there are others with the same name. I will tell you again, I never met Daniel Reed, and I did not have an appointment with him." Aguilar snorted his disbelief, but otherwise remained silent. "I was in New York, and unless you think I am able to be in two places at once, Daniel Reed was not meeting with me. If you think I murdered Quinn's husband, you are mistaken. All you need to do is check with my client in New York, and the hotel. I ate dinner in the hotel dining room. I paid with a company credit card."

"Just because you were in New York, doesn't mean you couldn't hire someone else to do your dirty work." He watched the other man closely for any signs of guilt. There was only anger radiating off him.

"I did not hire anyone to do it for me. But I imagine you will be checking my financials to see of any large payments coming from my accounts to unknown parties trying to prove my guilt."

Caught at his own game, Doug changed the direction of the conversation.

"Why would someone else use your name to set up an appointment with Reed?"

"When you find that person, you will have to ask him." In the meantime, he thought, he would do a little checking of his own. Marconi had been trying to get him to join the "family business" for years. If he thought murder would force him to join, Sergio had little doubt he would try. He had never discovered how the man always seemed to know where to find him, or how the police always discovered who he was related to. It was time for him to do a little digging of his own.

"What are you doing in Denver?" Maybe he could rattle the guy by changing the subject. The other line of questioning hadn't produced anything helpful.

"This is my home."

"What exactly do you do for a living?"

"I own a computer security company."

"Oh, that's rich. I'll bet your old man has made use of your services over the years."

"My old man as you so crudely put it, is dead. You might want to use a computer sometime to check that out."

Doug faltered for a second. Had the senior Marconi died? No, that would have made the news. "I don't think so. He's alive and well, and still running his illegal businesses in this country and others."

"If this person is doing something illegal, then you should arrest him and stop harassing me. I have done nothing wrong. I run a legitimate business, pay all the taxes due, and do nothing against the law." Denying knowledge of Antony Marconi wasn't working for him this time.

Damn, the guy is good, Doug grudgingly admitted. Sometimes getting a suspect angry was a good thing. They often let something slip, but not this guy. If he was following in his old man's footsteps, he was being awfully cagey about it.

"I would like to ask you something, Detective." He waited for a nod of assent before continuing. "Do you know that Quinn Reed is being followed? I do not believe it is one of your own."

Doug's stomach rolled. "How do you know someone's following her?" His tone was sharp.

"Because I have seen them. Quinn was my friend for a long time. Her husband has just been murdered; I wanted to make certain that she was safe. I believe someone might want to harm her."

Doug's first thought was Eunice Reed. That woman hated Quinn with a passion. He wouldn't put it past her to try something like this if it meant getting rid of the younger woman. "Can you describe the person following her?" Why was he asking this man for help, he silently questioned?

Without a word, Sergio took the cell phone off his belt. Pulling up a picture, he handed it over to the detective. It wasn't Eunice Reed. He couldn't hide his disappointment.

He would love to hang something on that woman. "Email that picture to me. Please," he added, a second too late to be polite. He handed Sergio his card. The man in the picture wasn't familiar. "I'll check it out. In the meantime, you might want to stay away from Quinn." He left without another word.

Sergio slumped down on the couch, resting his head against the dark leather. Hiding and running had never worked. What would the police think if I went to them with the truth about my birth, my life, he wondered? There was proof that he hadn't had any contact with Marconi until four years ago.

He gave a humorless laugh. That meeting had not been a pretty sight. Marconi had been surrounded by his three daughters, and many of his lieutenants for protection. What did they think he was going to do, kill their boss? The desire was there, but he would not put himself on the same level with the man. Those daughters were as deadly, or more so, than the men he had surrounded himself with. At least one of them was. Memory of those empty eyes sent a chill through him even today. What had made her change so much? Or had she always been like that, and he had been too young see it? He didn't have the answer to that question.

~~~

The dark figure watched from the safety of the car as the detective went inside, a gleeful grin on the otherwise complacent features. "I have waited a long time to see him pulled out in handcuffs. He thinks he is so much better than us."

Waiting was torture in the sweltering car. "How does anyone live in this hell hole?" The September sun beat down on the car, turning it into an oven. Even with the air conditioning going at top speed it couldn't keep up with the heat of the sun. Who knew Denver could be this hot?

Twenty agonizing minutes later the detective walked out of the building empty-handed. "What the hell! Why didn't that stupid detective arrest him?" If anyone had been watching, they would have seen the small figure having a temper tantrum in the car, hitting the steering wheel. If possible the figure would be kicking and screaming, but the economy car didn't allow much room to move around. "What do I have to do, put the body in his living room in order to get his ass arrested? He needs to learn his place."

When the detective's car disappeared, the figure slammed the car into gear, peeling away from the curb. "Maybe I'll do that next time."

~~~

First thing Monday morning, Eunice Reed walked into the sheriff's department like she owned the place. "Where is the man who's supposed to be handling my son's murder?"

The desk sergeant looked up from his paperwork, a frown pulling his light colored eyebrows into a straight line over his eyes. "Who's your son?" He didn't know there had been a murder overnight.

"What do you mean, who's my son? Don't you keep track of murders around here? Isn't that what the police are for?" She was disappointed when he wasn't intimidated by her haughty tones.

"Ma'am, there wasn't a murder in the county overnight. Exactly who are you looking for?"

"I'm not talking about last night, you dunce. My son was murdered a month ago. I want to talk to the man who is supposed to be arresting his murderer."

"Which detective is handling the case?"

"I don't know. Don't you know what's going on in your own department?"

The young man heaved a heavy sigh. "What was your son's name, ma'am?"

"His name was and still is Daniel Reed." By now she was screeching, drawing the attention of anyone within hearing distance.

Detective Aguilar stood up, looking over the cubicle

44

wall separating his desk from the others surrounding him. Seeing her, he wished to heaven he'd stayed seated, and pretended he wasn't here. Facing this woman was never pleasant. He could only guess what she was here to complain about this time. Until now, he thought he'd seen and heard everything families of victims would pull. He'd been wrong.

"What can I do for you, Mrs. Reed?" The implied 'this time' hung in the air between them.

"You can do your job and arrest *that woman* for murdering my son."

"What woman is that?" he asked innocently.

"You know what woman; that hussy who married my son!" She was screeching again, causing those closest to Aguilar's cubicle to cringe, at the same time making them very glad they hadn't caught that case.

"I have no evidence against the youn…um against your daughter-in-law," he amended quickly, remembering what Quinn had said about Eunice Reed hating anyone comparing the two women's ages.

"Stop calling her that! My son is gone; she is no longer my daughter-in-law, and she doesn't have the right to use his name."

He wasn't going to get into a debate over the rights of a widow to use her deceased husband's name. "I have no reason to arrest Quinn Reed." He didn't admit that at this point he had no evidence period.

"I told you to arrest *that woman*, she had my son killed, but you wouldn't listen. My son has been gone a month, and she is already cavorting with men of all sorts. If that doesn't say she's guilty, I don't know what does."

"And you know this how?" Detective Aguilar raised one eyebrow slightly. He itched to wipe the haughty, know-it-all smirk off her too-smooth face. She'd had one too many face lifts. Instinct told him she was behind the person Marconi or DeCosta, whatever his name is, said is following Quinn. Until he got his hands on the guy, he couldn't prove it. Would she slip up and tell him?

"You'd be surprised by what I know. What I don't know is why you haven't arrested that harlot."

"Be careful what you say about people, Mrs. Reed. There are laws against defamation of character and slander. There are also laws against harassment and stalking. You might want to think about that."

"There are laws against murder as well, but you seem to be ignoring them. Maybe she's cast her spell over you as well." She stood up, glaring down at him. "In that case, I will just have to take care of this myself."

"Taking the law into your own hands will land you in jail. That isn't a place you'd like very much." She ignored his warning, marching out with her head held high.

So he thinks he can throw me in jail, Eunice fumed. Just because he couldn't see the truth when it was right under his nose, didn't mean she was blind to who killed her son. That woman had never loved Daniel the way he deserved. Even if she had to manufacture the evidence to get her put away, she was willing to do it.

CHAPTER SIX

Sorting through the advertisements from her mail box, Quinn stopped at one envelope. Even after all these years she knew that special script. Sergio had the most beautiful handwriting of anyone she had ever known. Why was he writing to her? Hadn't she made it clear she didn't want to hear from him again? Slicing open the envelope, she withdrew the fancy stationery.

My dearest Quinn,

I wanted to tell you again how very sorry I am for causing you any pain. I would never do that intentionally. You said we all have choices, but I had no choice when I left Denver all those years ago. It is too much to try to explain in a letter. Maybe someday you will find it in your heart to let me explain in person. Until that day, know that I have never stopped loving you.

Please be careful, my darling. There is someone watching you, following you. I tried to tell that detective when he questioned me, but I do not know if he believed me. Again, please be careful.

All my love,

Sergio

A card was enclosed with the name of Sergio's company and his telephone number. On the back he had written his cell phone number. She remembered it well. It had been his when they were in high school. How had he kept it this long?

A sad smile curved Quinn's lips as she read the letter through once more. He even wrote with an accent, she thought. He had never gotten the hang of using contractions. She didn't know what to make of the letter. Why would someone be following her? What could they hope to find out? Eunice would delight in catching her doing something nefarious. Whoever it is, they're going to get pretty bored, she thought. The most excitement she'd had all day was picking up her mail. Even Tom hadn't bothered her.

Maybe Detective Aguilar decided to have her followed after all. She didn't know if he believed what she had told him about her history with Sergio. He'll get pretty bored as well. I've had it with men, she silently declared again. They were more bother than they were worth. So far, she hadn't been able to convince her heart of that fact. Since entering her life again, Sergio was never far from her thoughts. If he really was part of some crime family, she wanted no part of him. She didn't want to believe the boy she had loved was a criminal. The old familiar ache she'd suffered for so long continued to plague her though.

Her mind was still occupied with thoughts of Sergio the next morning. When she pulled into the parking lot at school she failed to notice Tom standing beside his car. Leaning into the back seat for her book bag, her head was inside while her backside was sticking out. She sensed more than heard someone approach her. Before she could move, something touched her bottom. Jerking away, her neck connected hard with the edge of the door frame. She saw stars and her head swam from the sharp blow.

"Hey there, Quinn, take it easy. It's just me." Tom chuckled, but he didn't move away. She could feel his arousal touching her. "I didn't mean to scare you." His chuckle said otherwise. He knew exactly how she would react.

"Get away from me!" Her sharp words attracted the attention of two teachers as they got out of their cars. Instead of approaching to help her, they just stared at the scene unfolding in front of them.

He stepped back, holding up his hands in mock surrender. "I was just trying to help you." Innocence radiated from him like this was one big misunderstanding.

With him no longer right up against her, she pulled her head out of the car. She was still stuck between the car and door. To move she would have to brush up against him. That was something she was unwilling to do. "You can help me by stepping back and leaving me alone," she hissed. More teachers were arriving, standing around to see what was happening. Her cheeks were flaming hot, the embarrassment and humiliation were almost more than she could tolerate.

Tom continued his innocent act, bowing and sweeping his arm in front of him as he stepped back. "By all means, I didn't mean to cause you any harm." He was playing to the audience they had attracted. Who would they believe? Probably Tom, she thought. She'd heard the whispers before Daniel was killed. Because she didn't join in when they bet on who would win this or that reality television show, or go out for drinks after work on Fridays, they thought she was a snob. Since his death, although they offered their condolences, they avoided her like the plague. Did they think murder was catching?

"Just stay away from me." She kept her voice low. The others already had enough to whisper about. Pulling her book bag off the back seat, she headed for the office with her head held high. She'd done nothing wrong, and she wasn't about to cower under their harsh stares.

The morning had been a disaster. She felt like every teacher in the lounge was whispering behind her back. Why was she the one being ostracized because of something Tom had done? Swallowing her sandwich in a few quick bites, she headed for the playground. It was her turn for outside duty.

"I know what you tried to do this morning. I suggest you leave Tom alone," Tina Croft, another teacher, came up behind her. "You've had your man; don't try to take mine."

Giving a startled jump, Quinn turned to see the angry woman glaring at her. Why did people feel the need to sneak up on her all of a sudden? "He's all yours. Just tell him to leave me alone."

"Don't try to put the blame on him. I heard what really happened. He was just trying to be nice and help you, but you tried to make it look like something dirty."

"I don't know how you feel about someone standing close enough that you can feel their arousal pushing against you, but I don't like it," Quinn countered

"How dare you accuse Tom of something like that! He's an honorable man. He would never do that." Tina was angry enough that Quinn thought she might attack her right there in front of the students.

"Well he did. I told him, and now I'm telling you, he needs to keep his distance. He is all yours. I want no part of him."

"Tom would never do such thing!" Tina insisted again, standing ramrod straight, fury burning in her clear blue eyes. "If he touched you at all, it was an accident. You had to make a big deal out of it.

Quinn shrugged, "It was a big deal to me. I don't want him touching me." Were all men dogs, she wondered? Didn't any of them stay true to one woman? She thought about Sergio's words in his letter. He had never stopped loving her, but that didn't mean he hadn't been with other women. Of course, they had no longer been involved, so that didn't count, did it?

Focusing on Tina again, she tried to reason with her. "I'm sorry if this hurt you, but I'm telling you the truth. Just tell him to stay away from me."

"I'm telling *you* to stay away from *him*," Tina hissed. "Don't think you can get him fired either. He's been here longer than you have." She stalked off, leaving Quinn visibly shaken.

"What have I done that's so wrong, God?" she whispered. "Why am I being punished?" It had been a long time since she'd talked to God. Maybe that was the problem.

What if Tom filed a complaint against her? She couldn't prove what had really happened that morning. Could she lose her job over it? She kept telling herself that she'd done nothing wrong, but there wasn't anyone to stand up for her. How easy would it be to find another job? Being fired from a teaching position was a big deal. No other school would want to hire her.

June Veracruz came into her room at the end of the day. She had made a habit of checking on Quinn each day to see how she was faring. Today was no different. "I heard what happened this morning, honey." She took Quinn's trembling hands. "Don't let it get you down. Tom has hit on all the women at one time or another. No one takes him seriously. No one but Tina," she amended.

"But that's sexual harassment," Quinn whispered. "Why hasn't someone reported him?"

June shrugged. "No matter what people say, this is still a man's world. I've heard of cases where a woman reports a man for harassment, and he's promoted but she's fired. It's not fair, but that's the way it works sometimes. Just hang in there. In time, he'll move on."

Quinn couldn't believe other women would let him get away with something like this. She couldn't believe the administration would let him.

Thoughts of Sergio were never far away, now was no different. What had his life been like after he left Denver? He said he loved her, but was he capable of being faithful? Was any man?

As juniors in high school, they hadn't slept together, taking a vow to wait until they were married. But it had been seven years since she last saw him. For all she knew, he could have been married and divorced several times. He could even be married now. The hurt that thought caused just about brought her to her knees. Whatever the case, she doubted that he'd remained celibate all these years.

Sergio had warned her that someone was following her. What would prompt them to do that? What did they hope to see? She hadn't noticed anyone, but that didn't mean it wasn't so. Had Sergio been hoping to frighten her, thinking she would turn to him? Would Eunice stoop to something like that? What would it accomplish? Her life consisted of work and home. She went nowhere and saw no one outside of school. If Tom was following her hoping to catch her alone, that was a no-brainer. She was always alone. Maybe that incident in the parking lot would convince him to cool his jets, and leave her alone. Her thoughts were spinning out of control, leaving her dizzy and confused.

~~~

The longer a case went without being solved, the less likely it was that they would ever find the murderer. Doug Aguilar went over his notes and the sparse evidence found at the scene. The mountain road was well-traveled at rush hours. In the middle of the day there was very little traffic. Whoever shot Daniel Reed had to know he would be traveling on that road at that particular time. They must have been following him. There was no evidence of the other car though. With no witnesses, the case was stalled.

Ballistics had also come up empty. The gun used to kill Daniel Reed had never been used in another crime. It was probably at the bottom of some landfill or the bottom of that ravine by now. It was all very professional, which led him right back to Dominic Marconi.

But Doug could find nothing to link him to this crime or any other. That didn't mean he was innocent, he reminded himself. It just meant he hadn't been caught yet. Why did the man insist that his legal name was Sergio DeCosta? If he had changed his name, Doug hadn't found the court records in Denver. The man was a mystery, and Doug didn't like mysteries he couldn't solve.

He didn't know who was following Quinn either. The picture Marconi emailed him hadn't turned up on any of the criminal data bases. It seemed a little farfetched to think Marconi or anyone connected to him would put a tail on her, then let the police know about it. This entire case was nothing but one tangle after another.

Another possibility was that Eunice Reed had someone following her former daughter-in-law. That woman would do just about anything to see Quinn behind bars, even if meant manufacturing evidence. Hopefully he was smart enough not to fall for that game.

~~~

The figure watched in the rearview mirror as Quinn made her way up the winding street. The dark windows prevented anyone from noticing if there was someone was sitting in the car. All the same, a sense of self-preservation had the figure turning away as Quinn passed. Had she taken notice of the car? Did she wonder if someone was watching her? An evil laugh escaped through parted lips. Let her worry. This game was just heating up, and becoming fun.

~~~

It had been two weeks since Rick Frost brought her the insurance check. It was still sitting in the safe in her bedroom closet along with the money she'd found. She couldn't explain why she hadn't deposited either of those items. What are you waiting for, she asked herself for the hundredth time? There were bills that needed to be paid. Her paycheck wouldn't cover half of them. If she didn't want to lose the house, her car and most of the furniture, she would have to decide soon what she was going to do.

She knew depositing that much cash would raise a red flag at some federal agency. How long would it be before Detective Aguilar showed up asking questions she couldn't answer? If she deposited the insurance check, would it get reported to someone? Why did Daniel have that much insurance without telling her about it? Did the company pay the premiums or were they taken out of his check? They'd been strapped for money, barely meeting their monthly payments. If he was paying the premiums, how could he afford it? She had asked herself these questions over and over without coming up with any answers.

Maybe next month she would have a clearer picture in her mind what to do about the insurance check from Mr. Frost. Until then, she had to do something about the current bills.

With shaking hands, she counted out part of the money in one bundle. She would deposit enough into her account to cover this month's bills and give her a cushion besides. She wasn't sure why she was hesitating, but if Daniel had been doing something crooked, the money didn't really belong to her.

She stopped what she was doing. Where had that thought come from? Just because he was unfaithful to her didn't mean he was a crook, did it? She couldn't come up with any other explanation for all that cash though. Her thoughts continued to whirl around in her mind.

Rick Frost had called several times since delivering that check, asking if she'd found the papers Daniel had taken home. With each call, he sounded a little more desperate. "I really need those papers," he insisted. "Are you sure you've looked through all of Daniel's things?"

"Yes, I'm sure. There's nothing here. Maybe he had the papers with him when he was..." Her voice faltered. Even after two months, Daniel's death seemed surreal to her. She would catch herself wondering when he was coming home for dinner, only to realize he was never coming home again. The thought wasn't as devastating as it should be, leaving her feeling guilty.

"No, that's not possible," Rick Frost argued, bringing her thoughts back to the present. "Please keep looking. I need to have them back as soon as possible." If Daniel had had the papers with him at the time he was killed, the police would have found them, and he'd be behind bars by now. He needed to get them back.

"I've looked everywhere. There isn't any place else to look." What was so important about those papers, she wondered? Wasn't everything backed up on computers?

"Did he keep things in a safe at your house?" he suggested, "Or maybe a safe deposit box at a bank."

"Why would Daniel put something from work into a safe deposit box at a bank?" He wasn't making any sense.

"Oh," he gave a nervous laugh, "that's not what I meant.

I…I meant to say his desk at home."

She hesitated. Eunice had kept Daniel's desk when she cleaned out the house. Had he put papers pertaining to a client in one of the drawer? If Eunice had found them, why hadn't she called Daniel's office? They weren't of any use to her.

At her continued silence, Mr. Frost grew suspicious. "What?" he snapped. "Did you remember where those papers are?"

"Um, no, of course not. I told you, I've looked through everything I have that belonged to Daniel. He wouldn't leave important papers lying around. He was very careful not to risk confidentiality." She hoped she sounded convincing. If there were papers somewhere, she had little doubt Eunice had them.

As soon as she hung up from Rich Frost, she dialed Eunice's number. When the other woman answered, she tried to be pleasant. "Eunice, this is Quinn." Click. She pulled the receiver away from her ear, staring at it. "She hung up on me," she announced to the empty room.

Redialing, she tried again. This time the line was busy. Eunice must have taken the phone off the hook. What do I do now, she asked herself? If Eunice has the papers Mr. Frost needs, why would she keep them? They would mean nothing to her. It would be just like the woman to demand money to give them back. Should she tell him there was a possibility Eunice had what he was looking for? That didn't sound like a good idea. Something about this didn't feel right. Why didn't he have copies of the paperwork?

She waited for another hour before calling again. Eunice couldn't keep the phone off the hook forever. On the third ring, the woman snatched up the receiver, growling at her without any greeting. "What do you want? I thought I was finally rid of you."

This wasn't going to be easy or pleasant, Quinn told herself. "Daniel's boss is looking for some important papers he may have brought home from work."

"What has that got to do with me?" Eunice interrupted, not giving her a chance to explain further.

"You have Daniel's desk. I just wondered if you had gone through the drawers and found anything from his work."

"That desk belonged to my son, not you. What I've found or haven't found is none of your business. Don't call here again, or I will file charges against you for harassment." She slammed down the phone so hard Quinn's ear smarted from the sound.

"Wow!" Hatred radiated off that woman in waves. If she had found the papers Mr. Frost needed, why wouldn't she turn them over? Again she wondered if she should tell him that Eunice might have what he was looking for. Intuition told her to keep that information to herself. At least for now.

Slamming down the phone, Eunice grabbed her purse, heading for her car. If Daniel's boss was looking for important papers, maybe they were important enough that he would be willing to pay to get them back.

The large storage locker where she had instructed the movers to put everything from Daniel's house was nearly empty. Only his clothes, his personal items and his desk remained. Where would he hide something? "Certainly not somewhere for *that woman* to find," she announced to no one. She systematically searched each drawer in the desk, but found nothing worthwhile. After an hour of fruitless searching, she still came up empty handed.

"Where would you hide something you didn't want *her* to find?" she asked the empty locker. "It has to be in here." She looked at the desk again. She began removing everything from the drawers. If it wasn't *in* the drawers, maybe it was *under* one of them.

Her persistence finally paid off! Turning one drawer over, a piece of wood that looked like the bottom of the drawer fell out along with a small stack of papers. Reading through them, she giggled with glee. She might not understand everything on them, but she knew enough. Something fishy was going on at the firm Daniel worked for. "Thank you, Daniel," she whispered. This was going to be her payday!

CHAPTER SEVEN

The parent-teacher conferences ran longer than necessary. Occasionally parents weren't willing to help their child, and wanted to argue with her if their child was falling behind. It wasn't their fault, the teacher needed to work harder. Those same parents didn't care that she had worked half of the day with the students and the other half and part of the night talking with parents. It was now after nine; she was tired and hungry. She hadn't even had a break to eat. Most of the parents were pleasant to deal with, but little Bobby Tucker's father wasn't one of them.

"Bobby is having trouble with spelling and math. He needs a little extra help. Is it possible for you to help him in the evening?" She was careful to phrase the question without sounding accusatory, but Mr. Tucker took exception to it all the same.

"Look, lady. I work hard all day. When I get home, I just want to relax. The kid needs to do his own work." She could smell liquor on his breath, giving her a pretty good idea how he spent his time relaxing.

"What about your wife? Is she able to help Bobby?"

"Don't go prying into my home life. It's none of your damn business."

"If Bobby could stay over for an hour two afternoons a week, there is an after-school program to help students who are having trouble." Before she finished talking, Mr. Tucker was shaking his head.

"I can't afford no after-school program," he growled. She tried to explain it was a free program, but he wasn't listening. "The kid needs to get home to watch his brother so the sitter can leave. I can't afford to pay her no overtime."

Quinn was shocked at this revelation. Bobby was only six years old. What parent in his right mind would expect a six-year-old to take care of a younger sibling? This could explain why Bobby was falling farther and farther behind in school. Reasoning with the man was useless. Her next option was talking to the principal. In her opinion, this was nothing short of child neglect and abuse.

The garage door slid shut before she got out of the car. Since Daniel's death, she had become more cautious. Coming home to an empty, dark house still spooked her. Several times she had considered getting a dog, but she was gone more than she was home. That wouldn't be fair to the dog.

Moving quickly into the laundry room to get out of the cold garage, she tripped over something on the floor. Catching herself on the edge of the washer to keep from falling, she switched on the light. A gasp escaped her lips at the chaos she faced.

Everything from the cupboards above the washer and dryer was on the floor. Even the clothes she had put in the dryer that morning were on the floor. Cupboard doors and drawers in the kitchen stood open.

Common sense told her to back out of the house and call the police from somewhere safe. Anger overcame her common sense. If Eunice had emptied her house for a second time, she was going to press charges.

Quinn marched through the house almost hoping to find the person who did this hiding somewhere. She was ready for a fight. Every drawer, closet and cupboard was standing open. Clothes were moved around in the closet or dumped on the floor. But nothing seemed to be missing. What were they looking for? If Eunice was behind this mess, she would have taken things like she had the first time she cleaned out the house. But there was nothing of Daniel's left for her to take.

Fifteen minutes later, a police car pulled up in front of the house. She met the young officer at the front door. "Nothing was taken?" Officer Bret Thompson asked a few minutes later. Quinn shook her head. "What were they looking for?" he asked.

"I have no idea." This was a waste of time.

"The lock on the arcadia door has been jimmied." He pointed at the broken lock. "There are special locks you can put on these doors that can't be opened as easily. You can also get a heavy dowel to put in the track. If they get the lock opened, the door will only open a few inches." These were good suggestions she should have thought of before now, but they didn't do her any good tonight. "Do you have someone who can stay with you tonight?" he asked.

She shook her head. "I'll be fine, and I'll get that dowel tomorrow."

"That won't be necessary. I keep some in my trunk." He kept a supply for instances just like this. Within minutes he had the dowel in place. "You'll be safer tonight, but get the extra lock this weekend," he advised. "Those dead bolts should also have a key on both sides." He pointed at the knob on the inside lock to the front door. "Do you lock the door to the garage when you leave?" She shook her head again, feeling like a misbehaving student receiving a scolding from a teacher. "You might want to rethink that," he said.

When he left, she sagged against the breakfast bar. Now she was not only tired and hungry, she was humiliated. "First things first." Speaking out loud gave her the feeling that she wasn't quite so alone. Her head was pounding, probably from lack of food. She hadn't eaten anything since a quick sandwich at lunch many hours ago.

Taking a cup of yogurt from the refrigerator and pouring herself a glass of wine, she sank down on the bar stool. While she ate, she tried to decide if it was worth staying up late to clean up the mess, or wait until tomorrow. She had more parent-teacher conferences in the morning. Thankfully it was only until noon. Then she had a three-day weekend. "This mess can wait," she said. "I'm going to bed."

She needed to talk to the principal in the morning about Bobby Tucker. That was a talk she wasn't looking forward to. Would Mrs. Grant agree with her assessment? Since the incident with Tom in the parking lot, everyone including the principal had given her a wide berth. Tom had won this round.

Stripping off her clothes, she slipped beneath the silk sheets. It was time to put warmer sheets on the bed. November nights were beginning to get cold. So far, they hadn't had any snow, but it wasn't far off. Trying to conserve energy and keep her heating bill down, she hadn't turned on the heater yet.

Just beginning to drift off, the phone rang, jarring her awake. Her heart jumped into her throat. Who would call at this time of night? Late night calls meant something bad had happened somewhere. She and her sister, Ginger, had been calling on a regular basis since Daniel's death. Had something happened to her or the baby? Maybe her husband? Fear gnawed at her in the few seconds it took to answer the phone. "Hello?"

"Quinn, are you all right?" Sergio's softly accented voice tickled her ear, allowing her to relax.

"Yes, I'm fine. Why are you calling so late? Is something wrong?" Her mind took her back to high school when she was comfortable talking to this man who had meant so much to her.

"I just heard about the break-in at your house. What happened?"

"How did you hear about it?" she asked, a frown drawing her brows together.

"One of my employees called me. I am in Los Angeles on business, or I would be there to make certain you are all right. I will be home tomorrow. Will you let me see you?"

"Sergio, how did your employee know about the break-in?" She tried to ignore his question.

"Forgive me, *mi amour*, but I could not let you be alone without protection. I have an employee patrolling your neighborhood. He saw the police car at your house."

"What do you mean you have someone patrolling my

neighborhood? Why are you having me watched?" Indignation brought her off the bed, moving the blind aside to look out at the empty street.

"No, not watched. I just want to make certain you are safe. But I did not do a very good job today."

"Sergio, you can't have someone watching me."

"You need to have an alarm system installed in your house. Will you let me do that for you?"

"No, I can't have you doing things for me."

"You still have not forgiven me. Please let me explain why I had to leave."

Quinn released a sigh, debating with herself. Did she want to know? Yes, she did, but not right now. If Detective Aguilar was right, and Sergio was connected to the mob, she wanted nothing to do with him. "Maybe someday, Sergio," she said softly. "Please, don't have anyone watching my neighborhood. What if one of my neighbors sees them and calls the police? I don't want to get anyone in trouble." Least of all Sergio, she added silently. Of course, her neighbors weren't exactly close. In Greenbrier, there were small hills and twisting roads between each house.

"I will wait until you are ready for me to explain. Sleep safe, my love." He hung up without agreeing not to have someone watching out for her.

She collapsed against the pillows. "What am I supposed to do now?" If someone really was following her, what would Sergio do if he found out who it was? She didn't want anyone getting hurt because of her.

Sleep was slow in coming, but she finally fell into a troubled sleep only to awaken several hours later. "Mr. Frost," she spoke aloud in the empty room. "Would he break in to look for the papers she couldn't find? Was he that desperate?" Realizing she was talking out loud again, she gave her head a shake. That was becoming a habit. People will think I'm nuts if I keep this up. This time she kept the thought in her head.

The rest of the night she tossed and turned, trying to fall asleep again, but it was no use. Her thoughts wouldn't let her relax. It was still dark when she gave up trying to sleep. Turning on the coffeemaker, she headed for the shower. Let's get this day started, she told herself, so it can finally be over. She was looking forward to a relaxing weekend.

The meeting with Mrs. Grant went better than Quinn expected. The older woman sided with her on this issue. She called Child Protective Services, giving them the necessary information. Quinn had a stack of papers to fill out and would have to give a statement, but she hoped they would be able to keep her name out of it as much as possible. She had enough people against her; she didn't need to add a drunk and angry father.

~~~

"Mr. Frost, I think I have something you want."

"Who is this?" Rick Frost snapped. He wasn't in the mood for games.

"We'll get to that in a minute." She gave a girlish giggle. "First we need to discuss how much these papers are worth to you." She had disguised her voice, even though they had never met.

"Is this Mrs. Reed?" Eunice gasped. How had he guessed? "Quinn Reed, you need to turn those papers over to me right now."

At this, Eunice laughed. This was even better than she first planned. She could get a lot of money, and be rid of that woman all in one step. "You'll get the papers back just as soon as you give me two hundred and fifty thousand dollars."

"What?!" His shriek was loud enough to shatter glass. "You're holding my own papers for ransom? How dare you do this to me! Your husband was in this the same as me. If you don't want his name splattered all over the news, you'd better turn them over right now."

Eunice sputtered, but stopped in time so she didn't reveal her true identity. He was going to pay for hinting that Daniel had done anything wrong. "The price has just gone up, Mr. Frost. You now need to give me three hundred thousand dollars."

"What?!" he sputtered again. "You have a lot of nerve."

She giggled once more. "Yes, I do. Now, are you through stalling? I've read these papers, and I think the authorities would be very interested in them."

"You bitch." He growled at her. "It's going to take time to get that much cash together. I'll call you when I have it. Then we can set up a meeting place."

"Oh, I'm not foolish enough to give you my phone number or meet you face to face. That wouldn't be very safe for me, now would it?" She giggled again, she was enjoying this immensely. As long as he thought she was Quinn, he would go after her when he didn't get his papers back. Then she would be rid of *that woman* once and for all. "I'll call you in two days. Have the cash ready. I'll give you further instructions then. Oh, and I want that all in twenties. Have a nice day, Mr. Frost." She disconnected the phone.

Who would have thought watching all those cop shows on television would give her all the ideas she needed to pull this off? She'd bought a 'burner phone' at the local electronics store so the number couldn't be traced back to her. When she had her money, she would decide on her next move. Right now, she had to figure out where to have him leave her money. It was always in a trash can in some public place on television. But there was too much chance that he would catch her. For this to work to her advantage, she had to remain hidden so he would go after Quinn instead of her.

CHAPTER EIGHT

Preoccupied with the mess she was facing inside, she started to get out of the car before the garage door was fully down. The door reversed direction when someone stepped into its path. Her heart was pounding rapidly when she turned to face Tom Barton. She could smell the liquor on his breath, and he wobbled as he stood in front of her. He'd been drinking to get up false courage. "You're drunk. You need to leave now." She hoped she sounded far braver than she felt.

If she could get back into the car and lock the door, she'd be safe. Her mistake was turning her back on him. He was on her in a matter of seconds. Pressing himself up against her, grinding his hips into her back side, her chest was pressed against the edge of the car.

"You always thought you were better than the rest of us, didn't you?" His whisper was harsh against her ear. "You wouldn't join in on the after-hour parties with the rest of us." He waffled between anger and petulant little boy.

"I couldn't go out partying; I had a husband waiting for me to come home." That wasn't the complete truth. Most days Daniel didn't arrive until long after she was home. She struggled to remain calm now. Fighting wouldn't do any good, even drunk he was stronger than she was.

"Well, you aren't married anymore, so what's your excuse now? I just want to show you how much I care about you." He ground his hips against her again.

"My husband has been gone just a few months. I'm still in mourning."

He laughed. "I doubt that. I've seen the men coming and going around here. You attract men like honey attracts bees." He stepped back enough to move her away from the car, turning her around to face him. "Well, it's my turn to get a little of that honey."

He pulled her to him, his wet mouth crushing down on

hers; his arms were like steel bands holding her prisoner. She began to struggle in earnest, but to no avail. He tightened his grip, his mouth and hips grinding against her. When she stopped struggling, he relaxed his hold just enough that she could move her leg. In one swift movement, she raised her knee, connecting hard with his groin.

With a strangled scream, he fell to the floor, holding his privates, the color drained from his face. Tears of pain and fury ran from his eyes.

"Get out of here right now, or I'll call the cops. Don't you ever touch me again!" She wiped her hand across her lips to get the feel and taste of him out of her mouth. Nausea rolled in her stomach.

He managed to pull himself to his feet, still clutching his crotch as he limped to his car. He had sobered up fast. "You'll be sorry for this." He could barely catch his breath, his words holding little threat.

After making sure he was gone, Quinn closed the garage door, grabbed her book bag, and hurried into the house.

That night her house was broken into again.

~~~

Sergio's warm brown eyes gazed down into her own, his fingers threading through her silken hair. He lifted his wine glass in a silent toast, before... the glass shattered. Quinn sat up in bed; her eyes darted around the room searching the dark for what had wakened her. No light shone through the blinds, the small light she kept on in the hall was out. Activated by the dark, it should be on unless the power had gone off. It wasn't unheard of to lose power during a storm, but there hadn't been one last night. She tried to remember if it had been on when she went to bed.

Straining to hear any sound, all she could hear was the rapid beating of her own heart pounding in her ears. A dark shape appeared against the slightly lighter darkness of the doorway, moving towards her. She opened her mouth to scream when something hard hit her on the temple, knocking her off the bed. Stars flashed in front of her eyes, and her head spun. "Who are you?" she whispered. "What do you want?"

"Bitch," a voice hissed close to her ear. "Did you really think you could get away with this?" He hit her again and again. Darkness finally claimed her, delivering her from the punishing blows.

When she opened her eyes again, she was greeted with nothing but blackness. She hurt in every bone in her body. The house was eerily quiet; the only sound was a steady beeping close to her ear. Whoever did this was gone. Groping in the dark to find the source of the noise, her fingers closed around the phone.

Fighting to remain conscious, she managed to hang up the phone and pick it back up. She fumbled to press the right buttons in the dark. When the familiar voice answered, her throat clogged with tears. "Sergio, help me." Darkness claimed her again, the phone fell to the floor beside her. She didn't hear his panicked voice calling her name.

She lay still, aching in every part of her body. The bed beneath her was hard. Her head and knees were raised. This isn't my bed, she thought, but where am I? Two men were talking quietly; one of them was holding her hand, softly caressing it. She was in a curtained room somewhere, but she had no idea where, or how she got there.

"Where am I?" Her voice came out in a hoarse whisper. "What happened to me?" She couldn't get her eyes to open properly.

"Quinn, darling, oh thank God you are alive!" Sergio leaned over, placing a soft kiss on her swollen face.

Detective Aguilar stepped up to the other side of the bed. "How are you feeling, Ms. Reed?"

"Terrible. I hurt everywhere. Where am I? What happened to me?" she asked again.

"We were hoping you could tell us that. You're in the

hospital. What do you remember?

It took her a minute before she could get her thoughts in any kind of order. "Someone broke into the house," she began, stating the obvious. "He wouldn't stop hitting me." Tears gather in her eyes, but she refused to let them fall. "Why are you here?" She turned her head slightly, looking up at Sergio.

"You called me, darling. All you said was "Help me." I was out of my mind to get to you."

"He was smart enough to call me before heading to your house from Denver," Doug Aguilar added. In the few minutes the two men spoke before Quinn awoke, he had gained a grudging admiration for the younger man. That didn't mean he believed everything he had to say. "Can you tell me who did this?" She started to shake her head, but stopped when the movement increased the pain. "What do you remember?"

"I was dreaming about," she looked at Sergio, but didn't finish the sentence. "The sound of glass shattering woke me up. The house was dark, too dark. A shadow came into my room, and he started hitting me." She couldn't keep the tears from spilling over now.

"Detective, please, is it possible to wait for any more questions." Sergio tried to remain polite, but he didn't want this to continue.

Doug ignored him, pressing Quinn with more questions, hoping one would shake something loose in her memory. "Can you think of anyone who would do this?"

"Several," she admitted.

Now they were getting somewhere, he thought, his pen poised over the small pad in his hand. Before letting her offer her suggestions, he looked at the younger man, giving a slight nod at the curtained entrance to the cubicle.

"You would like me to leave the room?" Sergio asked, raising one eyebrow. He thought they had come to an understanding, but apparently not.

"No!" Quinn gripped his hand, fear tearing though her.

"If I promise not to kill someone for doing this to Quinn, will you let me stay?" His tone was sarcastic; a self-deprecating smile tilted his lips.

For a long moment, Doug considered the younger man. Giving a slight nod as though coming to a decision, he turned back to Quinn, waiting for her to explain.

Telling what Tom had tried the previous afternoon, her cheeks burned with humiliation. Neither man said a word until she finished with the tale. "Why didn't you call the police?" Doug asked. "We would have picked him up for attempted sexual assault."

She shuddered at the reaction that news would receive at school. She couldn't say he was the one who had attacked her last night. She didn't want to think about that right now. "Eunice Reed would love to have me permanently out of her life," she put in, hoping to redirect the conversation. "But the person who hit me was a man," she added. In her mind, that excused Eunice.

There was one other likely person. She had stayed after parent-teacher conferences were over, talking to the police about Bobby Tucker's father. If they had gone to his house, and told him the complaint came from the school, he would know she was the one who turned him in. There's no telling what the man would do in a drunken rage.

She didn't think to mention Rick Frost. He was desperate, but she didn't think he was violent. Besides, she had reported the break-in from the previous night, so the detective should know about that.

A doctor pushed the curtain aside. "I think that's enough for tonight, folks. Ms. Reed needs to get some rest."

"Why can't I go home? What's wrong with me?" She didn't want to stay in a hospital.

"You have a concussion and two broken ribs, along with various cuts and bruises. We're just going to keep you overnight for observation." Hearing the extent of her injuries, Sergio's grip on her hand tightened momentarily before forcing himself to relax.

"I'd rather go home," she objected, trying to remember what they would do for her in the hospital that she couldn't do for herself at home.

"I can't let you go home alone," he insisted. "Someone has to watch you for the next twenty-four to forty-eight hours."

"If you will let me stay with you," Sergio spoke softly, "I will watch over you."

The detective in him wanted to object, but Doug knew Sergio, or Dominic, or whoever he was, would take good care of her. He would defend her with his own life if the need arose. But he couldn't say the person who attacked her would be safe if he found out who did this to her. There was still a lot about this man he wanted to know, but now wasn't the time to press the issue.

Convincing the doctor to release her into Sergio's care hadn't been easy, but eventually he let her go home. Sergio wanted to carry her into the house, but she wouldn't have it. She was going in under her own power. She also objected when he wanted to put her directly to bed. "Tell me what you found when you came to get me. Didn't he trash things?" She had just gotten the house back in order after the first break-in when this happened. She expected black fingerprint powder to be everywhere, but the house was in pristine condition.

He insisted on getting her settled on the couch, fluffing the pillows behind her back, and covering her with a soft blanket before answering. "Yes, he had ransacked the house. Your television was taken. You will have to check to know if he took anything else."

"But there's my TV." She pointed at the television hanging on the far wall where it had always been. Then she did a double take. This one was bigger than the one Daniel bought just a few months before he died. "Sergio, what did you do?" A small smile lifted her lips and her spirits.

He looked a little shame-faced now. "I just replaced the

television you lost."

"With a bigger one. You also had someone come in and clean up after the police were finished." He must have had the window replaced as well. Caught again, he nodded. Sitting down at the opposite end of the couch, he pulled her feet into his lap, absentmindedly massaging them.

They had never been uncomfortable with each other, and now was no exception. She rested her head against the back of the couch, closing her eyes. This is what life would have been like if he hadn't disappeared seven years ago.

"Will you tell me why you went away, Sergio? Why didn't you ever let me know you were all right?"

"I am sorry that I hurt you, *mi amour*, but it could not be helped. My mother and I had to leave. If he had found out I was in love with you, you would not have been safe either."

"Who are you talking about?"

Drawing a ragged breath, Sergio looked across the room as though he was looking into the bowels of hell. "His name is Antony Marconi. He is my birth father." She sucked in a breath, but otherwise remained quiet. He needed to tell his story, and she needed to hear it. "My mother was sixteen when she went to work as a maid for Antony Marconi. Everyone in the village knew he was part of La Cosa Nostra, the Mafia, but she needed to work to help her family.

"Marconi was in his forties at the time. My mother was a beautiful young girl, and he wanted her as his mistress." Quinn gasped, but said nothing to interrupt him. "You do not refuse someone like Marconi," he said quietly. "You just do as you are told.

"He had three daughters with his wife, but no son. A son is very important in La Cosa Nostra. His youngest daughter, Sophia, is just a year older than me. Mrs. Marconi and her two older girls hated my mother and me. She would do anything to rid herself of us."

"Did she know about her husband's affair," Quinn

asked quietly, "that you were his son?"

He gave a bitter chuckle. "There was never any doubt of paternity. His name was on my birth certificate. To my regret, even as a child I looked very much like the man. She wanted to send us away, but he wouldn't hear of it. I remember the fights."

"When I was eight, my mother became very ill." His words were so soft; Quinn had to strain to hear him.

"He wanted me to stay, but she wanted me gone as well as my mother. She said she would kill me and my mother if he kept me there."

Quinn gasped again. "Are you saying she tried to kill your mother?" These people were ruthless.

"Yes, she tried, but when we got away from that toxic place, my mother got well. Marconi wasn't concerned with what his wife was doing to be rid of her rival, but he didn't want the same fate for his son. Reluctantly, he let both of us leave. That was the last time I saw the man until I was grown.

"When I was ten my mother married Gino DeCosta, and he brought us to America. He adopted me, changing my name. When I was sixteen, Marconi found us in Denver. He contacted my mother. He wanted to see me. My adopted father had passed away the summer before I met you, but as far as I was concerned he was the only father I had or wanted."

"Why did he want to see you?" she asked quietly.

"To men like Antony Marconi, family is very important, especially sons. He had let his only son go; now he wanted him back, to bring him into the Mafia 'Family'." He spoke as though he wasn't talking about himself. Maybe in his mind, he wasn't the son of this criminal. "My mother wouldn't let that happen. We had to disappear before he could take me away from her.

"He came to my college graduation. He still believed he could bring me into his family. I told Marconi to leave me alone or I would tell what I knew about his business dealings."

Quinn frowned. "How did you know about his business if you weren't involved with them?"

Sergio gave a humorless laugh. "I was young when we left his house, but I was not stupid. His people paid little attention to me or his daughters. I could come and go while they were discussing business. All that was said, I remembered. I told Marconi he would leave me and my mother alone, or I would go to the authorities with what I knew. I have nothing to do with Marconi or his illegal businesses. He has not given up trying to see me, but I hold the cards now."

"Where is your mother? Does she know he has tried to contact you?" Occasionally, I catch myself talking with the slight accent he has, and not using contractions.

He smiled. "Yes, she knows. But she knows I will never live the life he has. She lives in Alaska now with my step-father. She was still young when they married, and they have two little girls. She is very happy. Marconi knows nothing of where she is, and cares nothing for her. He is only concerned with seeing his son now that he is an old sick man. God's justice will find him soon enough and he will pay for eternity for what he has done."

"So you were never actually in the Mafia?" She spoke so softly, he almost didn't hear her.

"Not actually or anything else," he chuckled, tickling the bottom of her feet. "Enough about that man. He is nothing to me. Detective Aguilar was not very forthcoming about the investigation into Daniel's death." He changed the subject. "Do they have a suspect other than me?" He said it in jest, but there was an underlying current of sadness in his voice. Would he always be a suspect because of an accident of birth?

She lifted one shoulder. "It's been three months, and they don't know much more than they did when he was killed. Detective Aguilar still stops by, but there isn't much he can tell me."

"Do you think it was that teacher who attacked you last night?" He was asking the same questions the detective had with the same results.

"He was limping when he left here. I thought he'd be using an ice pack for the rest of the weekend instead of attacking me."

"Good for you." A smile lifted the corners of his sensuous lips, and Quinn caught herself remembering the innocent kisses they had shared in high school. Innocent yes, she thought, but stirring all the same. What would those lips feel like now? They were both adults. The kisses would no longer be innocent. Butterflies filled her stomach at the thought.

"It is time for you to rest." Standing up, he bent down to place a kiss on her forehead. Knowing what he intended, she tipped her head just enough so their lips met. Leaning in to him, she allowed him to deepen the kiss. Fireworks went off in her head. What she had felt for him in high school was magnified a hundred times now. He would have swept her into his arms, if she hadn't moaned at the movement. "Oh, forgive me, darling. Did I hurt you?"

Sergio spent the weekend caring for her, letting her out of bed or off the couch only long enough to use the bathroom. He delivered breakfast to her in bed, while lunch and dinner she ate sitting on the couch. Following the doctor's orders, that night he woke her every two hours to make certain she was all right. He slept in the overstuffed chair in her room. The other nights she insisted he would be more comfortable if he slept in the guest room.

After lazing around for three days, she was ready to do something Monday morning. She wanted to go to work, but Sergio wouldn't hear to it until she'd seen a doctor again. This time, the doctor came to her. It was nice having a doctor on the payroll.

Once she was pronounced fit for work as long as she took it easy, she could go back to school the following day. The stitches could be covered with bandages, and her

74

bruises were already turning a putrid yellow. They weren't as easily covered, but makeup helped.

"What happened to your face, Mrs. Reed?" Bobby Tucker asked quietly when he came into the room first thing in the morning. "Did you fall, too?" He was sporting a cast on one arm and a bruise on his cheek.

"No, Bobby, I didn't fall." Fury surged through her. She would bet money his injuries weren't caused by a fall any more than hers were. "How did you fall?" She took his small hand in hers. That was about all the physical contact a teacher could have with her students anymore.

Tears welled up in his sad eyes. "I didn't fall either," he whispered. "But you can't tell anyone," he added quickly looking around to make sure no one else could hear them.

"Did someone hit you like they did me?" she whispered back.

His eyes got big. "Yes. I didn't know big people got hit." That was a concept he didn't understand.

"Bobby, you need to tell the police. They will stop the hitting."

"No, the police only make it worse." For a six-year-old little boy, he seemed so defeated.

Her heart broke for him while fury burned inside. She wanted to stop that monster from hurting Bobby again. "Did the police come to your house last week?" His head bobbed up and down, but he didn't say anything. "Is that when you broke your arm?" He nodded again. Child Protective Services wasn't doing a very good job of protecting this child. The classroom door opened as six-year-olds poured into the room chattering happily.

Bobby scurried to his seat to avoid the other children's questions. Another call to the police was in order, but it would have to wait until lunch.

"You have a lot of nerve sending the police after me, after what you did," Tom hissed from his position in the doorway of the teachers' lounge during lunch. "You just about broke my balls." When she looked up from the papers she was working on, he drew in a sharp breath. "I didn't do that to you!"

"I didn't say you did. Someone broke into my home that same night and did this." She waved one hand in front of her face, while holding on to her broken ribs with the other. "When the police asked if I had any enemies, I told them what you tried to do that same afternoon."

"But I would never hit you," he insisted, sinking down on a corner of the couch by the door.

"No, you were drunk and wanted to rape me!" Thankfully they were alone for the moment.

"No, I wasn't going to rape you! I just wanted to persuade you to go out with me." He sounded like a pathetic little boy now.

"Well, force isn't going to work on me or any other woman. I just want you to leave me alone." Gathering her papers to leave, she was spared when two other teachers joined them.

"What happened, Quinn?" June Veracruz sat down beside her, taking her hand. She glared at Tom who had stayed when the others walked in. "We heard you'd been injured, but this wasn't an accident, was it?"

Giving an abbreviated account of the break-in and beating, she hoped the school gossips would now leave her alone. Although she had a good idea who her attacker was, she made a point of saying she couldn't identify him.

That night Tom was attacked, sending him to the hospital with a severe concussion, broken ribs, and various other broken bones. He fared much worse than Quinn had.

CHAPTER NINE

"Hello, Rick. Do you have my money?" Eunice was enjoying the cloak and dagger very much; too much to stop now.

"My money you mean, but yes, I have it. Now tell me where you want to meet. I want my papers." The last words were ground out. She was enjoying herself, but this was no fun for him.

"Oh, we're not going to meet. You're going to take a little ride with my money."

"What are you talking about?" She giggled that stupid little laugh that was beginning to grate on his last nerve.

"I've decided where I want you to drop off my money. Tomorrow morning you're going to take a little ride on the light rail. I'll call you somewhere along the route. All you have to do is walk off, leaving behind the briefcase."

"Briefcase my ass," he interrupted. "Do you know how big three hundred thousand dollars all in twenties is? I've got it in a gym bag. Do you also know what I went through to get this much cash all in twenties? If the bank hasn't notified the IRS or some other federal agency, it would surprise me. Now just tell me where you're going to leave my papers."

"Not so fast, Ricky boy. Once I have the bag and verify that my money is all there, I'll call to tell you where you can pick up your papers. Get on the light rail downtown with my bag of money. Be sure you get on the last car, not any other. Put the bag under the seat, sit back and enjoy the ride. When I'm satisfied that you haven't got the cops waiting for me to pick it up, I'll call you. Then you can get off. Of course, you'll leave your little donation to my health and welfare fund behind."

"What if someone else picks up the bag before you get it after I'm gone?"

"That sounds like a personal problem to me, Rick.

You'd just better hope that doesn't happen. If it does, we'll just have to start this process all over again."

He started yelling obscenities at her, but the dial tone buzzed in his ear. "That bitch hung up on me." What was he supposed to do now? Sweat popped out on his forehead. He had little choice but to do as she said. Once he had his papers securely in his hands, he was going to enjoy ringing her pretty little neck.

Eunice giggled as she danced a little jig. Who knew crime could be this much fun? She had already picked out what she was going to wear to this little party. He'd never in a million years recognize her. Of course, he'd be looking for Quinn, not her. She giggled again. "I just wish I could see what he's going to do to that bitch when he doesn't get his papers back. She shrugged, well, we can't have everything.

After Barnard left for work the next morning, Eunice took the bag with her disguise hidden inside and headed for Denver. She had rented a room at a small hotel not far from Union Station. She dressed carefully for her little charade. Daniel had been built slim like her; even so his clothes were a little snug in spots. For what she had in mind, they would do. She had hemmed his pants to accommodate her shorter legs, and she rolled the sleeves of his shirt up to her elbows. Pulling on a baseball cap to hide her red tinted hair, she was ready to go. For the first time in years, she went out in public without any makeup. She was supposed to be a man; makeup would only draw unwanted attention.

She had never used any form of public transportation in the past, adding to the nerves she was experiencing over this little adventure. If she could pull this off, she would have a nice bundle to add to her 'retirement' fund. She giggled as she walked to the station. She was retiring from being the wife-in-name-only of Barnard Reed. Of course, she was going to need more than she received today to live the life she was accustomed to. Without realizing it, Barnard had been contributing to that fund for years. She giggled again, ignoring the stares her maniacal laughter garnered from the people around her. She really was very clever, she congratulated herself.

Getting on the light rail at the start of its route, Eunice sat down at the back of the car. That way, she could keep track of the people entering and leaving. She wasn't taking any chances that he had called the police. Of course, he didn't want them involved any more than she did. Holding a newspaper in front of her face, she wanted to discourage any conversation. She had a long way to go before they reached the stop where Rick Frost would board. Getting on this early was just a precaution, she told herself.

If he followed her directions to the letter, she could keep a close watch on him and her bag of money from where she was sitting. He would be looking for Quinn; he might even think she would be in disguise. But he wouldn't be looking for an old man.

She settled back in the seat. It would be a while before they arrived at his stop. She pretended to read every article on each page of the paper. As people came and went at the different stops, she watched them carefully No one paid her the least bit of attention.

At last, Rick Frost boarded the car, looking around at each passenger before taking a seat. Nerves attacked her stomach. Would he be able to see through her disguise? She kept the paper high enough that he couldn't get a good look at her face. They had never met, but she belatedly remembered the picture of herself she had given Daniel for his office desk. What had happened to that?

For a moment she lost focus as fury boiled up in her again. *That woman* probably threw it away when she got the things from his desk at work. She should have all of his personal effects, not *that woman*.

When her fingers began to crumple the papers she was holding in front of her face, she forced herself to relax. There was time enough to exact her retribution on *that woman*. Right now she needed to concentrate on Rick Frost.

He sat down, placing the bag under his seat as instructed. The bag with her money, she mentally rubbed her hands together in anticipation. He continued to scan the faces of each passenger, his gaze passing quickly over her. So far, her disguise was holding.

They were almost at the end of the route before she felt safe enough to let him get off. The car was nearly empty now. Everyone who had boarded when she had, had already gotten off. Those getting on with Rick Frost were also long gone. No one would remember that he brought the bag sitting under his seat with him.

Pulling the burn phone out of a pocket of the loose jacket she was wearing, she dialed the only number programed into the phone. She hoped no one paid any attention to his phone ringing at the same time she was making a call. But everyone seemed to be on their own cell phones, paying no attention to those around them. When he answered on the first ring, she spoke softly so he wouldn't know she was in the car with him. "Leave. Now." She disconnected, keeping her eyes diverted, but watching him out of the corner of her eye.

Rick walked to the door, waiting for it to open when the train came to a stop. He stood on the platform, watching to see if anyone moved towards his vacated seat. No one moved, and the train was quickly out of sight.

As soon as they left the station, Eunice moved to his seat before someone else sat down. She would ride back to the origination point before getting off with her money.

~~~

"Where were you last night?" Doug Aguilar was at Sergio's loft at daybreak. Technically, assaults weren't in his jurisdiction, but if this latest attack was tied in with Daniel Reed's murder, he was going to investigate.

"Good morning, Detective. Would you like a cup of coffee?" Sergio turned from the door, letting the older man close it as he headed to the kitchen.

The rich aroma of fresh brewed coffee made Doug's

mouth water. He'd been at the crime scene for two hours before spending another hour with Tom Barton at the hospital. When Sergio placed a steaming cup in front of him along with some sort of French pastry, he had to force himself not to pounce on both at the same time.

Taking a careful sip of the hot liquid, he asked again. "Where were you last night?"

"Right here in my loft, alone."

"Can anyone verify that?"

Sergio chuckled. "I was alone, so I suppose the answer to that is "No." But the garage attendant can tell you I left my car there at roughly six-fifteen. I did not use it again for the rest of the night. The doorman can tell you I never left again after I came home. There are cameras on all entrances to the building; you can check them as well to see I never left after arriving home. What is this all about? I know Quinn was not hurt again since I just spoke to her on the phone."

"Tom Barton was attacked last night around ten o'clock. His attacker was a 'big Italian dude.'" He made air quotes around the description.

Sergio shrugged. "What does that have to do with me?"

"Well, you're big, at least six feet tall." Sergio nodded affirmatively, and Doug continued. "And you're Italian."

"So is any number of men in Denver. Does that mean whenever someone of Italian descent commits a crime, you will be at my door the next morning?"

"I imagine you know a fair number of those men. Any chance you hired one of your buddies to teach Barton a lesson after what he tried to pull on Quinn?" He'd resisted long enough; he picked up the mouthwatering pastry, barely able to suppress the moan as it melted in his mouth.

"No chance of that. What Quinn did to his masculinity should be enough to keep him away from her. If he gets other ideas, I'm certain you will be able to convince him it is in his best interest to leave her alone."

He had to give the guy credit, Doug thought. He was

one cool customer. He didn't rattle easily.

"You haven't had a little talk with Antony Marconi lately? Maybe telling him what Barton did to your lady love?"

"Detective, I have only seen that man once since I was eight years old. That was when I graduated from college. I will tell you what I told him. I want nothing to do with him, his family, or his money. If I had to be a pauper for the rest of my life, I would not take a dime from him."

"That's easy to say when you own a million-dollar company. I wonder how you managed to get that company. You're what, all of twenty-five years old, and already a millionaire? You sure your old man didn't set you up?"

"My *father*," he emphasized the word, "was Gino DeCosta, a successful man in his chosen profession. He had nothing to do with the likes of Antony Marconi. He adopted me, changing my name, when I was ten. He passed away when I was fourteen. He left his money to my mother and me. I have put that money to good use starting my own company. I have also tried to protect myself and those I care about from Antony Marconi."

"That doesn't change the fact that Marconi is your biological father."

"An accident of birth, I assure you. It takes more than a sperm to make a man a father. I am not involved with him in any way. I had nothing to do with Daniel Reed's death, or the assault on that teacher. You should be questioning him regarding his attempted sexual assault on Quinn."

"So you're saying he deserved what he got?" Doug Aguilar raised one eyebrow in question. Could he be so lucky to have Marconi slip up and admit to that assault?

Sergio smiled serenely. "Nice try, Detective. If you have proof I have done something wrong, arrest me; otherwise I am finished speaking." He stood up indicating the interview was over.

Nice try indeed, Doug thought as he walked out. How much of that tale could he believe? He had begun to like the man, but if he was behind the attack on Barton, he wasn't the man he portrayed himself to be.

~~~

"What is wrong with that detective?" The car was parked close enough to see the man as he left the building, but not close enough to draw attention. *"If I could get inside his apartment, I could make certain that stupid detective arrested him."* Getting inside was the problem. That place was like a fortress. I'll bet another attack on his darling Quinn would bring out the Marconi genes.

~~~

"How could you do that to him?" Tina stormed into Quinn's room before class started.

"Do what? What are you talking about?" Tina looked distraught and ready to kill.

"Don't play dumb with me. I know what you had your boyfriend do. He almost killed Tom. How could you?" she said again, a sob tearing from her throat as she sank down on one of the student desks.

Quinn gasped. "I had nothing to do with that. Why would you think I did? Is he going to be all right?" Ignoring any fear of the other woman, she wrapped her in a hug.

For a minute, Tina forgot to be angry, leaning in to the comfort Quinn offered. "He will be, but he's hurt bad." Remembering who she was talking to, Tina pulled away again. "Your boyfriend did this to him."

"I don't have a boyfriend. Tell me what happened."

Tina stared at her, trying to decide whether to believe her or not. "Tom's seen you with him. He's at your house all the time." Her tone was uncertain now instead of hostile. "He said a big Italian guy attacked him."

"Sergio wouldn't do something like that," Quinn insisted, a frown drawing her arched eyebrows together. "How does Tom know who is with me or when? Has he been spying on me?" She stood up, glaring down at Tina.

"Of course not! Why would he spy on you?" Uncertainty clouded her blue eyes though. She didn't know what to believe anymore. "This isn't Tom's fault. Your boyfriend attacked him." Her voice held a lot less heat than it had when she entered the room. If she said it often enough, maybe she could make herself believe it.

"Tina, believe me, Sergio wouldn't do something like that, but you have to tell Tom to stop following me." Tina tried to object, but Quinn talked over her. "The only way he could know I've been seeing someone is if he's been following me."

Tears streamed down Tina's face again, tears of hurt instead of anger. "Why would he do that? He says he loves me."

Because he's a dog like a lot of other men I know. Quinn kept that thought to herself.

When the first bell rang, Tina escaped out the side door to avoid the students. She needed to fix her makeup before she could face them.

"Will this ever stop, God?" Quinn whispered quietly.

~~~

"Who killed Reed? What's going on with the rest of this mess?" Doug Aguilar sat in his lieutenant's office going over the investigation. Or he should say investigations. The original murder investigation had turned into a whole handful of cases, related or unrelated, he couldn't say at this time.

"It's a toss of the dice at this stage. We have suspects coming out our ears, and they all have motives for any number of crimes." He began naming off the different suspects. "Reed was murdered, you always suspect the spouse, but in this case, she didn't have a motive. I've checked their financials; they were broke, living paycheck to paycheck. The company he worked for carries a small insurance policy on all their employees, but it wouldn't cover even a quarter of the debt that Reed had gotten them into."

"Are you aware Ms. Reed deposited a check for a hundred thousand dollars just before Christmas?"

"No, I wasn't aware of that." His voice was calm, but inside anger ate at him. What had he missed regarding Quinn Reed? Was she behind this all along? "Where did the check come from?"

Lieutenant Beck produced a copy of the check, pushing it across the desk to Aguilar. Looking it over, a frown drew his bristled brows together. "Why would Reed have a hundred thousand dollars insurance? His boss told me the company carried only twenty-five thousand on their employees."

"Maybe Reed paid extra for higher coverage," the lieutenant suggested. It was one more inconsistency in a case full of them. He'd have to make another trip to see the widow Reed. "Getting back to motives? Who else is there?"

"The Securities and Exchange Commission has been investigating that entire company, including Reed, for the last six months before his death." His stomach was beginning to burn, and he wished he had a roll of antacids in his pocket instead of his desk.

"What are they looking for?" Lieutenant Beck's thick brows formed a straight line above his grey eyes. This investigation had more twists and turns than the road leading up to the fancy house.

"Security fraud," Aguilar answered, "a Ponzi scheme, I'm not really sure. They aren't very forthcoming."

"Then there's the drunken teacher who came to her house to 'show her' what a good lover he is. For his efforts, he got his balls kicked up to his throat. Serves him right, he needs to learn that no doesn't mean maybe. But he didn't deserve the beating he took at the hands of some big Italian dude. His description, not mine," he chuckled.

"Another drunk in this mix is that miserable excuse of a father. He got all pissed when Quinn Reed called Protective Services on him. After the second call, he lost his kids, and is sitting in a jail cell awaiting trial for child abuse, child neglect, burglary, and assault. He's the only one I'm sure committed which crime. He beat the crap out of Quinn, trashed her house and stole her television. The guy isn't very smart. We found the TV in the living room of his crappy apartment.

"Then there's Reed's mother," he gave a frustrated sigh. "If it was illegal to be a bitch, that woman would have been arrested a long time ago. She gives mothers-in-law everywhere a bad name. As it stands, that's all I have on her." He ran his hands through his already rumpled hair.

"Back to Reed, where do you stand on the murder?" The lieutenant drew him back on point. "Where does Dominic Marconi or Sergio DeCosta, or whoever he is, fit in with this?"

Doug shrugged. "I don't have the answer to that question. I've checked his company every way from straight. There is no connection to Antony Marconi or any other mob figure. His adopted father was clean, and from what I can find, he's also clean." He actually liked the guy, but he wouldn't admit that to the Lt. "The man is so in love with Quinn Reed, he just about falls over himself wanting to help her." He drew in a deep breath.

"If Reed was being investigated by the SEC, anyone in the company he worked for could be a suspect," he continued with his list of suspects and their motives. "The SEC is playing this so close to the vest, I can't even find out who in the company they're investigating. I don't have the names of any of the women Reed had affairs with other than the last one, but the boyfriend or husband of one of them could be a suspect." He gave another frustrated sigh. Every cop has one case that haunts him; this one might be his.

The next day, he paid a visit to Quinn Reed. He wanted an explanation for that insurance check. He thought her husband had left her nearly destitute. "Can you explain this, Ms. Reed?" He handed her a copy of the check she had deposited.

"It's an insurance check from Daniel's company." She

thought it was rather obvious since it was stated right on the check.

"But that company only carries twenty-five thousand dollars on their employees. Why did you receive four times that amount?" Suspicion darkened his eyes as he glared at her.

"I...I don't know," she stammered. "Mr. Frost just said it was from a company insurance policy."

"Why so much?" he pressed. If she had anything to do with her husband's death, he damn well wanted to know. This case had him twisting in the wind.

If he thinks this was excessive, what will he think of the cash she'd found in the safe, she wondered? "I need to show you something. Will you wait here for a minute?" She stood up, not waiting for him to answer before disappearing up the stairs to her bedroom.

Pressing the hidden panel to expose the safe door, she stared at the combination for a second. After Daniel's death she'd stopped the practice of leaving the dial set on ten as he'd insisted. It seemed a little silly. Now, the dial was on ten. Had she left it there out of habit, or was it just a coincident that it fell on that number when she turned the dial the last time she closed the door?

Giving her head a shake, she twisted the dial to put in the combination. Pulling open the door, she took out what was left of the money. When she turned around, Detective Aguilar was standing in the doorway, his hand resting on the gun on his hip.

Her heart jumped into her throat, the color draining from her face. "Wh...what are you going to do?" she whispered, her frightened eyes locked on the gun.

"What do you have there, Ms. Reed?" He took his hand off his gun. Stepping back into the bedroom, he headed for the staircase. He hadn't been willing to take the chance she was going after a gun. He still had a lot of living he wanted to do, and he wasn't about to let some sweet young thing get the drop on him.

Seated in the living room again, she handed him the cash. "I found this in a safe. I had no idea Daniel kept money in there, especially that much. I don't know where he got it either. There was fifty thousand dollars." Her hands were shaking when she handed over the remaining twenty thousand dollars.

His expression remained neutral, but his mind whirled. He had enough suspects and motives to fit every crime he was investigating. "Why haven't you deposited this?"

She gave a humorless laugh. "You came here today ready to accuse me of murdering my husband because of a hundred thousand dollar insurance check. If you knew I also had fifty thousand in cash, what would you think?"

His face colored slightly at being caught at his own game. "Besides that, why haven't you deposited this?"

She lifted one shoulder. "I didn't know if it was really mine."

"Why wouldn't it be yours?"

"What if he stole the money?" She was speaking to her lap now, her voice no more than a whisper.

"Where's the rest of the cash?"

"I deposited it a little at a time. We were so far in debt, and some of the bills were overdue. If Daniel stole that money, I'll find a way to repay it. I just didn't know what else to do." Tears sparkled in her eyes, slipping down her pale cheeks. Was he going to arrest her now? What had she done that had been so wrong? Please, God, tell me what I'm supposed to do, she silently prayed.

"The insurance money wasn't enough to pay off all your debts?" He knew the answer, but he wanted to see if she would admit it.

She gave a bitter laugh. "Not hardly. The payment on this house alone is over two thousand a month, and my car payment is five hundred. My paycheck doesn't cover half. I'm putting the house up for sale. A realtor is coming over this afternoon." She hoped the house sold quickly or she'd be in trouble. The hundred thousand dollars had taken care of most of their bills, but she kept finding others she hadn't known about. How had Daniel kept all of those bills hidden from me, she wondered yet again?

"I'll be paying Mr. Frost a visit to find out about the check from his company." His comment brought her back to the present.

"He's called me several times asking about some papers Daniel brought home from work. I didn't find them, but I don't think he believes me." She paused for a minute before continuing. "I'm afraid Eunice might have them. She didn't return anything of Daniel's, including his desk from here."

Doug shook his head. That woman was a piece of work. He left a few minutes later satisfied once again that Quinn Reed had nothing to do with her husband's death. He hoped to God he was right. He'd never been taken in by a suspect before. He didn't want this to be the first time.

CHAPTER TEN

Why was Rick Frost still asking about papers Reed brought home months ago, he wondered? If they were that important, couldn't they be reproduced? Don't most companies back up everything on a computer or keep copies of all important documents? It was something else that didn't make sense in this tangled case.

"What can I do for you, Detective?" Rick offered him a seat before sitting down himself. He tried to control the nerves that were eating at his stomach. The SEC was still combing through any files they could get their hands on; he didn't need a homicide detective breathing down his neck as well.

"I've come into information that I find rather puzzling." He paused, letting the tension build up. Sweat was beginning to pop out on the other man's forehead. "I was under the impression that your company carried a small life insurance policy on all of their employees."

"Yes, that's right. We felt it was a nice benefit for their families. I hope we haven't done anything wrong by offering that."

"No, most companies give their employees that option. But I don't understand why Daniel Reed had such a large policy when I was told you carried only twenty-five thousand on each employee."

Frost mopped at his forehead. "Well, Daniel was a valued member of our team. For our top employees we increased the amount of insurance they have."

"You're sure all of the other executives have the same hundred thousand dollar policy? Daniel wasn't the only one?"

"Why would Daniel have a larger policy than the other executives? That doesn't make sense." He was trying hard to hold himself together. If they started investigating the insurance policies on all the employees, he would be in even more trouble. He'd increased the amount he'd given Quinn Reed, hoping that would be incentive for her to return his papers. Then she started blackmailing him. He had to get them back before it was too late.

Doug Aguilar shrugged his broad shoulders. "See, that's what has me puzzled." He waited some more while Frost squirmed in his seat. "Well, I'll let you get back to work. Thanks for your time." He stood up, extending his hand to the other man. He'd made no mention of the papers Frost had been looking for. He wanted to make the man sweat first. And he was sweating big time. He'd come back with more questions later.

Stepping out of the office, Doug pulled his hanky out of his pocket, wiping his hand. Rick Frost was sweating bullets over something. It would be interesting to know what. In the meantime, the murder case had stalled. He had multiple suspects with multiple motives for any number of crimes, just not one for Daniel's murder. Yet.

~~~

Putting the house on the market was easier than she expected. Now if it would only sell. She sank down on the couch, trying to look at the room through the eyes of a prospective buyer. Plush carpet covered the floor here and in the four bedrooms. The kitchen and four bathrooms had ceramic flooring. The rest of the house had hardwood floors, beautiful to look at but a pain to care for. The multi-levels each had a door taking you to a patio at ground level on the hillside home.

The ostentatious house hadn't been her idea. Daniel had committing them to buying it without even consulting her. The house and mortgage were staggering, but it had been too late. He had already committed them, all she had to do was sign on the dotted line. She should have refused, she thought now. "How had I missed all the warning signs?" she whispered. All the advice columnists say a controlling person isn't a good mate. They'd been right on the mark with Daniel. How had she been so blind?

Living in Greenbrier hadn't been her idea either. She had wanted to live in Denver, closer to Daniel's work, and her friends. She had wanted to get a teaching position there as well. But Daniel had other plans. He wanted to be close to his parents, he'd said. She doubted that was the true reason. He really wanted to stash her far away from where he had his many girlfriends. The more time that passed, the more she was finding out about the man she had been married to. Most of it wasn't good news.

Someone was leaning on the doorbell, pounding their fist on the door. When Eunice began screaming to let her in, Quinn wished she could just hide. That wasn't an option though. The woman was persistent if nothing else.

"What is the meaning of that sign?" Eunice screeched as soon as Quinn opened the door. "Why doesn't my key work? Let me in!" She rattled the decorative screen door.

"Your key doesn't work because I changed the locks. The sign should be obvious. I'm selling the house." She made no move to let the woman in.

"You have no right to sell this house. It belongs to my son." She talked about Daniel like he was away on a trip, and would be returning at any time. The woman was delusional.

"I have every right to sell this house. It belongs to me." If the screen hadn't been between them, Eunice would have grabbed for her. As it was, she pounded on the screen, trying to get through.

"Go away, Eunice. I have nothing more to say to you. If you don't leave me alone, I will press charges. I don't think you want to end up in jail."

"What charges," she sneered. "I haven't done anything to you." The silent "yet" hung in the air. A shiver crept up Quinn's spine. She had little doubt the woman could be homicidal if provoked.

"Go away, Eunice," she said again, shutting the door in her face. Quinn leaned against the heavy door, making certain her former mother-in-law left. Her parting words were clear.

"You're going to be sorry. I'll see to it."

"What else can happen?" she asked the empty house. Moving out of this house and this town couldn't happen fast enough for her.

~~~

"Where are my papers?" he growled. He didn't bother with a greeting. He knew who was on the other end of the line. "You've got your damn money, now give me my papers." Daniel had been dead four months now. The SEC was breathing down his neck. If they got their hands on those papers, he'd spend the rest of his life behind bars. If someone else got their hands on them, he was a dead man. Now that detective was looking at him like he was a murder suspect. How much did he already know? How much was he guessing at?

"In due time. Right now we have something else to discuss. I've gone over those papers you want so desperately. It looks like you've made millions off your scams. I want my share."

"Your share," he screamed, nearly breaking her ear drum in the process. "You don't have a share."

"No, but you claimed Daniel did. I want his share."

"You need to remember I know where you live. You'll never know when I might decide I've had enough."

For a long moment, Eunice remained silent. Her stomach rolled, the big lunch she had just shared with her friends at the country club threatening to make a return appearance. But he wasn't talking about her, she reminded herself. He still thought he was dealing with Quinn.

"And you need to be careful. I still hold all the cards; I should say all the papers." She giggled.

He really hated that giggle. He'd always thought Daniel's wife was rather mousey and quiet. She was pretty enough, but there wasn't much behind that pretty face. He couldn't imagine thinking she was pretty ever again.

"I want fifty thousand dollars a month deposited in a

numbered account in the Cayman Islands." She gave him the account number. "Are you writing that down? I don't want you to make a mistake. When I decide you've given me Daniel's share, I'll mail the papers to you." He was still sputtering when she quietly closed the burn phone, cutting him off.

She had spent the holidays in the Caymans taking care of business. Years before she had started her little retirement fund there. It was growing by leaps and bounds now, but it wasn't nearly enough for her to live on for the rest of her life. It would be, before she finished with Mr. Rick Frost. He was even going to take care of *that woman* before she did her own disappearing act.

~~~

With his finger poised to ring the doorbell, Doug paused. Someone inside was singing. He couldn't make out the words, but the tuneless sing song was clear enough. Eunice Reed didn't strike him as the type to dance around singing to herself. When the chimes from the doorbell sounded, the singing stopped. He waited for her to open the door, but nothing happened. After another minute, he rang the bell again. Did she think he would give up and go away if she ignored him? Did she even know who was at the door?

A shadow moved at the window. Someone was looking out to see who was there. He gave a little finger wave, smiling benignly at the shadow. It took another minute before she finally opened the door.

"Hello, Detective. What can I do for you?" She had always presented a calm but angry exterior. Now she looked... he tried to decide exactly what her demeanor was.

"I just have a few more questions for you. May I come in?"

She seemed to debate the question, but finally stepped aside to let him enter. "What do you need to know now? You haven't believed anything I've told you before, why would you believe me this time?" She didn't offer him a seat.

"Well, you've tried to make out your daughter-in-law as a killer, and that just doesn't fly with me. Now I have some different questions."

"She is my *former* daughter-in-law. I would appreciate it if you'd remember that. Have you changed your mind about her?" She was still unwilling to say Quinn's name. With her arms wrapped around her waist in a gesture of protection, she rocked from one foot to the other. She was nervous about something, he decided.

"No, I still believe she's innocent. But I was wondering if you had returned everything you took from her house."

Her face grew red with suppressed anger. "What I took and what I kept is none of your business. Everything in that house belonged to my son. She had no right to it. Now she's selling my son's house." Tears of fury momentarily blurred her vision.

"I'm not here to debate that with you. I want to know what you kept." His tone held a measure of threat now.

"I kept my son's clothes. Would you like me to give them back to her? She would just throw them away since she's already seeing another man. Or didn't you know that?" She acted like she'd just given him the answer to this murder.

"And how would you know what Mrs. Reed is doing? Are you having her followed?"

"Stop calling her that! I am Mrs. Reed."

"Are you having her followed?" he asked again, his tone more forceful. He could see her inner debate.

With an exaggerated sigh, she finally answered. "No, I'm not having her followed. I just happened to see her in a restaurant with a man."

Doug didn't buy that answer. He knew Quinn didn't frequent the same eating establishments as this woman, even if she was with DeCosta. For now, he let that subject drop. "I was speaking with your son's boss today. He said some papers are missing from Daniel's office. He's been looking for them. I was wondering if you knew anything about that." The sudden change of subject drained the color from her face, leaving red circles of makeup on each cheek. "I...I don't know anything about any papers. I had nothing to do with Daniel's work." She paused, her mind working hard to figure a way out of this mess. "Maybe my husband would know. They're in the same line of work." She thought it was a brilliant idea to throw her husband under the bus, throwing the detective off the scent at the same time. She didn't believe for a minute that Rick Frost had spoken to the detective about those papers. They would put him behind bars, or worse, if they came to light.

"Well, if you happen to find them, give me a call." Her hands were shaking as she reached for the card he offered.

~~~

"Will you go to Alaska with me this summer to see my mother?" Sergio asked. "She is excited to see you again after all these years." The realtor was holding an open house that weekend, making it necessary for her to leave. Anywhere they went in Greenbrier there was the possibility of running into Eunice. That wouldn't be good. Instead, she met Sergio in Denver for dinner. Would the first person to look at it, buy it? Could she be that lucky?

Quinn considered his question. She'd done a great deal of soul-searching since Daniel's death. She hadn't loved him the way he deserved. Maybe he had sensed that, and had gone looking for love in the arms of the other women. Or maybe he was just a dog like his father, she thought. Either way, he had deserved better than she'd given him. It was a certainty he wasn't the man she'd thought he was. She would wait until Detective Aguilar said the case was hopelessly stalled before giving up on finding out who killed him. Then she would move on.

Leaning in to place a kiss on his sensuous lips, she gave herself up to the love Sergio had to offer. "I've never stopped loving you," she whispered. "Please be patient with me. I have to see this through. Then I will go anywhere you want. I love you."

It was much later when she rounded the last curve to her drive. Once again the street light was out. "Why can't the county get that fixed?" Every other week that light was out. Something had to be wrong with it, but no one bothered checking it out.

Inside Quinn looked for a note from the realtor but there was nothing. She sighed, it had been too much to hope that the first person to look at the house would want it, but she'd hoped anyway. She wanted to be out from under the huge mortgage payments. Give it time, she told herself, making her way to the bedroom. She was tired. A shower would have to wait until morning.

Within minutes of lying down, she began sneezing. Something was wrong. She turned the light on again, moving the covers and her pillow. Rose petals fell out of the pillow case. "What the...? Who would do that?" She was allergic to roses; already her eyes were itching and her nose was running. She gave a violent sneeze.

The only way to be rid of the scent after lying on the pillow was to take a shower and wash her hair. Sleep would have to wait.

~~~

Sitting in the dark car, she watched Quinn come home, making her way through the house light by light. When the bedroom light went out and moments later come back on, she chuckled. She found the rose petals. I hope she chokes on them. Starting her car, she left Quinn alone for now. She had other plans for the woman.

~~~

"Who did you bring here yesterday? Did you leave them alone in my room?" She called the realtor the next morning, ready to find out how those rose petals got in her pillow case.

"I don't give out the names of the people I show the house to, Ms. Reed. Everything is confidential."

"Did you leave them alone in my room?"

"Are you accusing me of something?" Her voice turned

indignant.

Quinn gave a frustrated sigh. "I'm saying that someone put rose petals in my pillow case. I want to know who you brought in here, and if you left them alone in my room."

"I'll speak with my client, Ms. Reed, but I assure you, I only deal with the upper class of clients. No one would do something like this. My other line is ringing, I need to go."

Before she could say anything else, the realtor hung up, leaving Quinn hanging.

PART TWO
CHAPTER ELEVEN

It had been eight months since Daniel's murder. It seemed like a lifetime ago and just yesterday, all at the same time. The days had crept by, but were gone so fast. School would be out in four short weeks. I still hadn't given Sergio an answer about visiting his mother this summer. The thought of another mother-in-law like the last one was enough to give me hives. The Mrs. DeCosta I remembered was sweet, but I hadn't been a threat then. Marriage had been a long way off for us. How would the woman react now to having her only son getting married?

My hopes that the house would sell fast were gone. I was still waiting to be rid of the albatross. No one wanted to pay what I was asking, but lowering the price wouldn't help me. Without my knowledge, Daniel had forged my signature and taken out a second mortgage with deferred payments for a year. That year was up. Now the bank was expecting monthly payments. Instead of digging my way out of debt, I was getting farther and farther behind. "Thank you, Daniel," I muttered.

The investigation had gone nowhere. There had been other murders, ones with obvious suspects, with evidence left behind. Detective Aguilar hadn't given up yet, but as other murders were committed, Daniel's case was pushed to the bottom of the pile. I couldn't expect him to ignore the recent cases to work one that had been a dead end so far.

Will this end up as one of those cold cases that don't get solved for twenty years? That thought was always with me. I wanted to put this behind me, but how could I while a murderer was loose? I needed to know why Daniel had been killed and who killed him.

He had been far from lily white. It was bad enough to know he had cheated on me, as well as burying me in debt, but to learn he was possibly a crook? That was almost more than I could stand. I hadn't known at the time of his death that the SEC had been investigating him and his entire company. They didn't know, or weren't telling me, if he had been a part of the scheme to defraud their clients, or if he was trying to stop it. I wanted to believe the latter, but I wasn't convinced of that fact. Daniel had been many things, certainly not the man I thought he was when I married him.

~~~

Someone was leaning on the doorbell waking me out of a sound sleep. Stumbling out of bed, I headed for the front door. Whoever was there refused to be ignored. But I wasn't ignoring him. It was still the middle of the night, and I'd been sound asleep.

Stopping with my hand on the door knob, I remembered to check the security peep hole to see who was there before opening the door. Rick Frost, Daniel's former boss, was leaning drunkenly against the house. Even through the small peep hole I could tell anger was boiling through him.

"Mr. Frost, what..."

"Give me my damn papers," he shouted, cutting me off. "I've given you the last dime you're ever going to get."

"You're drunk. I don't know what you're talking about." I could smell alcohol even through the screen door.

"I told you I want my papers. I'm through paying you. Blackmail is against the law, you know." He rattled the screen, trying to get in.

"Blackmail? I don't know what you're talking about. Go home and sleep it off." I started to close the door. His next words stopped me cold.

"I've paid you a half million bucks. That's all you're getting," he growled. "Now give me my damn papers." He pounded on the screen. It wouldn't take much more punishment before he put a hole in it. Then what would I do?

"I don't have your papers. I've told you that, and I don't have your money either. I don't know..." My words ran out when a light bulb went off in my mind. "Eunice, did she..." Her name came out on a breathy whisper. Had she been blackmailing him, letting him believe I was the one doing it? That sounded like something she'd do.

"Eunice? Who's Eunice?" I hadn't meant for him to hear me, but it was too late.

"Go home, Mr. Frost. You're drunk." The alcohol fumes coming through the screen were strong enough to knock me over as his breath heaved out. I shut the door, hoping he would take my advice and sleep it off. Maybe he would forget this whole conversation in the morning.

Sleep didn't come easily for the rest of the night. Whatever papers he'd been searching for, Eunice must have had them the entire time. Whatever was on those papers had to be incriminating for him to give her five hundred thousand dollars in an effort to get them back. Was this the evidence the SEC had been searching for? Would it prove Daniel's innocence or his guilt? Did I even want to know?

Barnard Reed called three days later asking if I'd heard from Eunice. It was only seven in the morning, and I was far from being mentally alert, but his question didn't make sense. "Why would she call me? She hated the very ground I walked on."

"She hasn't been home for the last three nights. I'm beginning to worry about her." He sounded distraught. Was he really worried? Their marriage was contentious at best, hateful most of the time. Although they'd been married for close to thirty years, Barnard had been cheating on her most of that time.

"Did you call the police to file a missing persons report?" He made some noise I couldn't understand. "She enjoys going to the Caribbean," I suggested. "Maybe she went there for a vacation."

"Vacation from what?" he snapped before gaining control of himself again. "She's never worked. What does she need a vacation from? Besides, all of her clothes are still here. None of her luggage is missing either. Quinn, I'm afraid something terrible has happened to her."

Maybe I had misjudged him. He was more upset than I'd ever known him to be. "If she's been gone for three days, you need to let the police know."

"Will you go with me to see them?"

"Why would you want me to go with you?" I objected.

"Just call them. Someone will come to you, or they will take the information over the phone. I don't know how this works."

"You've dealt with the police before, Quinn. I don't want to do this alone." Was this all for show? Was he more concerned about Eunice or himself?

"Barnard, I can't take time off from work. If you think something has happened to her, you need to call them now. Has she been sick or depressed lately?"

"For a long while after Daniel's death she was very distraught, but lately she had been acting…" He paused, trying to find the right word. "Squirrely is about the only way I can describe how she has been. You mentioned the Caribbean; she's gone there twice since Daniel's death."

"Would she go there without taking any clothes with her? Do you have property there?"

He gave a snort of disgust. "Nothing fancy enough for her. We had a time-share, but that was never good enough for her. Every time she came home, all she did was complain about how provincial it was; that she deserved something better. I finally sold it. She wasn't happy about that either."

Now he sounded like the old Barnard. "Call the police. Tell them what you've told me, and let them handle it. I really need to get ready for work." Without waiting for him to argue, I hung up. I didn't understand why he had called me. He knew Eunice hated me. There was no way she would contact me about anything.

The conversation with Barnard ran through my mind while I put the finishing touches on my makeup. My hand froze in midair as I thought about Rick Frost's middle of the night visit. He heard me say Eunice's name. Did he know who that was? Were those papers so incriminating he would harm Eunice to get them back? Of course he would, I answered my own question. He'd paid her a half million dollars hoping to get them back.

"What do I do now? If Eunice has gone missing, it's a safe bet Rick Frost had something to do with it." I absently brushed my hair while I tried to decide what to do. I didn't think Detective Aguilar handled missing persons' cases, but he could point me to the right person. Had Barnard already called the police? It still didn't make sense for him to call me. What did he think I could do for him?

"Oh, crap." I put my brush down, and went to get the phone. I had to tell someone that Rick Frost might have done something to her.

"Detective Aguilar," he barked as he answered the phone. It had been a busy morning already, and the day didn't look like it was going to get any better.

"Oh, you're there." I was surprised he was at his desk this early in the morning.

"If you didn't think I'd be here, why did you call? Who is this?"

Although I had spoken to him many times over the past months to see if there was anything new on Daniel's murder, it had been several months since I last spoke to him. There was no reason he would expect a call from me now. "Um, this is Quinn Reed, Detective. I'm sorry to bother you this early. I was just going to leave you a message. I'm not sure if you're the person I need to talk to, but I didn't know who else to call." My mouth was running at top speed, and I couldn't seem to stop myself from babbling.

He drew a deep breath, releasing it slowly. "I'm sorry, Ms. Reed. I didn't mean to be so…rude?" It turned out to be a question instead of a statement. "What can I do for you this morning? Are you all right?"

My explanation about the call from Barnard was rather

convoluted. "If something happened to Eunice, Rick Frost probably did it," I finished, knowing I wasn't making much sense.

"Why don't you start at the beginning?" he asked with another sigh.

I hurried through my explanation about the papers Rick Frost had been looking for, and the five hundred thousand dollars he said he'd paid to get them back. I'd told him about the papers before, but apparently he'd forgotten about them. He was busy, and I still needed to get ready for work.

"Okay, I'll pass this information on to the Missing Persons' desk. Thank you for calling." I wanted to ask my usual question, but I also knew he would call if he had anything new on Daniel's murder. I was about to hang up, when his question stopped me "Are things going okay for you?"

"Ah, yes, I'm doing all right." I wasn't sure what he meant. He must know I was seeing Sergio. He had never been completely convinced of Sergio's innocence in Daniel's murder, but he couldn't prove it either. In my heart, I knew Sergio wasn't capable of something like that, but the police needed more than a woman's heart.

"Well, take care, Ms. Reed. If you ever need anything, don't hesitate to call." He gave a small chuckle. "I'll try not to bite your head off next time." He hung up before I could respond.

I barely made it through the laundry room from the garage that evening when someone began pounding on the front door, ignoring the fact that there was a doorbell. Why were people always pounding on my door? Why don't they leave me alone? I didn't think Rick Frost would come back.

"Open up, bitch. I know you're in there." I didn't recognize the voice. When he started pounding on the frosted window beside the door, I hurried to the foyer. Looking through the security peep hole, I groaned, leaning my head on the door. What more could happen today?

"I know you're in there, bitch," he yelled again. "I'm not going away, so you might as well open the damn door." He hit the thick glass again hard enough to make it rattle.

"Okay, okay, don't break the glass." I opened the heavy door as far as the chain lock allowed. Sergio had insisted I add it to my assortment of locks; now I was thankful. The screen door was locked, but it wouldn't take much for him to punch a hole through the decorative screening. "What do you want, Mr. Tucker?" Bobby Tucker's father glared at me. If looks could kill, I'd drop over right there.

"I wanted you to know I've served my time. I'm out, and you're going to be sorry you ever crossed my path."

"That sounds like a threat, Mr. Tucker. Do you want to go back to jail so soon after you got your freedom?" I tried hard to keep my voice from shaking. My heart was pounding hard enough to jump out of my chest.

"Oh, I'm not going back in. You took my kids away from me, and got me thrown in jail because I was defending my rights."

"I didn't take your kids away from you. The state took them away to protect them from an abusive father. What rights were you protecting when you broke into my house, beat me up, and stole my television?"

"Nobody's going to tell me how to make my boys mind what I say," he growled. He was getting more agitated the longer he talked. I wasn't going to change his mind about hitting those two little boys. Abusers rarely saw their actions as wrong.

"You need to leave, and never come back here. I *will* call the police, and you *will* be arrested again. Is that what you want?"

He punched the screen as though it was my face, a small tear appearing where his fist hit. Another blow like that, and he would be able to reach through for my throat. "I'm calling the police. If you don't want to be arrested again, I suggest you leave now." I shut the door, flipping the key in the lock. Two more fierce blows to the screen and his heavy fist landed on the inside door.

"Please God, let this stop. Make him go away." My whispered words were heartfelt and sincere. My cell phone was in my purse in the kitchen. I needed to call nine-one-one before he could break through the inner door.

"Nine-one-one, what is your emergency?" The calm voice on the other end of the line helped to calm me enough to respond coherently.

"Someone is trying to break into my house. I need you to send the police."

"What is your location, ma'am?" Because I was on my cell phone, she didn't know my address. "A car is on the way," she responded once I gave it to her. "I'll remain on the line until the officer gets there. Is there a safe place for you to hide in case he gets inside?" She continued calmly talking to me until I heard sirens, but it was too late. The pounding on the door had stopped. He was gone for now, but I didn't think I'd seen the last of him.

CHAPTER TWELVE

Eunice's body was found in a landfill outside of town three days after Barnard called the police. Rick Frost was arrested for her murder. "I'm sorry, Barnard." It was the only thing I could think to say. I didn't believe he loved her, but they had been together for a long time. He had to feel something, some loss.

"Thank you, Quinn." His warm, clammy hands gripped my much colder ones. Was he nervous about something, or just upset about losing his wife? "She wasn't the easiest person to get along with," he admitted, "but she was still my wife."

I didn't know what else to say. How do you show sorrow for someone you never liked? "At least they caught the person who did this." It didn't take a rocket scientist to know what I was thinking; Daniel's killer was still on the loose. Had Rick Frost also killed him? He had admitted killing Eunice, claiming self-preservation, not self-defense mind you, because she was bleeding him dry. I wasn't aware there was such a defense. Of course he denied having anything to do with Daniel's murder.

Barnard let go of my hands, moving across the living room to sink down on the white couch Eunice had let few people sit on. Maybe now he could sit comfortably in his own home. "Did they recover the papers or the money he paid her to get them back?"

He gave his head a shake, lifting one shoulder in a shrug. "I have no idea what they found. They aren't telling me anything. The SEC is all over that company like fleas on a dog. Daniel isn't going to come out of this mess looking very good either. I'm sorry about that, Quinn."

Against my better wishes, I spent the entire weekend consoling the man without figuring out why he was so distraught. Yes, his wife had just been murdered, but he had never acted like he cared for her. So why was he upset about her death? Or was it something else? He hadn't been this upset when Daniel died. I didn't know what to make of him. I didn't know why he wanted me with him either. He never seemed to care one way or the other about me.

The winding street was dark when I returned home Sunday evening. "What is wrong with these lights?" I asked the empty car. Every other week it seemed that one or more of the street lights on the twisting road were on the blink. At least the light in the garage came on when the door lifted to let me drive in.

After the second break-in, I had put motion sensor lights in most of the rooms. As I went from room to room I left a trail of light in my wake, giving me a sense of security. Walking down the hall to my bedroom, the faint scent of roses tickled my nose, bringing on a fit of sneezing. Roses again, I thought. Had the realtor brought someone to look at the house? When I had questioned her about the rose petals in my bed after her first and only open house, she denied any knowledge of it.

Waving my hand to activate the light before I went into the room, I searched for the source of that scent. Nothing was out of place; at least I didn't think so. I'm not as paranoid as Daniel had been, but I was getting close. Because the house was for sale, realtors could bring people through while I was at school. This wasn't the first time the scent of roses had been present when I came home. It always seemed to center around my bedroom. Once again I would be sleeping in the guest room to get away from the sickening scent.

~~~

Sitting in the dark car, she chuckled as she watched the light in the guest room come on. Tormenting her was entertaining, but it wasn't getting her what she wanted. She needed to concentrate on her main objective. He needed to know his place, to pay for what he had done. Getting that stupid detective to cooperate was the problem. A body in his car would certainly get his attention, and she knew just who to choose.

~~~

At Barnard's request, I went to Eunice's funeral with him. His insistence that I be with him so much still puzzled me, but without sounding unfeeling, I didn't know how I could refuse. He knew I was seeing Sergio, but he had asked that he didn't accompany me. "It would look bad if my daughter-in-law showed up with a date." He didn't seem to care that one of his mistresses came to offer her condolences. Her actions shouted out the intimacy they had shared.

She looked familiar, but I couldn't place where I'd seen her before. At barely five feet in her stocking feet, she was several inches shorter than me, but the four-inch heels put her at my height. The short, tight dress left little to the imagination, drawing the attention of every man in the room.

"Barnard, darling, I was so sorry to hear about what happened to your dear wife." She placed her slim hands on his shoulders to steady herself as she leaned up to place a kiss on his cheek. In those shoes, she had to be on her tiptoes already, but somehow she managed to get a little higher.

The woman held Barnard's hand a little longer than necessary before moving away. For a split second her eyes rested on me, but she didn't say anything. A shiver traveled up my spine at that look. Then a smirk lifted the corners of her pouty mouth. What was that about, I wondered? I was still having trouble remembering where I'd seen her before.

Barnard didn't bother to introduce her, or anyone else for that matter, which was just as well. There were a great many people that I didn't know and wouldn't remember if I was introduced to them. But that woman I wouldn't forget any time soon. I just wished I could remember where I'd seen her before. As she walked away, I sneezed as the sickly sweet scent of roses settled over me. Looking over her shoulder, she winked at me. "Bless you." Her voice was soft with a slight accent. Her laughter floated back to me as she walked out of the funeral home.

Barnard was enjoying the attention everyone was paying him, and didn't notice that my attention was now riveted on the young woman as she left. She'd been in my house; I just didn't know how to prove it.

"Who was that woman?" I tried to get Barnard's attention.

"Huh? What woman?" His mind was occupied with another beautiful young woman. Probably another mistress, I thought. He'd already forgotten the one who just left. Eunice was even farther from his mind.

~~~

"Will you marry me, Quinn?" Sergio's voice was a soft caress. This wasn't the first time he'd asked. He was trying to be patient.

"You must know I want to, but I need to know who killed Daniel and why."

He pulled me into his arms, kissing my eyes, my cheeks before placing a gentle kiss on my lips. "Are you willing to wait until the end of time for that to happen? I have spent every day possible with you since you were hurt. I would spend every night as well if you allowed me. I have loved you forever." This time his kiss was filled with passion and promise. By the time we came up for air, we were both breathless.

"I want to take care of you, protect you," he whispered against my lips. "Will you let me do that?"

"I don't need someone to take care of me," I argued, pulling back, looking up at him. "That isn't what a marriage is about. We take care of each other."

I took his face in my hands, placing my lips on his. He released the breath he had been holding. He playfully pulled me against him, holding me tight. "I have found you again, and I will never let go this time. I am through running." He grew serious, his dark eyes growing even darker. I didn't think he was talking about us now. There seemed to be a deeper meaning behind his words, but he didn't give me a chance to question him. He ran his fingers over my ribs, finding that special spot that was so sensitive, so ticklish. Within minutes we were rolling around on the couch, laughing like a couple of kids between the kisses we shared.

It was much later when he left. The good-byes were growing longer each time he left. I stood at the front door watching his car disappear into the night. The street lights were back on. But for how long, I wondered? I still didn't know why they kept going out. You'd think the county would be wondering that as well when they had to come out so often to fix them.

Turning to go inside, I stopped when car lights came on up the incline from the house. Mine was the last house on the winding lane. Why was a car parked up there?

Tom had been back at work for a while, and was avoiding me like I had the plague. Was he still spying on me? Who else would be watching my house? The dark-colored car crept past. The windows were so dark I couldn't even make out the silhouette of the driver. A shiver moved up my spine. There was something sinister about that slow-moving car. The click of the lock was loud as I twisted the key.

If you couldn't see the person inside, why are you so afraid, I asked myself. My heart was pounding, my hands shaking uncontrollably. "Get a grip, girl," I admonished aloud. "It was probably just teenagers taking advantage of the dark street to make out. They got spooked when they saw me standing at the door." No matter how many times I repeated that, I knew better.

Rushing to get my cell phone from my purse in the bedroom, I dialed Sergio. He needed to know someone might be following him. He couldn't be very far down the mountain yet. After the sixth ring, his phone went to voice mail. Why didn't he answer? He has hands free availability in his car. All he had to do was push a button on the steering wheel. "Sergio, I think someone is following you. Please be careful." I disconnected, redialing immediately. Again it went to voice mail after six rings.

Cell service in the mountains is spotty at best, but if neither of us had service, the call wouldn't have gone through at all. So why wasn't he answering? Had the driver of that dark car already run him off the road? Why would anyone do that? The easy answer: Antony Marconi was behind the wheel of that car. Would he harm his own son? I dialed Sergio's number again just to be sure. "Please God, take care of him," I whispered. "He's a good man, and I love him."

When voice mail picked up once again, I grabbed my purse and car keys. If I couldn't raise him on the phone, something had happened to him. The garage door moved in slow motion while I waited for it open. "Come on, come on," I muttered, tapping my fingers on the steering wheel as though that would make the door move faster.

After what felt like a lifetime, it was fully open, and I reversed out of the garage ignoring the speed limit once I hit the street. There was only one way from my house to reach the main road through Greenbrier. After that, there were several different roads leading to the highway. All of them were steep and winding. A misjudgment on a curve or a push from behind at the wrong time, and you go flying out into emptiness. I had no idea which one Sergio would take. How far had he gone in the short time since he left me?

This was like reliving Daniel's murder all over again, only now I was aware as it happened. Was Daniel's killer following Sergio? Why would someone want to murder both of the men in my life? I gripped the steering wheel tighter. I couldn't lose him after just finding him again. "Please God, keep him safe." I repeated my prayer over and over as I drove.

At each turnout, I slowed down hoping to find the dark car parked there. If it really was teenagers using the dark lane for a make-out session, they would stop to finish what got started earlier. Each turnout was empty. There were many areas where a car could go over, plunging to a certain death. The guard rails were all firmly in place, no breaks anywhere. That was a good sign, right? I asked myself. If that car had run Sergio over the cliff, there would be an indication somewhere.

By the time I reached the highway with no sign of Sergio's car or the dark one following him, I began to relax. Or had he taken a different road down the mountain? Was he lying in a heap at the bottom of another road? I hadn't seen the dark car anywhere along the route either. My hands began shaking again as adrenaline pumped back into my body. I had to make sure he was safe.

Should I turn back, taking one of the different side roads? Or keep going to his condo in Denver? I tried one more time to call him. Off the twists and turns of the mountain, my call went through with no problem.

"Hello, Darling." He answered on the first ring. "Do you miss me so much you couldn't wait for me to call when I got home?" he joked. "I am still close enough that I can come back if you like." To ease my fears, he called each night to let me know he made it home safely.

"Sergio, someone followed you when you left my house." Even to my own ears, that sounded more than a little paranoid. "Are you okay?" Assured that he was safe, the adrenaline drained from my body leaving me weak and sick to my stomach.

He talked me down off the edge of my fear, but I needed to see he was safe. The past eight months left me feeling fearful in the extreme. He waited for me at the first fast food joint, pulling me into his arms as soon as I shut the car off.

"Come home with me, *mi amour*, I do not want you driving up that mountain while you are still upset."

Finally able to laugh at my escapade, I touched his face. "I'm going to be fine. I've driven that road many times in the last few years. Besides, no one's after me. You're the one being followed. Or so I thought." I tried to laugh it off. "It was probably just teenagers looking for a lovers' lane, and I spooked them."

A few kisses later, we went our separate ways. In spite of my insistence I was safe, I kept a close watch on my rearview mirror. It was after ten by then. The roads weren't well traveled this time of night. Most sensible people stay off the unlit, twisting roads after dark. As I pulled into the garage, my phone rang. Sergio wouldn't be home yet, but he probably wanted to make sure I made it back safe and sound.

"Hello, Darling." My greeting was met with a harsh laugh.

"Well, hello, would you like me to come over now that your lover is gone?"

"Who is this?"

"Your darling, of course. Isn't that what you just said?" He gave that same harsh laugh, sending chills up my spine. I was still sitting in my car. The garage door was down, but I didn't feel safe. How easy would it be for someone to get through that door?

Shutting off the car also ended the call. I made a mad dash for the laundry room door. "Don't let him be in there, God." I found myself praying a great deal more since Daniel's death. It was something I needed to make a habit of doing, not just when I had problems, but all the time.

Everything was as it should be as I walked throughout the house, motion sensor lights clicking on as I went. I couldn't wait to be rid of this monstrous house.

~~~

"How long does it take to sell a house?" I complained to Jenn Jones, my realtor. It sounded like a phony name to me. I was in a foul mood. After the race down the mountain last night and the harassing caller, today had gone downhill from there.

Mrs. Grant, the principal at school, had informed me

that my contract wasn't being renewed for next year. No surprise after all that had happened. But it still hurt, and scared me to death. Most of what had happened wasn't my fault, but I was the one being punished all the same. What was I going to do? I still had more bills to pay than money, mostly because of this stupid house. I was really getting to hate it.

Jenn gave a phony little laugh to go with her phony little name. "These things take time. It hasn't been that long since you listed the house."

"I don't have time," I wailed into the phone. "I need to sell this place. Now." I wasn't going to tell her my tale of woe, but I needed to impress upon her how desperate I was getting.

"Then you need to lower your price."

"That won't help me out of the spot I'm in. You know I have two mortgages to pay off. The current price will just cover those, leaving nothing to spare." I wanted to add that her commission would take a big chunk, but wisely kept that thought to myself.

"I'm sorry, Quinn. I understand, really I do. The market is soft right now." There was a shrug in her voice. She didn't sound sorry at all. She didn't get that hefty commission unless she sold the house, so why wasn't she working harder to get the job done?

I hung up the phone a few minutes later, dissatisfied with the conversation. Her suggestion that I walk away from the house, letting the mortgage company and bank fight it out over who gets whatever they could sell the place for didn't sit well with me. What kind of realtor was she? She wouldn't get her commission, and I would get a giant black mark on my credit.

What else could go wrong with this horrible day?

CHAPTER THIRTEEN

I'd only been in the house a few minutes when the doorbell rang. I hesitated, undecided about answering. Too many things had been happening lately. When the bell rang a second time, I reluctantly opened the door. As long as the screen was locked, nothing could happen, I reasoned. I was wrong. He didn't have to touch me to turn things on end again.

"Hello, Mrs. Reed." The man standing on my front steps was in his seventies, maybe older; his white hair was still thick with a slight wave to it. His broad shoulders were beginning to droop with age or sickness. "Do you know who I am?"

"How would I know you? I've never seen you before." I played dumb, but there was no doubt in my mind who this man was. This is how Sergio will look in thirty or forty years, still handsome, still proud in his bearing.

"My name is Antony Marconi." He said it with pride, like the name should mean something to everyone.

"I'm sorry, am I supposed to know the name?" His shoulders drooped even further.

"My son hasn't mentioned me?" he asked hopefully.

"Your son? I'm sorry I don't know who you're talking about. I don't know anyone by that name." Sergio didn't want to have anything to do with this man. I wasn't going to help him in any way. If that wasn't reason enough, the man was a mobster. I didn't want anything to do with him either.

"You know him as Sergio DeCosta," he spit out the name like it left a foul taste in his mouth. "His birth name is Dominic Marconi, but he prefers to use another man's name. You tell him his father was here to see him." The fact that he knew of my relationship with Sergio and where I lived was unsettling.

"Why don't you tell him?" I worked hard to keep my voice from quivering.

"He will not see me." I could see how much that admission cost him. He turned back to the black limousine waiting for him in the drive. His back was ramrod straight, his shoulders stiff. Anger radiated off him in waves.

A chauffer opened the passenger door for him. Someone else was in the car waiting for him. I gasped, staring at the beautiful woman from Eunice's funeral. Her eyes locked with mine keeping me rooted to the spot. What was she doing with Antony Marconi? I had assumed she was one of Barnard's many mistresses, and that was why she been at the funeral. Was she now Antony Marconi's mistress? I was certain she had been in my house, but why? How had she gotten in? What did she have to do with me? A memory teased at my mind, but I couldn't grasp it long enough to see it clearly.

I hadn't told Sergio about my caller last night, but this was something I couldn't keep from him. He needed to know Antony Marconi was in town hoping to see him. Maybe he could tell me who the beautiful woman with Marconi was. I struggled to remember where I had seen her before Eunice's funeral.

I paced through the house waiting for Sergio to arrive. How should I broach the subject of Antony Marconi? With no clear plan of what to say, the words tumbled out as soon as he arrived.

"He didn't try to harm you?" His voice shook with barely contained anger. "What did he want?"

"He wanted to see you. He expected me to know who he was. In fact, he was disappointed when I played ignorant. He certainly has an inflated opinion of himself."

Sergio laughed, which was my intention. "He certainly does." Growing serious again, he drew a deep breath, letting it out slowly. "All my life I have avoided that man. Even when I lived in his house I avoided him. I have confused strength with violence. Instead I have been weak, a coward." He was talking to himself as much as to me.

Pulling him into my arms, I tried to comfort him, be

117

there for him, the way he's been there for me. "It takes strength of character to avoid violence when it's all around you, when people are trying to make you into something you're not. I'll always be there beside you, so will God." For the first time in a long time I felt God's presence with me, not because He had turned away from me, but because I had turned away from Him.

"That man always went to church," Sergio stated, "then he would spread his violence, his vile corruption everywhere he went. Another thing I confused because of that man. No more. I will see him, one last time; I will stand up to him."

That was easier said than done. Setting up a meeting with Antony Marconi was harder than getting an appointment with the president. He wanted Sergio to know he was looking for him, but he wanted to set the time and place. He didn't make it known where he was staying, and of course he hadn't left a number with me where he could be reached.

I could only imagine what Detective Aguilar would think of this latest development. Did he even know Marconi was in Colorado? Probably, I decided. If the FBI had been monitoring Sergio's activities when he came to see me the first time, they had to be aware that Marconi himself had come to see me.

I didn't have to wonder for long. Detective Aguilar was at my door bright and early Saturday morning. "Hello, Ms. Reed. I'd like to ask you some questions." He waited impatiently for me to unlock the door to let him come in.

It had been several months since we last spoke. There had been nothing new on Daniel's murder. Whoever killed him was still running around loose. But that wasn't why he was here this time.

"What can I do for you today, Detective? Would you care for a cup of coffee?" I hadn't had my first cup yet. This wasn't a social visit, but I needed caffeine to fortify myself. He gave me a curt nod, still without saying anything. The silent treatment must be a cop tactic to make a suspect nervous. I might not be a suspect, but I was nervous anyway. His stern expression told me he wasn't any happier about this meeting than I was.

"Why was Antony Marconi here yesterday?" he finally asked after taking a sip of his coffee. "And don't tell me you don't know who he is."

"He came to tell me he wanted to see Sergio."

"Why tell you? Why doesn't he just go see his son?" His dark frown said he didn't really believe me.

"Because Sergio won't see him," I lifted my shoulders in a shrug, like the answer should be easy to figure out.

"And what did DeCosta say about the message?"

"Why are you asking Quinn these questions when you should be asking me?" Sergio came in through the laundry room without either of us noticing until he spoke. He placed a light kiss on top of my head before turning back to the detective.

"All right, I'll ask you. What are you going to do about the message from your father?"

Sergio released a heavy sigh. "He is not my father. Call him a sperm donor, or anything else you want, but he is not and has never been a father to me. What I am going to do is go see him, if I can find where he is staying. That is top secret knowledge I am not privileged to. I suppose he will get in contact with me when he is ready to stop playing his little game."

"What game is that?" The detective lifted one dark brow questioningly.

Sergio gave a humorless laugh. "I wish I knew. He came to tell Quinn he wants to see me; then he is unreachable. This is how the man works. Keep people off balance, keep them on edge. Then when you least expect it, he springs his trap."

"What trap is he setting for you?"

Again Sergio shrugged. "Do you know where the man is staying?" he asked. "You and the FBI seem to know more about him than I do." He waited for the detective to answer.

It was his turn to shrug. "I'm not privileged to that information either. The FBI is stonewalling me." He didn't sound the least bit happy about that situation either. Without getting the answers he wanted or hoped for, the detective left a few minutes later.

I wanted to ask about the case against Rick Frost, whether they knew yet if he had killed Daniel, but decided this wasn't the time. There had been very little in the newspaper since his arrest. Had they found the papers he wanted? Had they found the money he said he paid Eunice? I hadn't heard from Barnard since Eunice's funeral more than a week ago either. Maybe I was finally through with that crazy family.

Pulling me into his arms, Sergio held me for a long moment. "I am sorry to drag you into this with that man," he finally spoke. "I wish I could whisk you away to someplace he would never find either of us. But like the long arm of the law, La Cosa Nostra also has a long reach." The American phrase sounded odd coming from him.

~~~

By Monday everyone knew which teachers wouldn't be returning the following year. Tina was jubilant over the fact that I was one of those who wouldn't be returning. "It's too bad you won't be with us again next year," she sneered. The smirk on her face told a very different story. "Do you have any prospects for next year?" If I told her the truth, I was sure she would do a little happy dance at my dismal-looking future.

Sergio had been asking me to marry him for several months, but I couldn't do that with this mess hanging over my head. My credit rating was in the toilet, and until I could sell that stupid house I wouldn't drag him down with me.

"Teachers are always in demand," I stated with a flippant shrug, hoping that would throw her off the scent of my blood. "It won't be hard to get another job." None of that was true. Schools are always the first things cut when state budgets are tight. Teachers are always the first to be let go when school budgets are tight. Administrators didn't have to worry though.

Tina must have known all that as well. She just smiled sweetly. "Well, good luck. I think you're going to need it." She made it a point to see me as often as possible for the remainder of the week, always with a happy sneer on her face.

Tom had a different reaction. "I'm sorry if anything I did or said had anything to do with the fact your contract wasn't renewed, Quinn." He didn't come all the way into my room at the end of the day. His voice was soft, and he looked truly sorry.

I tried to act casual about the whole thing. "It's all for the best. After everything that's happened in the past year, I need a change of scenery." Until I said the words, I didn't realize how true they were. Greenbrier didn't hold a lot of happy memories for me.

"Good luck. I hope life is better for you from here on." His shoulders drooped as he turned to leave.

~~~

It was the last day of school until the fall, *my* last day period. The knowledge that I was unemployed was frightening. I had no money coming in, but there were still bills that needed to be paid. Creditors didn't care that you were out of a job, they still wanted their money. If the realtor would do something besides give me a song and dance about how the market was soft right now and nothing was selling fast, I could get out from under all of this.

The fact that I had gone through one hundred and fifty thousand dollars and still didn't have all my bills paid off, left me dumbstruck. Why hadn't I known Daniel was digging us deeper and deeper into debt all the time? Why hadn't I paid closer attention to finances? Is that why he went along with the crooked scheme to defraud their clients?

I had learned the check Rick Frost gave me under the pretext that it was insurance money had really been an attempt to bribe me into giving him the papers, papers I didn't even have. Would the authorities ever be able to find where Eunice hid them, or find the money he paid her? I was grateful I didn't have to return the money from that check. That would have put me in an even deeper hole.

Stepping into the kitchen, I was still preoccupied with these thoughts when the cloying scent of roses caught my attention with a sneeze. "Bless you." I let out a startled squeal, whirling around to face the young woman who'd been in the limousine with Antony Marconi.

"Who are you? What are you doing in my house? How did you get in here?" The questions tumbled out one top of the other without waiting for an answer. My fists were braced on my hips. I sneezed again spoiling my angry glare.

She gave a trilling laugh. "Oh, I have been in here many times." She laughed again, enjoying my surprise and anger.

"That isn't what I asked. Now answer me!" Another sneeze shook me. By now the scent was making my eyes water and my nose run.

"Which would you like me to answer first?" She was making fun of me and enjoying it.

I sniffed, then sneezed again. "Why don't you just start at the top and work your way down?"

"Later. I came to tell you to stay away from Sergio. You are not part of the Family. You are not good for him. He needs to know his place; he belongs with the Family, not with someone like you." Her light blue eyes darkened with hatred as she stared at me.

"What am I like?" I didn't know what she was talking about, but for now I'd play along.

"You are not in the Family. You need to leave him alone."

"What family is that?" Keep her talking, I told myself; maybe she'll give away more information than she wants to.

122

"Why don't you explain what you're talking about?" I rubbed my eyes even though I knew that would only make them itch worse. I needed to get her out of the house along with the nauseating scent of roses.

"Listen to me, or you will be sorry. Stay out of Family business." The way she said family, sounded like it should start with a capital F.

"What business is that?" It was getting hard for me to breathe. The strong scent of roses was making my head feel like it was stuffed with cotton, making it hard to think.

"Never mind!" She snapped, slipping off the bar stool. "Tell Sergio I am through playing games. He is to come see his father, or he will be sorry. You will be sorry," she snarled. Without another word, she pushed past me, knocking me against the wall. I sneezed again. The front door slammed hard enough to rattle the windows.

With the door banging shut, the memory that had been eluding me clicked in, knocking me harder than she had. "She was at Daniel's funeral!" I whispered, sinking down on the nearest bar stool to keep from falling over.

Why had she been at Daniel's funeral? She knew Barnard; that much had been obvious. Had she come to Daniel's funeral to lend 'moral' support to Barnard, or was there a deeper reason? Had Daniel and Barnard shared her as their mistress? Had she killed Daniel, hoping to push the blame onto Sergio?

She said he was to go see 'his father'. It had been nothing short of an order. She didn't tell me where Sergio could find him though. Did the Mafia have women enforcers now? She was part of the Marconi Family, but where did she fit in? In the confusion after Marconi had paid me a visit, I failed to tell Sergio that she had been in the limo with him.

She looked about the same age as Sergio. If she just worked for that family, she wouldn't have known him before his mother took him away. How did she know him if he'd never had anything to do with them? Had he been lying to me this whole time? I felt like I was trapped in a whirlwind with no way to get out.

I put my head down on the breakfast bar. "What am I to do, Father? Please tell me if I've made another mistake. Are my heart and my head so easily led astray that I will believe anything a man tells me?" For once I was grateful Sergio was out of town on business. Before I saw him again, I needed to sort through this mess.

CHAPTER FOURTEEN

With no job and no immediate prospects until I heard from one of the schools where I'd sent my resume and application, I started packing. If that realtor didn't start doing her job soon, selling the house wouldn't be an option. The bank would come in and kick me out.

While I kept my body busy, my mind wouldn't cooperate and stay away from all my troubles. Sergio would be home today. He called last night after...I didn't even know her name. What was I supposed to call her?

The conversation with Sergio had been strained, but I couldn't think of anything to say without telling him about that woman's visit. I wanted to see his face when I told him about her, hoping to be able to tell if he was lying. Because of Daniel's betrayal with his many women, I was no longer a very trusting person.

It was clear she knew Sergio, but I didn't know how. She also knew Barnard and Daniel. Had she been mistress to all three of them? If I asked Sergio, would he deny it? Of course he would, I answered silently. What man in his right mind would admit to something like that unless he was caught red-handed, or with his pants down?

I hated where my mind was taking me, but what was I supposed to think? Her veiled hints had hit their target.

"Hello there, darling." A gruff voice came up behind me as I sorted through the few items Eunice had returned from the garage. It was hot for the first week of June, and I had the big doors open to let in some air. Unwittingly, I'd also let in someone looking to hurt me.

With a startled screech, I whirled around holding out the broom I'd been using like it was a weapon. Bobby Tucker's father stood between me and escape down the driveway. The house door wasn't close enough for me to reach before he would be on me. His nasty chuckle sent chills up my spine.

"What are you doing here? You need to leave." My voice quivered, despite my effort to keep it from doing so. I kept the broom handle pointed at him. I wasn't sure what I would do with it if he came any closer.

"I just thought I'd pay you a visit. You know, since you think I'm your darling and all." He took a menacing step towards me. He'd left several suggestive messages on my phone since I made the mistake of answering without checking caller ID.

"You need to leave, now," I emphasized.

"Not yet," he growled. "I came to tell you I'm getting my boys back, no thanks to you. The county don't want to take care of them no longer. I told you you'd be sorry for making me lose them, and getting me thrown in jail. Well, now it's time for payback." He reached out, grabbing the broom handle, yanking me towards him.

He didn't expect me to let go, and he fell backwards when I did, landing on his backside with a grunt. With the breath knocked out of him, he sat there just long enough for me to make it to the laundry room door. The lock clicked into place seconds before he reached for the door knob.

"You bitch; open this door or I'll break it down. You're gonna pay for what you did." He kicked or hit the door, then let out a strangled scream of his own. I had no idea what had happened. All I could hear through the heavy door was scuffling and crashing. Someone was being knocked into things in the garage.

As quietly as possible, I released the lock on the door, opening it just a crack. Sergio had Mr. Tucker by the front of his shirt, his fist drawn back to throw another punch. The older man already had a bloody nose and a split lip.

"Sergio, don't. Let him go." I grabbed his arm before he could throw the punch. He released his grip on the other man's shirt, giving him a shove.

"Stay away from Quinn, or you will be the one who is sorry." Mr. Tucker limped down the drive to the clunker sitting at the curb.

"Are you all right?" Sergio crushed me against his chest, kissing my hair before lowering his head to claim my lips in a hard kiss.

Forgetting my doubts about him and the mystery woman, I leaned in allowing him to deepen the kiss. His arms tightened around me, lifting me off the floor. I was caught between him and the door, his hands roaming over my body. When he finally lifted his head, we were both breathing hard. His dark eyes were even darker with passion held barely in check.

"Did he hurt you, *mi amour*? Who was that?" I strained to get my mind back on track.

"I'm fine. Where did you learn to fight like that?" He had said he had always stayed away from violence of any kind, but that isn't what I just saw. Going into the house, and locking the door behind us, Sergio led me into the living room.

"Because I never wanted to be like that man, I would back away from a fight. That does not mean I do not know *how* to fight. Who was he? What did he want?"

I had a lot of explaining to do, and so did he. I needed to know if he had anything to do with the Marconi family or that woman, whoever she was.

In a few short words, I explained about Mr. Tucker. I wanted to dispense with the man as quickly as possible, so I could ask about the woman from the previous night. "Why was he limping? What did you do to him?" All I'd seen was the blood on Tucker's face. What else had Sergio done to him?

He gave a humorless laugh. "I came up the drive in time to see him kick the door. It was more solid than he expected. He might have a broken bone or two in his foot."

That was all the time I wasted talking about the vile man. The woman who had been in my house last night was a different matter. Recounting her surprise visit, I watched his face for signs of recognition.

"What did she look like?" His voice shook with

suppressed rage. "What did she say?"

Describing her wasn't easy. "She was beautiful, exotic." Most men would be unable to avoid falling under her spell, I admitted to myself. Had Sergio been one of them? "Her hair is blue-black and her almond-shaped eyes are a very light blue." I repeated our short conversation as best I could, adding, "She was with Marconi when he came here." His face lost all color; his hands shook as he dragged them through his hair.

"Who is she?" My stomach was tied in knots, waiting to hear what he had to say about this woman.

"I wish you had told me you saw her when Marconi came here. I never would have left you alone for her to come near you."

"Who is she?" I repeated sharply, holding my breath, waiting to learn that she was his lover, or worse, his wife.

He stood up, pacing across the room. It took several minutes before he said anything while my mind conjured up the worst-case scenario. "She is Marconi's daughter, his youngest daughter," he clarified. I strained to hear his whispered words.

"The one you played with when you were little?" That would explain why she was with Marconi, and how she knew Sergio. It didn't explain why she had been at Daniel's and Eunice's funerals.

"The very one. Her name is Sophia. She is more dangerous than her father ever hoped to be. Even as a child she took delight in hurting animals." The breath I'd been holding escaped on a whoosh, relieved it wasn't what I'd been afraid to hear.

He sank down beside me again, taking my hands in his icy one. "Let me take you away from here, cara. She will do anything to get her own way." Too agitated to sit still, he stood up again, pacing across the room.

"But why did she come to see me? Why didn't she just tell you what she wanted?" Like her father she was passing her ultimatum through me instead of talking directly to

Sergio.

"She knows I am in love with you. That makes you a threat to her plans." Pulling me off the couch into his strong arms, he rested his forehead against mine. His eyes were clouded with worry and something akin to fear. "She always wanted me to join with her when she was torturing the animals. When I refused, she called me weak, that I needed to learn what it meant to be a Marconi. When her father allowed me to leave, she vowed that she would bring me back to the Family."

"How old was she?"

"I was eight, she was ten. Even then she took great delight in the fact that her father was feared by so many. She called it our legacy."

She had been a child, I thought. How would she know all that went along with being part of the Mafia? Did they even indoctrinate the children into that way of life?

"How would any of this convince you to join with them? I would think it would have the opposite effect."

He shrugged. "Not if I was accused of a crime, and needed their help to get out of trouble."

I felt like someone had punched me in the stomach, and it left me gasping for breath. "Did she kill Daniel hoping you would be blamed? Did she plan all of this?"

He nodded his dark head. "She is capable of doing something like that. She couldn't have known I left town on a business trip the same day Daniel was killed. It was an unscheduled trip. It proves she isn't capable of manipulating everything to her liking."

"I still don't understand why she was at Daniel's and Eunice's funerals?" Recalling the intimate looks she shared with Barnard, I could guess what her relationship was with him. But why had she gone to Daniel's funeral?

"Do you think she was one of Daniel's mistresses?" I couldn't stop from voicing the question. If so, why would she kill him? Had he known what she was? Who she was? I was still trapped in that whirlwind. My head was spinning with all the questions.

Unable to find the answers I needed, I turned my thoughts to another matter. "How did she get in here yesterday? I'm the only one who has a key. She's also been in here before." Explaining about the rose petals in my bed after the realtor showed the house for the first and only time, the answer was glaringly obvious.

"Somehow she got the combination to the lock box the realtors use. There's a key in there. That's how she keeps getting in." Anger boiled up inside me. Did Jenn Jones deliberately give her the combination, or had Sophia managed that on her own? It could also explain why Jenn had brought no one else to look at the house. Maybe Sophia was paying her not to sell my house. Whatever the case, I needed to fire that realtor and get a new one.

My head hurt from all the twists and turns in this mess. "Can we talk about something else for a while?" I rubbed my temples trying to relieve the tension.

"I know just the thing to make that headache go away." He waggled his eyebrows in a very American gesture. He moved me to the floor with my back to him. It wasn't what I expected him to do, but when his fingers began to work their magic, massaging my shoulders, my neck and my temples, every other thought disappeared from my mind.

I began to relax, really relax, for the first time in nine months. When my head dropped forward giving him better access to my neck, his lips took the place of his fingers. My eyes popped open. I was no longer relaxed. Now I was charged with energy, the kind of which I hadn't felt in seven years.

He moved to the floor beside me. Suddenly we were teenagers again necking on the living room floor in my parents' house. His kisses robbed me of any thoughts as his hands moved down my body exploring, teasing all the sensitive places.

Just when I thought I couldn't take another minute without fulfilling what he was silently promising, he sat up, turning away from me. His breath was as labored as mine. "I need to stop now, or it will be too late." His voice was gruff with reined-in passion. "I promised I would not sleep with you until you were my wife. I intend to keep that promise." He drew in a deep breath, releasing it slowly. "It might kill me, but I will keep it." He stood up, walking away until he had himself under control.

We were both adults with no one to hurt by giving in to our passions, but I knew he was right. We needed to wait. Rearranging my clothes, I drew in a few deep breaths of my own. Never before had I given myself up to passion, forgetting everything else. What did that say about my relationship with Daniel? Had I subconsciously known he wasn't what he pretended to be, or had I held a part of myself from him forcing him to look elsewhere?

For the remainder of the day, we managed to pack up the few things in the garage without bumping into each other. At least not very often. A brush of his hand, a fleeting look in his eyes, had passions smoldering just below the surface again. I wanted him to hold me, to tell me everything was going to be okay, that we would spend the rest of our lives together. But how could either of us know that?

Antony Marconi still hadn't resurfaced. He wanted to see his son, but we had no idea where he was staying. If the FBI knew, they weren't telling us either. I was getting tired of all the head games people were playing. Sophia Marconi was a wild card, or just plain wild. There was no telling what she would do next. Did she even know what she had planned for us?

By five o'clock, we were hot, sweaty and hungry. I was ready to quit. We both needed a shower. "Will you let me take you out for dinner?" Sergio pulled me into his arms, keeping his kisses light.

Until I was able to reach Jenn Jones, I was afraid to leave the house, and afraid to stay there. As long as Sophia had the combination to the lock box, she had free access to my house. I didn't want to walk in and find her waiting for me again.

Jenn wasn't returning my calls though. How do you fire your realtor when you can't reach her? The company she worked for wasn't very helpful either. Without the combination to the lock box myself, I couldn't keep Sophia out if she decided to visit me again. For now, we opted for delivery.

Much later, we took a long time to say good night. His nibbling kisses on my lips, along my jaw, were light, teasing. He was as reluctant to leave as I was to have him go. He could stay here in the guest room, but did either of us trust our will power to stay in the proper bedrooms? I had to chuckle at the thought.

"Care to share the joke?" He cocked one eyebrow at me. The foyer was dark with only the muted light from the living room, leaving everything in shadows.

"I was picturing us sneaking into the other's bedroom if you stayed here tonight."

He gulped. "Please, do not tempt me. I am trying to be honorable."

I placed a kiss under his jaw, nipping at his neck. "I know, and I do appreciate it. I think." It was his turn to laugh.

To guide my thoughts away from these carnal ones, I changed the subject. "What is she going to do next?" I didn't need to say who I was talking about. We had avoided the subject of Sophia long enough, but she was never far from our thoughts.

He lifted his shoulders in a resigned shrug. "There is no telling what she will do at any one time. Whatever it is, it is not going to be good for anyone."

We had no way of knowing how prophetic his words would turn out to be.

CHAPTER FIFTEEN

Sergio was supposed to arrive early the next morning to go to church with me. When he didn't show up, and his phone went directly to voice mail, panic gripped me by the throat, making it hard to breathe. No one had been parked in the dark to follow him down the mountain last night, and he'd called when he arrived home. So where was he this morning? I was filling up his voice mail box with panicked messages, but he still hadn't returned my calls.

Hearing a car door slam, I ran to the door hoping it was him, only to be disappointed. My heart fell to my toes when Detective Aguilar stepped out of his unmarked car. "Please no, God. Don't let him be dead." I whispered my prayer as tears streamed down my face unchecked. I wanted to slam the door, and not let him in. I didn't want to hear his bad news.

"It's not what you think, Ms. Reed. I just have a few questions." His serious expression told me whatever he had to say wasn't going to be good.

"Please, call me Quinn. Can I get you something to drink? I have fresh coffee." I wanted to delay the bad news as long as possible.

"Sit down, Ms. Reed, Quinn," he corrected. "Please." He took my arm, leading me to the couch. "I need you to tell me what happened yesterday."

"Yesterday? What are you talking about?" I was confused. "Where's Sergio? What happened to him?" With my arms wrapped around my waist in an effort to hold myself together, I rocked back and forth.

"He's all right; we have him at the police station. Please, tell me what happened yesterday," he pressed.

"Nothing happened yesterday. I was packing, getting ready to move. What does that have to do with Sergio?" He seemed to sag against the back of the chair, disappointed in my answer. "Why is Sergio at the police station?" I asked.

"Nothing unusual happened yesterday morning?" He ignored my question, asking more of his own. "You were here alone?"

"No, I wasn't alone. Sergio came here when he..." The confrontation with Mr. Tucker flashed in my mind. "Did that man file a complaint against Sergio? You can't believe anything he says." Unable to sit still any longer, I paced across the room much as Sergio had done the day before. "He came here thinking he could beat me up again."

"Who? Who are you talking about?" I barely heard his question, and didn't bother to answer. My mind was reeling with anger. How dare he file a complaint against Sergio!

"If I hadn't made it into the house when I did, he would have finished what he started months ago. Ask him why he was limping when he left here. Take a look at my door. He kicked it hard enough to put a dent in it and maybe even break his foot. It serves him right." I sank down on the couch, my anger spent for the moment.

"Who are you talking about?" Was he asking for information he already had, wanting me to confirm it?

"Mr. Tucker," I snapped. "I hope Child Protection doesn't give those two boys back to him. He'll just beat them again. What did he say Sergio did to him?"

"He's not saying anything, Quinn. He's dead."

"What?!" I jumped back up. "When? How?"

"That's what we're trying to determine. Please, tell me what happened. Was DeCosta here when Tucker tried to attack you?"

"No, yes," I stammered. "He got here in time to run the man off." I sat down again, trying to be calm. "Why is Sergio at the police station?" I asked again. "Please tell me what's going on."

"We're questioning him on suspicion of murder."

"Murder? You can't be serious." I jumped back up. "Sergio didn't murder anyone. He wouldn't do anything like that."

"Even if he thought you were in danger?" The detective

lifted one eyebrow.

"No, not even then. They exchanged punches, but Mr. Tucker was alive when he limped out of here."

"How did he get in the trunk of DeCosta's car then?" I was beginning to feel like a jumping jack as my legs gave out, and I sank down on the couch again.

"I don't know," I whispered, "but I know Sergio didn't do this." My mind was spinning. This was exactly what Sophia wanted to happen. If Sergio was in deep enough trouble, she thought he would turn to her family for help.

"They were in a fight," Aguilar said. "DeCosta has the bruised knuckles to prove it. Tell me what happened." This time it wasn't a request, it was an order.

To make him understand, to make him see that Sergio wasn't capable of doing something like this, I had to start at the beginning. He had to know about Sophia, and what she wanted. I had to give him credit. He listened to my tale without interrupting unless to clarify a point I was making. Finally I fell silent waiting for him to say something, anything.

"If she wants to get her brother back into the family fold, why would she frame him for murder?"

I collapsed against the couch. He didn't believe me. How could I make him see the truth? "You don't understand."

"You've got that right. What you're saying doesn't make sense."

"Yes, it does! She thinks she can force Sergio to ask her father..."

"His father, too," he interrupted.

"That's what she's trying to impress upon him. She thinks if he gets in enough trouble, the only way he'll be able to get out of it is by asking *her* father for help. She might be the killer you're looking for, and not just for Mr. Tucker. Maybe she killed Daniel thinking Sergio would be blamed." I didn't say anything about the possibility of her being Barnard's, maybe even Daniel's mistress.

He shook his head. "That doesn't make sense. How could Marconi get him out of a murder charge?"

"I don't know," I said with a sigh. "Did you know she was at Daniel's funeral as well as Eunice's?" I asked. "She's also been in here several times." I drew a deep breath, hoping I was convincing him of what I was saying.

"I know this all sounds implausible," I said at his questioning expression, "but it's true, all of it. She's been in here several times."

"How do you know? How could she get in? Were the locks jimmied, anything taken?"

I slumped back on the couch, resting my head against the cushion. This was going to sound even more far-fetched. If he didn't believe what I'd said so far, how could I get him to believe this? "I don't know how she's gotten in, but I know she was in here."

"How do you know if nothing was taken?" he pressed, skepticism coloring his voice.

I drew a deep breath. Well, here goes, I thought. This will really seal the deal; he'll never believe me now. I tried to explain as concisely as possible about my allergy to roses, ending with the fact that she was in here when I came home on Friday.

"Okay, but none of this explains who killed Tucker, and how his body got in DeCosta's trunk." I suppose it was his police training to question everything, but why couldn't he see what was right in front of him?

"Sophia Marconi did it. I know you think I would say anything to give Sergio an alibi and point the finger at someone else, but I'm telling you the truth. She was sitting in my kitchen Friday when I came home." I'd told him this already, but I went over it again just to drive home my point. "Mr. Tucker was alive when he left here."

"How would she even know about Tucker?" he asked. "Why would she kill him?"

I raised my hands letting them fall into my lap in frustration. "I don't know! Why does she keep getting in my house? What does she hope to gain? None of this makes sense, but it makes perfect sense." That sounded like a contradiction, but in a roundabout way it was true. You can't explain a psychopath.

For a long moment, he remained silent while he digested everything I'd told him, twice. Refocusing on me, he gave a little nod. "All right, say that I believe you, how do we prove any of it?" My heart gave a little jump. He said "we," that meant he was going to let me help. "Tell me again what happened beginning with Friday until last night. I want to know exactly what she said to you, and what happened with Tucker." For the first time, I felt some hope.

I recounted my conversation with Sophia Marconi, wishing I could have recorded it. When I finished, he shook his head. "This is just crazy enough to be the truth. What time did Tucker get here yesterday? When did DeCosta arrive?"

"I'm not sure of the exact times. I was working in the garage. I had the big doors open because it was warm." Once again, I repeated myself, trying to remember any details I'd left out. "Sergio was with me the entire day after Mr. Tucker left," I finished. "It was after ten when he left here last night. When he got to his place, he called to let me know he was safe. It took him the same length of time to reach his loft as it always does."

Detective Aguilar frowned at me. "Why wouldn't he be safe? Were you expecting trouble? Have you had more problems?" After Sophia's visit, I expected trouble every day. I kept that thought to myself.

I needed to go back even farther to make him understand, but would it help or give him even more reasons to question what I was saying? After I told him about the car that followed Sergio off my street, he frowned at me. "Nothing happened though, right? It wasn't her?"

I lifted my shoulders in a shrug. "I don't know if it was Sophia, or why she would be sitting on my street watching us." Once again, I felt like I was being blown about by an errant wind, with nothing to latch onto to steady myself.

He took his time digesting everything I said. I prayed that I was finally getting through to him.

"How is everything else going for you, Quinn?" His change of subjects caught me off guard. "Did that hundred and fifty grand help you out of your financial hole?"

I gave a harsh laugh. "A hundred and fifty thousand dollars doesn't go very far when you're in debt to the tune of more than a half million dollars."

I thought it was impossible to surprise the seasoned detective, but I was wrong. His mouth dropped open, but no sound came out for a full minute. "That much?" he finally asked around a gulp. "How did it get so far out of hand? Did you try to stop him?"

"It happened because I'm stupid and gullible," I snapped unnecessarily. "I'm sorry," I apologized. "I don't mean to take it out on you." I drew a steadying breath. "Whenever I asked Daniel about our finances, he told me not to worry; he was taking care of everything. He was investing in the future. Get that, *the* future, not *our* future? It was like he was giving me a pat on the head and sending me off to play, leaving everything to the adults. I was dumb enough not to press the issue."

I drew another deep breath, releasing it slowly, trying to calm myself. "It seems that women weren't the only problem we had, I just didn't know about the rest until it was too late. After he had promised to change if I would take him back, he took out a second mortgage on this place." I swept my hand around. "Somehow he got the payments deferred for a year. He was already dead when I got the news on that bit of betrayal. The bank is going to foreclose on me if I can't sell the house. And I can't sell it if my realtor won't show it." Anger had replaced my tears several months back. Daniel had lied to me about everything. I no longer mourned for him.

"I hope you aren't betrayed again, Quinn," Detective Aguilar said softly. "As yet, I don't have enough to charge

DeCosta, but he's a long way from free of suspicion."
When he left a few minutes later I sank down on the couch
feeling like my entire life had been one giant fiasco. How
could this be happening? Why was it happening? "Please
God, show me what to do. Have I entrusted my heart to
another man who doesn't deserve it?" The answer seemed
to come to me as if someone right in the room was
speaking to me. Sergio wouldn't do those things. Now I
had to help prove it.

~~~

A very shaken Sergio arrived a few hours later. His hair
was mussed like he'd been combing his fingers through it
repeatedly. He pulled me into his arms, burying his face in
my neck. Holding me without speaking for a long moment,
he finally drew me away looking down at me. "I don't
know what you said to Detective Aguilar, but for the
moment he believes I did not kill that man. At least I think
he believes it." He drew a shuddering breath. "If I live to be
one hundred, I will never forget what it feels like to be
dragged in by the police."

"Did they handcuff you?" I asked, horrified. I couldn't
imagine what that would be like.

"No," he sighed. "I thank God for that."

"How did they even know to look for a body in the
trunk of your car?"

He shrugged. "Detective Aguilar said they received an
anonymous tip." He gave a harsh laugh. "Of course, Sophia
would want to make sure they found the body before I did.
She wouldn't want me to be able to dispose of it first."

"Why would she think you were dumb enough to leave
a dead body in the trunk of your own car?"

"Detective Aguilar is asking some of those same
questions. After he spoke with you, he asked me all sorts of
questions about Sophia."

"When you came here the first time, he was on my
doorstop the next morning. The same when Antony
Marconi came here. Why didn't he know about Sophia's

visits?"

He lifted one shoulder in a shrug. "I do not think he even knew she existed until you told him of her."

"But why didn't he? He said the FBI had told him about you. Why didn't they tell him about Sophia? Is it possible they don't know who she is?"

Again he shrugged. "I cannot believe the FBI does not know of her existence, but she is able to hide what she does from the eyes of the authorities."

We could discuss this until eternity, and not come up with a good explanation for what was happening. It was too late to go to church now. To distract ourselves from thoughts of Sophia and Mr. Tucker, we resumed packing. It wouldn't be long before I needed to move. Why wait until the last minute?

CHAPTER SIXTEEN

That night the police made it official; Jenn Jones, a young realtor was missing. Her family and friends hadn't seen her for a week, and she hadn't checked in with her office in that length of time either. I wasn't sure why no one had reported her missing before this. Didn't anyone care?

What would Sophia Marconi gain by getting rid of Jenn? Unless, of course, she could finger Sophia as the person who kept getting into my house when I wasn't home, giving credence to what I had told the police.

Would they ever find her body, I wondered? Was Sophia that good at her evil game? According to Sergio, she was that good and better.

The body of a man found in the trunk of a car barely made a blip on the evening news-cast. The police didn't release the man's name or the identity of the owner of the car in which his body was found. At the time, all the police were saying was that they were investigating, and they had several 'persons of interest' they were seeking.

My heart went out to Bobby Tucker and his little brother. I didn't know where their mother was. When I had asked Mr. Tucker about his wife, he hadn't confirmed or denied one even existed. Foster care wasn't ideal for those small boys, but it would be better than they were getting from an abusive father. At least I hoped it would be.

Since the police had little or no information on Sophia Marconi, I decided to pay Barnard a visit. He had to know something about the woman. He had wanted me to hold his hand through initial investigation into Eunice's murder and her funeral. Since then, I'd heard nothing from him. I wondered if he'd discovered the papers Eunice was using to blackmail Rick Frost.

His trial wouldn't be until sometime in the future. First the SEC had to finish their investigation into everything

Rick and probably Daniel had been involved in. Would the federal government's case take precedence over the state's murder case?

Rick was still claiming to be innocent of Daniel's murder. His attorney called almost daily, requesting I go visit Rick at the county jail. "You won't have to be in the same room with him," Ted Burns, the attorney, kept telling me. "You'll speak to him on a phone and see him on a monitor."

"Why does he want to see me? What does he think I can do for him?"

"I'm not sure." There was a shrug in the man's voice. "He hopes to assure you that he didn't kill your husband."

"I'm not the one he has to convince," I argued. "He needs to convince the prosecutor."

"Yes, I know, Ms. Reed, but Mr. Frost wants to talk to you. Please, go see him. I've arranged with the prosecutor and the jail for you to visit."

I meant to say "no." There was nothing to be accomplished by seeing him. "All right I'll go see him." Who said that? I looked around to find myself alone. Where did those words come from? I wanted to recant, but curiosity spurred me into going.

As it turned out, another man had lied to me. Considering my track record with men, I guess I shouldn't have been surprised. He hadn't just arranged for me to talk to Rick Frost. He made it look like I was one of the attorneys working with him.

I was led into a small room with no windows. The only furniture was a table and two chairs. This wasn't the way the attorney described it would be. What happened to the monitor and phone, I wondered?

When Rick was brought into the room I stood up so fast, the chair fell over backwards. This man was a self-confessed murderer; I didn't want to be in the same room with him. The guard gave me a disinterested look before making sure Rick was seated and the shackles were bolted to the floor. Without a backward glance he left, closing the door behind him.

"Wait!" I finally regained my voice. "I want out of here." I wasn't sure if the guard could hear me, but he didn't return.

I recoiled when Rick reached out his cuffed hands to me. "Please, Quinn. Listen to me. I didn't kill Daniel. I don't know what the police have told you or what's being said on the news, but I didn't do everything that's being said about me."

"You defrauded your clients, you paid blackmail so you wouldn't get caught, then you killed Eunice. That's what's being said about this whole mess. You did those things. There's nothing left to be said." I was still standing by the door, hoping the guard would return to let me out.

"Daniel did those things," Rick whined. "He got me in this mess."

"Daniel didn't blackmail Eunice, or kill her. He was already dead. Did you kill him?" I stomped back to the table, slamming my hands down to lean over, glaring at him. Anger made me forget to be afraid of him.

"No, no, I didn't kill him. I meant to say that he got me involved with his scheme to defraud our clients. That's all I meant."

"It's rather convenient for you that he isn't here to defend himself. If you were so squeaky clean, you wouldn't have gotten involved in any kind of scheme in the first place."

"You're right, I know you're right. But it didn't sound so bad when we first started. He said it was foolproof, and we'd be rich."

"Why did you kill Eunice?" I hoped someone was listening to this. Maybe they could figure out what had really happened.

"It was self-defense. She was robbing me blind." He'd changed his mind from self-preservation to self-defense. I didn't think either excuse would get him off the hook.

I finally up righted the chair and sat down in it. Chained to the floor the way he was, he couldn't do anything to me. "How did this all start? *Why* did it start? I thought your company was doing so well." If I could get him to tell me why Daniel had gotten into this mess, maybe I could begin to forgive him and move on.

"It was doing well. But that's before...things happened," he hedged. "Daniel's mother spoiled him rotten." He paused like that explained everything.

He was right about that, but it didn't explain anything. "What's that got to do with what the two of you got mixed up in?"

"Like I said, his mother spoiled him; she gave him everything he wanted, while his old man kept telling him what a screw-up he was. He wanted to prove to both of them that he could make it on his own. He kept spending, getting deeper in debt. He was investing in risky projects, using clients' money until it all started to collapse on him."

"In the end, he proved his father right. He was a screw-up." I didn't bother to hide the bitterness in my voice. "He also followed in his father's footsteps. They were both incapable of being faithful to one woman."

Until that moment, Rick had maintained eye contact, I suppose in an attempt to prove how sincere he was. Now he looked away, unable to meet my hard glare. "What? What do you know that you aren't telling me?"

"Ah, I just wanted you to come here so you would know I didn't kill Daniel. That's all I have to say."

"Not so fast, buster," I snapped, slapping the table one more time. "What do you know about Daniel's girlfriends? Or is it Barnard's girlfriends you don't want to talk about?" His eyes looked everywhere but at me.

"Ah, um," he stammered some more, still looking elsewhere. I slapped the table again, finally drawing his attention back to me. By now my hand was hurting, but I wasn't going to let him know that. "Um, well, his girlfriend was the one to help set us up."

144

"Oh, which girlfriend was that?" My stomach was on fire, my head was spinning. I was about to learn more about my late husband than I really wanted to know.

"The last one," he whispered. "She was something else." He shook his head at the memory of the woman.

"Tiffany Sanchez? A cocktail waitress?"

He gave a harsh laugh. "Not hardly. I don't know what Daniel told you about her, but she wasn't any waitress. That woman was smart. She knew more about investments and how to make them work for her than anyone I ever met."

"You met her? Can you describe her?" Now we were getting somewhere. I had a funny feeling I knew who he was talking about.

He shook his head though. "I'm not describing her to anyone. I know better." Fear now darkened his eyes.

"Have you told the police any of this?"

He gave a harsh laugh. "I'm not telling them or the feds anything until I get a deal on the table. I want protection."

"Protection from whom? Who are you afraid of?"

He crossed his arms over his chest, his thin lips clamped tight as if to keep any more words from coming out of his mouth.

"If you won't tell the police this, why are you telling me? You know I'm not a lawyer. I can turn around and tell Detective Aguilar everything you've said to me."

He smiled serenely. "Go ahead. I'll deny it all. It will be your word against mine. The only thing I'm admitting is doing away with that bitch who was robbing me blind. She deserved what she got."

Why did I even go see him? I asked myself as I left the jail. There were no more tears left in me for Daniel, but I didn't want to spend the rest of my life hating him either. Hate hurts you, not the person you hate. Besides, he's no longer around to care.

Was Tiffany Sanchez really Sophia Marconi? She wasn't a cocktail waitress like she and Daniel told me, that much was certain. Had Daniel known who and what she was? Was Barnard also involved with her? Would he tell me the truth if I asked him?

Leaving the jail, I called Sergio as I promised I would. "What did he have to say? Was it helpful?"

I gave a heartfelt sigh. "I'm not sure. I'll tell you everything when I get home. Where are you?"

"I will meet you at your house. I love you." He disconnected without another word. My heart fluttered. He didn't say where he was. What did that mean? With so many people betraying me recently, suspicion crept over me. Could I trust my heart when it came to men? "Please, God, give me some sign whether I can trust him," I whispered my prayer as I started my car.

Trying to put these thoughts aside, I attempted to digest everything Rick Frost had told me, and read between the lines of what he hinted at. I was on autopilot as I drove the winding roads into the foothills. I had more questions than answers. The whirlwind I was trapped in just kept getting stronger, spinning me into space.

The roar of a big SUV brought me out of my fog and back to the present. It was so close all I could see in my mirror was the front grill of the big vehicle. The sun glinted off the chrome, nearly blinding me. Was the sun blinding him so he couldn't see my car? If that was the case, he needed to slow down before we both went over the edge.

I tapped the horn, hoping he would back off. When he stayed on my bumper, I pressed the gas pedal to put some distance between us. He kept pace with me. "What is wrong with that guy?" On the first straight stretch of road, I hit the blue tooth button on my steering wheel. "Sergio, where are you?"

"*Cara*, what is wrong?"

"Someone's following me. I think he's trying to run me off the road." I was panicking, praying that I'd be able to keep the car from going over the edge on one of the many twists on the road. The heavy SUV wouldn't have any trouble pushing my small Lexus over.

"I am just a few miles behind you. I will be there as fast as I can. Please be safe." His whispered words came through the speaker almost as a prayer.

How had he gotten here so fast? I tried not to dwell on that thought. I needed to stay focused on the road and the big vehicle behind me. Keeping my eyes on the twisting road, I also tried to watch the SUV in my rearview mirror. Only minutes later I caught a glimpse of Sergio's car rounding a curve behind us. He was here! I wasn't sure what he could do to stop whoever was driving the SUV, but it was comforting to know he was there.

The other driver must have noticed Sergio as well. At the first opportunity, the big vehicle roared past me, rounding the curve of the mountain. Just that quick he disappeared.

I sagged in my seat, drawing a cleansing breath. When my phone rang, I jumped as though I'd just taken a jolt of electricity. "Are you all right, *cara*?" Sergio's softly accented words washed over me the instant I pressed the connect button.

I could feel the adrenaline begin to seep out of my veins, leaving me feeling weak and shaking. "I am now. How did you get here so fast?"

"I couldn't be with you when you went to see that man, but I could be waiting when you left him. I was close when you called. I am sorry I was not closer."

Was this the sign I'd asked God to send me? Sergio was trying to protect me. He remained on the phone with me. At the first available place to pull over, we turned off the highway. He was out of his car almost before he had the motor shut off, pulling me into his arms. We were both trembling with the aftermath of this little scene. "Could you see the driver?" he asked, finally finding his voice.

I shook my head, releasing a pent up breath. "Even the front windshield was darkened. I could only see a shape behind the wheel. Did you get a license number?"

His sigh was pure frustration as he shook his head. "Mud was crusted on it. Are you certain you are all right?" He tugged me into his arms again as if to prove to himself that I was really safe. Finally calm enough to get behind the wheel again, we got back on the road. He stayed close behind me, not leaving room for other vehicles to get between us.

Safe at home with the doors locked, I poured a large glass of wine for each of us, hoping it would help calm our shattered nerves. My mind was filled with what could have been. Was this how Daniel had spent the last seconds of his life, fear choking him as the car sailed over the edge of the cliff? Detective Aguilar said he'd been shot. Was he dead or unconscious when his car went over the cliff? Had he died before the car caught on fire?

"What did Rick Frost have to say?" Sergio's words broke in on my troubled thoughts.

"I don't know how much of what he said to believe." I shook my head. "He says he didn't kill Daniel, and he doesn't know who did. He claims it was Daniel and his girlfriend who came up with the scheme to defraud their clients."

"He met her?" His excitement matched mine when Rick first told me.

"Yes," I nodded, "but he couldn't and wouldn't describe her. I think he's afraid to tell what he knows. He said he would deny telling me any of this if I went to the police. He wants a deal and protection before he'll talk." I took another big swallow of wine. So far, it wasn't helping me relax.

"You still need to tell Detective Aguilar," Sergio insisted. "Maybe he can convince Frost to tell what he knows."

Reluctantly, I picked up the phone. What good would it do to tell the police, if Rick Frost denied saying anything to me? If he couldn't describe Daniel's girlfriend, we still wouldn't know who she was.

"What do you mean you *saw* Rick Frost?" Detective Aguilar's astonished question vibrated through the phone. "The government prosecutor isn't letting anyone but his attorney near him. I can't even talk to him."

"That damn man," I muttered. I was getting really tired of people lying to me.

"What man, Ms. Reed, Quinn?" he corrected. "Where did you see Frost?"

It took several minutes to explain how my meeting with Rick Frost had come about. He was clearly unhappy that I'd been allowed to talk to the man, but maybe, just maybe, I had given them the break they needed. Now they had to get him to talk.

But Rick Frost wouldn't be talking to anyone. That night he was found dead in his cell, an apparent suicide. He'd hung himself. Or had he? Just how long a reach did Antony Marconi and his daughter Sophia have?

CHAPTER SEVENTEEN

My visit to Barnard had been postponed long enough. If he could tell us anything about this woman Daniel had been working with, he needed to talk to the police. I had no proof, but I had little doubt Tiffany Sanchez was really Sophia Marconi. What I didn't know was why she had called me. If she hadn't made that call, I wouldn't have known about his current round of cheating. I would have gone blissfully on in my ignorance. I needed to know if Barnard had also been sleeping with her, and if he knew who she was although, I didn't know what difference it made now.

I waited until the end of the day before going to see him. It had been three weeks since Eunice's funeral. He would be back to work by now, if he even took time off. The curtain on the front window moved slightly while I waited for him to answer the door. He was home, so why didn't he open the door? More determined than ever to talk to him, I rang the bell again. I wasn't going to give up and go away.

After five minutes the lock clicked, and Barnard opened the door. He was dressed in a smoking jacket right out of a fifties romantic comedy movie. "Hello, Quinn. How are you doing?" He didn't bother inviting me in.

"I'm fine. I haven't heard from you since Eunice's funeral. I was beginning to worry about you." I looked him up and down. "But I see you're doing all right for yourself. May I come in?" I reached for the handle on the fancy security door.

"Um, this isn't a good time. I, I'm kind of busy," he stammered. "Why don't we get together over lunch someday?"

Was that the well-known 'someday' that never materializes when someone is giving you the brush-off? "Oh, I'd like that. When are you free? I'm out of school for the summer, so any day is good for me." I didn't bother telling him I was out of a job, thanks to all the drama that had surrounded me for the past year. He wouldn't care anyway.

"Oh, ah, um, I'll have to check my calendar to see what day I'm available. I'll give you a call. I really am busy right now, Quinn. It was good seeing you." He shut the door without another word.

"I'll bet you'll call," I muttered. "What is it you're hiding, Barnard?" Was Sophia in there? Now that he didn't have a wife to hide his many affairs from, was he keeping a mistress in his own home? He was being awfully brazen, whatever he was up to. There was more than one way to skin a cat though. If he wouldn't see me at home, I'd go to his office.

The next day the real estate firm Jenn Jones had worked for sent out a new agent to take over the listing on my house. "I'm so sorry we weren't aware of the problems you were having," Barbara Swanson stated. This woman looked all business. No showcasing a trim figure in fancy clothes. Sophia would have a hard time pulling the wool over this one's eyes. She made no mention of the fact that Jenn Jones had disappeared. Did she even care?

"I would like to have a different lock box on the door, one with a different combination." She frowned at my request, but didn't argue. "I'm also very allergic to roses," I went on. "Please don't let anyone come in here with rose-scented perfume." If she thought I was putting some silly restrictions on her, she kept those thoughts to herself.

With a new realtor, someone who was actually trying to sell my house, maybe they would begin to generate some interest. She had an open house scheduled for the following weekend. It couldn't happen fast enough to suit me. I needed to get out from under the enormous mortgages Daniel had saddled me with. Even with that, I would be in a world of hurt if I didn't get another job soon.

~~~

I waited three days before driving into Denver to the

fancy offices of Baker, Reed and White, Barnard's investment firm. I had been to Daniel's office several times during the course of our marriage. At the time I thought it was rather pretentious, trying too hard to impress potential clients. The lobby of Barnard's company was understated elegance, giving the impression of old money and lots of it.

"Welcome to Baker, Reed and White. How may I help you?" The receptionist behind the cherry wood desk was in her forties. Her makeup was perfect, and there wasn't a hair out of place. No sexy young woman to advertise here, I thought. It was all elegance and class.

"I'm Mr. Reed's daughter-in-law. I'm in town for the day and thought I'd surprise him by taking him to lunch." That sounded plausible to me, but apparently she didn't agree.

"I'm sorry, Mr. Reed isn't in." The look she bestowed on me now was no longer cordial.

"Oh, that's too bad. Will he be back later today? I'll be in town for the afternoon."

"Mr. Reed will be out of the office for an extended period of time." The temperature in the room had dropped several degrees since I walked in. I couldn't help but wonder about the cause.

"Oh, I'm sorry to hear that. When I saw him a few days ago, he didn't say anything about being out of the office. We were going to have lunch the next time I was in town." I was making this up as I went. "At the time, I didn't know I would be coming in so soon. I'll give him a call at home tonight." I tried to think of something that would convince her to be a little more forthcoming with information. Nothing came to mind though.

"I'm sorry for your loss," she belatedly added as I started to turn away.

"Thank you." I gave her a weak smile. "It's been a rough year for both of us."

"Yes," she agreed. "I suppose that's why Mr. Reed decided to retire early. You never know how long you have on this earth, enjoy it while you can."

"Um, yes, I suppose so." I struggled to keep my mouth from dropping open. "Thank you." I escaped out the door before she guessed how surprised I was by this announcement. Why was Barnard retiring? He was only fifty-five. What was he going to do, spend the rest of his life going from one mistress to another?

I had no idea of his financial status. Eunice had lived like they were millionaires, and that's the way Daniel tried to live. I know where that had gotten him. Or me, I corrected. If Daniel was murdered because of his manipulations at work, he'd gotten the worst end of it.

Had Barnard discovered where Eunice put the blackmail money she'd received? Had he found the papers the SEC was looking for? The company had been shut down, so there was no one else to blackmail. Was Sophia Marconi still involved with Barnard?

The forty-mile trip down the mountain had been a waste of time. I had nothing but time, so it didn't really matter. I'd also wasted a lot of gas in my useless round trip. Money was one thing I couldn't afford to waste. Something needed to break soon on a job for the next school year.

The highway leading back to Greenbrier had limited traffic in the middle of the day. I kept a careful watch on any cars that came up behind me. I didn't want a repeat of my last trip down the mountain. No one seemed at all interested in my small car though.

Back in Greenbrier, I drove past Barnard's house hoping to find him outside, or see something useful. I wasn't sure how useful it was, but it was certainly surprising. A For Sale sign was planted in the front yard.

Parking across the street, I waited to see if Barnard would come outside. There was no movement that I could see. Maybe he had already left town, even before the house was sold.

There'd been no sign in the yard just three days ago, and he hadn't said anything about moving or retiring. Why the sudden desire to move? Where was he going? Why had he suddenly decided to retire? I needed to talk to him about Sophia before he left, but I couldn't sit in front of his house all day. Hopefully, it wouldn't be much longer before I could move, and I had packing of my own to get done.

~~~

Sergio had asked me to marry him, but with a possible murder charge hanging over his head, his life was also in limbo. How had life become so complicated? Our personal lives would have to be put on hold until this could be cleared up. Daniel's murderer was still running free. The authorities had no suspect. Pointing them to Sophia Marconi wouldn't help since I had no proof to offer.

Sergio went about his business as usual, traveling when necessary, just not out of the country. I was getting desperate in my job search. Had the principal put me on some sort of a black list? I knew I was being overly dramatic, but desperation does that to a person. Marrying Sergio would solve my money problems, but I wouldn't marry him only to bring his credit rating into the dumps with mine.

Sergio spent every evening he could with me. I was no longer the widow in mourning. After all the things I had learned about Daniel, I no longer cared what other people thought of me.

As we left a restaurant one evening, dark clouds scudded across the sky. It wouldn't be long until rain washed the air clean. Summer showers were common in the foothills around Denver. Coming abreast of a dark limousine, a man stepped out, moving into our path. I gasped, taking a step back as I recognized him. At the same time, Sergio moved in front of me in an effort to protect me.

"What? You think I am going to harm you and your lady right here on the street? I want to talk to you, to get to know my son." The man stood defiantly in front of Sergio. "I have that right."

"You have no rights concerning me, and I am not your

son," Sergio countered. "I want nothing to do with your murdering, corrupt way of life."

Marconi's eyes grew dark, a muscle jumping in his cheek as he tried to control the rage building in him. My heart was in my throat. What would he do to Sergio for speaking to him like that? Then he pulled himself up to his full height which matched Sergio's. "I have left that life. I am a sick old man now, and I want to know I have left something behind, something worthwhile."

"You have three daughters; one I know is following closely in your corrupt ways. I am certain that pleases you."

Marconi waved his hand dismissively. "She goes her own way. I want to know if you have children."

"What business is that of yours?" Sergio's temper was held in check by a thread.

"I want to know if I have grandchildren."

"You will have to ask your daughters in Italy that question. Sophia has always been more interested in following in your footsteps than in being a wife and mother.

"I am talking about a namesake, another Marconi to carry on the name. Do you have children?" he growled.

"I have never been married. Does that answer your question?"

The old man gave a harsh laugh. "One does not have to be married to have children, or you would not be here."

I gripped Sergio's arm, or he would have lunged at the older man. "What you did to my mother was rape. She was sixteen! You would have allowed your wife to kill her to be rid of her. She would have killed me as well."

Marconi waved his hand again, dismissing Sergio's words as though they meant nothing to him. "I never would have allowed that to happen. When you do get married," he looked at me with a gleam in his eyes, "what name will you give them?"

I could feel my face growing warm, but I refused to rise to his bait, letting Sergio handle the conversation. "I will give them my name," he stated simply.

A hopeful look lifted Antony Marconi's tired features. "Your name is Dominic Marconi."

It was Sergio's turn to give a harsh laugh. "Not anymore. As you well know, when Gino DeCosta adopted me, he changed my name. I have a new birth certificate to prove he was my father. More than you ever could have been."

"You would be wise to be careful of what you say to me. I may be retired from my old profession, but I am still a Marconi. I do not take insults lightly."

Sergio lifted his hands in a palms-up gesture. "You make my point for me. You retire, but you are still the same Mafioso you always were, always looking for a violent solution. Violence is still your answer for everything." He drew a deep breath, releasing it slowly. "Now you know what I am like. You need to leave. Never come near Quinn or me again. When we have children, you will *not* be a grandfather to them." He moved to step around the other man. "Tell Sophia she is to leave us alone as well. The police know she is in this country, and that she has committed many crimes here."

Marconi's expression darkened. "What crimes do they think she has committed?" When neither of us said anything, Antony Marconi's smile was smug. "Just as I thought, they have nothing. The police will do well to leave Sophia alone, and not try to make up phony charges. She is still my daughter, as you are my son."

"That sounds like a threat, Mr. Marconi." I spoke up for the first time. "Do you generally threaten the police, or anyone who doesn't do as you wish? Did you have Daniel killed because he wanted out of the little scheme Sophia had cooked up?" I'm not sure where that idea came from, or what gave me the courage to voice it.

He gave a snort of derision. "You do not know what you are talking about. I did not kill him."

"Maybe Sophia did then," I suggested.

"As I said, you know nothing of what you are saying." His cryptic words puzzled me. Saying nothing more, he turned, laughter rumbling in his chest. A chauffeur materialized seemingly out of nowhere, opening the door of the limousine for Marconi. He couldn't even open his own doors.

CHAPTER EIGHTEEN

Sergio's puzzled frown mirrored my own. "What did he mean by that? Does he know who murdered Daniel?" We watched as the big car disappeared into the night. "How did he know where we were?" Fear zipped through my veins. "Is he having us watched?" It wasn't a comforting thought to have a member of the Mafia keeping tabs on our whereabouts.

Sergio pulled me against his side, placing a kiss on my temple. "Possibly, but he is trying to get on my good side. Harming you would put an end to that forever." The dark clouds chose that moment to open up, releasing huge drops down on us.

Laughing, we ran for his car. It wasn't far, but we were soaked to the skin by the time we got there. Thoughts of Marconi were washed from our minds by the sudden downpour. The temperature dropped twenty degrees in a matter of minutes. Even in June, there was the chance of snow in the Rocky Mountains. Hopefully that wouldn't happen tonight.

The heater in the car had barely taken away our chill by the time we pulled into my garage. "We need to get out of these wet clothes." My teeth were chattering hard enough to crack a tooth.

"Do you still have any of Daniel's clothes for me to change?" Sergio was shaking as hard as I was.

Giving my head a shake, I pushed him into the bathroom "You can wear one of my robes. Toss me your wet clothes, and I'll put them in the dryer. I'll bring you a robe to put on." I chuckled at the look of horror on his face. I knew he was picturing a flowing, see-through negligee.

"Do you have any sweat pants I could wear?" he called through the closed door, panic edged his voice.

I laughed at the idea of Sergio in any of my clothes, my sweats, or a robe. His six-feet-two-inches, would make my sweat pants hit him around the knee, if he could even pull them over his hips. There isn't an ounce of fat on his lean frame, but my five foot three one hundred pounds are much smaller than him. Even my longest robe would be short on him.

Pulling on a pair of sweat pants and sweat shirt, I took my wet clothes to the laundry room before handing a robe around the bathroom door. "Oh, please, Quinn, not this. You have nothing of Daniel's?"

I laughed. "Not a thing. Eunice kept everything of his. It won't take long for our things to dry; then you can put your own clothes back on."

"I will stay in here until they are dry then." I guess he thought his masculinity would be in question if he wore the flowered pink silk robe I'd given him.

"It's not see-through," I chuckled. "Come on, cowboy up, and put it on so I can put your clothes in the dryer."

"A cowboy would not be caught dead in this pink thing," he muttered before tossing me his wet clothes.

It took him several minutes to gather the courage to leave the bathroom. When my lips twitched, he turned back to the safety of the bathroom. "Oh, come on. It's just us. No one will ever know you wore my robe." As I suspected, it hit him mid-calf. The shoulder seams were pulled tight across his broad shoulders.

"I would rather have on your sweat pants," he grumbled. I'd never seen him so self-conscious before. He had always been very confident in himself.

Wrapping my arms around him, I placed soft kisses along his jaw, before settling on his full lips. "I think you look cute," I whispered.

"Grrr." He growled playfully, deepening the kiss as he walked me backwards into the living room. We tumbled down on the couch, forgetting that the robe was held closed with only a sash. His hand moved under my sweat shirt, skimming across my bare skin. Goose bumps traveled up my spine. I couldn't get close enough to him.

We both froze when the robe parted, exposing his naked frame. "Um, ah." My mind wasn't working very well at the prospect of what could happen next. Is that what I wanted? Right now, in the middle of everything that was happening to us?

The decision was taken out of our hands. The doorbell I had always considered melodious sounded like a cowbell clanging in my head.

Sergio jerked away, grasping the edges of the robe together. "Do not open that door," he hissed. I'd never seen him move that fast as he tore down the hall to the bathroom. Before the door closed behind him, whoever was at the door impatiently pressed the button again.

"Hold your horses," I mumbled. My heart was still pounding rapidly against my ribs by what could have been. I couldn't decide if I was sorry for the interruption, or grateful. Checking the security peep hole, I leaned my head against the door. What would Sophia do if I continued to ignore her?

"I know you have my brother in there with you," she shouted as her fist hit the screen. "I will not go away until I see him." Did she think I was holding him hostage? The woman was a psychopath. There was no telling just how crazy she could get.

"Just a minute." I ran for the dryer in the laundry room. She couldn't see Sergio in my robe. That would certainly send her over the edge. "It's Sophia," I whispered as I shoved his still-damp clothes around the crack in the door. "Get dressed."

"Do not open the door until I am there."

Ignoring his command, I unlocked the heavy door, leaving the screen locked. "What do you want?" I sneezed when the breeze blew in her signature perfume of attar of roses. Did she bathe in the stuff?

She chuckled. "Are you catching a cold? That's too bad. Let me in so I can talk to my brother."

"I am not your brother. Go away and leave us alone."

Sergio came up behind me, placing his arm around my shoulders in a protective gesture. Another sneeze caused her to chuckle again. The rain had stopped, but the wind was still howling, carrying her rose scented perfume into the house.

"Go away, Sophia, or I will call the police. I do not think your father would like to have their attention brought down on you."

"You would call the police on your own sister?" That sounded like a new concept to her, something never done in the world she grew up in.

"I will say it again, you are not my sister. Even when I lived in your father's house, I was never treated as a family member. Go away and leave us alone. I have told your father the same thing. I am *not* a Marconi."

My eyes were beginning to itch and my nose was running, but I wouldn't leave Sergio standing there by himself. What if she had a gun, and decided to shoot him? The screen door wouldn't offer any protection at all.

"No matter what you think, there is Marconi blood running through your veins. Blood always stands with blood. You would do well to treat our father with respect."

"And what will you do if I refuse? Will you kill me? What would your father think of that?" My heart was pounding against my ribs. Why was he baiting her?

She shifted her hateful gaze to me, ignoring Sergio's taunt. "I told you to leave my brother alone. Why did you ignore me?" Her bright gaze traveled down my body, a sneer curling her lips. "What took you so long to answer the door? Did I catch you seducing my brother?"

Seduction hadn't been necessary. What happened was by mutual consent. Still she was very close to the truth. A few minutes longer, and she might have caught us in the middle of something much more passionate than the groping that had just begun. I hoped the dim light in the foyer hid the blush on my face.

Deciding to change the subject, I asked a question of

my own. "I know you were sleeping with Daniel," I bluffed. "Were you also sleeping with Barnard? Are you still sleeping with him?"

She gave a harsh laugh. "You know nothing." She sneered. Turning away, she looked over her shoulder at me. "You know nothing at all." A 'cat that ate the canary' smile tilted her full lips. I sneezed one more time before she disappeared into the dark night.

"What did she mean by that? Does her whole family speak in riddles?" I waited to hear a car start before closing the door, but there was nothing. "Where's her car? She couldn't walk here." There was no car in the driveway or in front of the house. It was like she walked into thin air.

I finally closed the door to shut out the cold night air. "She and her father know what's behind everything that's been happening around here." I said, thinking out loud.

"If that is true, they will never tell, unless it is to their advantage. Could we forget those two crazy people for a little while? I would like to pick up where we left off." He pulled me against his hard chest, nibbling on my neck.

Before things could advance to the point of no return, his cell phone chirped in his pocket. We both groaned. "Do you think God is telling us that we are not supposed to be doing this yet?" The pledge we took as impressionable teenagers couldn't be held against us now, could it? His sigh was filled with frustration. He rested his forehead against mine as the phone chirped again. Whoever was calling wasn't going to go away. While he answered his phone, I headed to the kitchen to make coffee. It looked like it might be a long night. I had no idea how true that thought would turn out to be.

All romantic thoughts had to be put on hold. Someone had broken into his office. "I feel that the universe is against us," he whispered, his dark eyes probing mine. It was harder to say goodnight each time he left, but tonight it was necessary. There was no telling what he would find when he reached Denver. Still, neither of us was ready for him to leave.

I gave a strangled laugh. "So it seems. Please, be careful driving down that mountain. Call when you get to your office." We lingered over our kisses one more time. Since that night when someone had followed him as he left, I watched for an unknown car to appear out of the dark night. All was quiet as it should be.

I still didn't know where Sophia had gone when she left. She could be lurking around a bend in the road waiting for a chance to do something. Would she really harm Sergio because he was with me? I couldn't answer that question. The woman was a complete mystery.

It was too soon for Sergio to reach his office when my phone rang a short time later. Maybe he just wanted company on his drive into town. The strange voice on the other end wasn't what I expected though.

"Ms. Reed, this is Officer Fontaine with the Highway Patrol." My heart rate went into overdrive. There was only one reason for a call from them. "Mr. DeCosta asked me to call you. He's been in an accident, and is being taken to the hospital in Denver. Would it be possible for you to meet him there?"

"Of course, which hospital are they taking him to?" My voice was shaking as well as my hands.

"I can send someone to pick you up."

"No, I'm fine, just tell me which hospital, and I'll be there." I didn't sound fine, but I wasn't going to wait around for someone to come get me."

As I passed the accident scene, my heart jumped into my throat. The Highway Patrol was still investigating the accident, but the ambulance was gone. This was the second time someone I cared about was hurt or killed on this winding stretch of road. I wanted off this mountain. I didn't care if I ever drove here again.

It felt like forever before I got to the hospital, but I made it in record time. Sergio was still in the emergency room. He was conscious, but just barely when I pushed aside the curtain in his cubical. A tortured gasp escaped my lips at the sight of the man I loved more than life itself. A nurse was cleaning blood from his face; there was a splint on one arm, and multiple cuts everywhere. One pant leg had been cut to give the paramedics access to his leg. There was more blood than seemed possible for the person still be alive. He was alive, wasn't he? The thought just about brought me to my knees.

"Careful there, ma'am," the nurse looked up at me as my knees threatened to give out. "Sit down before you fall down. I don't need another patient to take care of." She was all business when talking to me, but her touch on Sergio's face was gentle. That's all I cared about. Watching for the slow rise and fall of his chest to make sure he was still breathing, I sank onto the chair beside his bed.

"I am all right," his voice was only a whisper, taking a great deal of effort just to say those few words. I reached for his hand not held stationary by the splint. It was my turn to hold his hand while we waited to hear the extent of his injuries.

"What happened?" I leaned close so he wouldn't have to speak too loud.

"There's time enough for that later," the nurse admonished. "Let's get him cleaned up for the doc."

An hour later, Sergio had been x-rayed, poked, prodded, and examined. He had a broken leg, a broken breastbone thanks to the seat belt, his wrist was sprained but not broken, a head laceration along with a mild concussion, and many cuts from flying glass. But he was alive and would live. That was the best news ever.

Finally alone, I held his uninjured hand, as I brushed the dark hair that had fallen across his forehead. He was groggy, but conscious. "What happened, honey? Can you tell me?"

Before he could answer, the curtain closing us in was pushed aside as a young deputy strode in. The man was very impressed with his own importance if the expression on his face meant anything. "That's my question, Miss. Can you step out so I can talk to Mr. DeCosta?"

"You can ask me anything you like while Ms. Reed is right here. I have nothing to hide."

He didn't look happy about it, but didn't press the matter. "Were you drinking before you started down the mountain?"

The censor in his voice had the hackles on my neck raising. "This wasn't his fault! Someone tried to run him off the road." I was as certain of that as though I had been in the car with him. He was a careful driver. He wouldn't have an accident without a reason.

"You know this how?" He lifted one eyebrow in question. "You weren't in the car with him."

Sergio patted my hand, a slight smile on his face. "It is okay, *cara*." He looked back at the young officer. "I had one glass of wine with dinner. That was several hours before I started down the mountain."

"Then what happened? Why were you in such a hurry to get back to Denver? You said something about your office being broken into?"

Why didn't he wait for Sergio to answer one question before asked two more? The teacher in me wanted to reprimand him, but I clamped my lips shut, closing off the words.

Sergio released a weary sigh. "A large SUV turned onto the highway cutting me off." I gasped, but refrained from saying anything. "I do not know if he saw me, or just did not care. His vehicle was much bigger than mine. I managed to stay on the road, but he kept pushing me toward the cliff. Instead, I hit the mountain. I was in a hurry as you say because I received a call that my office had been broken into."

"But that didn't happen," the officer contradicted. "I called security at your building. Everything was fine, no problems."

I gasped again. Someone had lured Sergio onto the

highway in the hope of sending him over the cliff. This had to be Sophia's doing. But why would she try to kill him when she was trying to bring him into her family? I received a dark glare from the officer to shut me up again. He really wanted me out of the room. Did he think he could intimidate Sergio into admitting something that wasn't true?

"If you find a dark-colored Chevrolet Yukon with damage to the front of the truck, you will find paint from my car. If you actually investigate, you will also find dark paint on my car as well. My car was silver, not dark." His tone was sharper than I'd heard him use before. It must be the pain meds, I decided. They had loosened his tongue enough to make him say things he normally wouldn't say to a police officer.

"Yes, well, there will be an investigation." His cheeks had reddened slightly at Sergio's reprimand. "I'll leave you alone for now." He backed out of the cubical, getting tangled up in the curtain before he made it through.

When I was sure he was out of earshot, I leaned against the bed. "Was it the same SUV that followed me? Would Sophia do that to you?"

He started to shake his head, but winced and held still, closing his eyes for a minute. There was a commotion in the hallway, and the curtain was ripped aside. A white faced Antony Marconi stood there, his chest heaving. "What happened? Who would do this?"

"Ask your daughter," I snapped without thinking. Fortunately, he ignored me.

"Sir, you need to leave." A nurse stood behind Marconi, her face flushed with anger. "Mr. DeCosta needs to rest."

He ignored her as well. "Tell me who did this."

"It is okay," Sergio spoke to the nurse. "He will leave in a minute."

"Like hell I will," the older man ground out. "Not until I know who tried to kill my son." The nurse backed out of the room, but didn't look happy about it.

Sergio gave a world-weary sigh. The man just didn't get it. Sergio wanted nothing to do with him. He would never be the son Marconi wanted. "Someone tried to run me off the side of the mountain. It was the same vehicle that would have run Quinn off the road not many days ago. You might want to ask Sophia what she has been up to tonight, and what kind of car she was driving."

"She would not do something like that to you when she knows how much you mean to me." Both Sergio and I gave a snort of disbelief. The woman was crazy. There was no way to predict what she would do.

"Maybe she would do it for exactly that reason," I spoke softly. "She might not like the feelings you so blatantly profess. Maybe she's jealous enough to want to do away with the person she considers her rival for your affections."

His dark eyes rested on me for a minute, and a chill passed through me. He wasn't a nice man, but he didn't appear to be insane like his daughter.

A man in a chauffer's uniform pushed aside the curtain, speaking to the older man in Italian.

Turning back to the room, Marconi looked at Sergio with a sad expression. "I will talk to you another time." With that, he disappeared down the long hall.

"What did the chauffer say to him?" I was watching to make sure Marconi didn't come back.

"A detective is asking about me. The old man needed to leave before he arrived." The ER was busier than Grand Central Station tonight.

CHAPTER NINETEEN

Antony Marconi and his chauffer had been gone only minutes when Detective Aguilar pushed aside the curtain. A nurse followed him in. "Sir, can't this wait until morning? Mr. DeCosta needs his rest." Apparently she wasn't used to dealing with the police, because she backed off when he sent her a dark glare for her efforts.

"What in the hell is going on?" he growled. "The two of you seem to be in the middle of more things than anyone else in this county." I bristled at his words. We weren't the ones causing all this trouble. He needed to find Sophia Marconi. Put her away, and he would solve any number of crimes he was investigating.

For the next half hour, Sergio went over the events of the evening again. This time he started with Marconi's visit outside the restaurant, Sophia's visit to the house, and ending with the phone call and crash into the side of the mountain.

"How did you avoid going over that cliff?" Aguilar looked skeptical.

"At one time, I thought I wanted to be a race car driver. I took many lessons on how to avoid a crash." The pain meds were beginning to wearing off, sweat beaded along his hairline and above his lip as he tried to control the pain with sheer will power. With all the interruptions, the nurses hadn't been able to attend their patient the way they should.

While the men had a staring contest, I pushed the nurse call button. It was time to put a stop to this for one night. "All right, my patient needs to rest." A grizzled doctor came instead of a nurse. "I've put up with the revolving door to this cubicle long enough. No more visitors." He glared at the detective first then at me, daring either of us to argue.

Reluctantly, Aguilar nodded assent. "I'll be back tomorrow to talk to you again. Are you coming, Ms.

Reed?" A slight smile tilted one corner of his mouth. His demeanor over the last few months had taken several different turns. I wasn't sure what he was thinking about me now.

"No, she is taking me home," Sergio spoke up. The doctor had other ideas, but Sergio wouldn't listen. An hour later, the nurse wheeled him out with a brace and sling on one arm, a flexible cast on his leg, stitches in his head and a sack full of pain pills. We both knew the routine needed to watch for problems during the first forty-eight hours after a concussion.

The long ride from the hospital back up to Greenbrier was accomplished without any incidents. By now, the accident scene had been cleared. The only evidence that something had happened was glass on the side of the road that glittered in the car's headlights, and a long scrape on the rock face. "I'll be so glad when I don't have to drive this road anymore." I whispered softly in case Sergio was sleeping.

"Move in with me, *cara*. Then you won't have to. There are two extra bedrooms in my loft if you are not comfortable sleeping in my bed yet." The offer was very tempting. I had no one to answer to, no one who would condemn me if I did. No one but God, I corrected. What would He think? Living together but separate couldn't be so very wrong.

"We'll talk about it in the morning. Tonight, we need to get you in bed." I spared him a quick glance. In the glow from the dashboard lights, he wiggled his eyebrows suggestively. The movement pulled on the stitches in his forehead, and he stopped in mid-wiggle.

"Bed sounds good," he sighed. "It has been a long day."

A long year, I thought. I felt like I had lived a lifetime in the space of that year.

The rest of the night was uneventful. Sergio's biggest problem was sleeping with the heavy cast. He wasn't supposed to put any weight on his leg until after he'd seen his doctor. That would be sometime later in the day. Having a doctor on call came in handy in emergencies.

True to his word, Detective Aguilar was at my door before we'd had our first cup of coffee. Without asking if he'd like any, I brought in a tray with three cups, a thermal carafe of coffee, and all the fixings. Placing that on the big coffee table in front of the couch where Sergio sat with his leg propped up; I went back to the kitchen for a plate of pastries. We might as well eat while the detective put us through another interrogation.

Sergio calmly repeated his account of what happened the previous evening while I was chomping at the bit to put in my two cents worth.

"Why are you treating us like we're the suspects here?" I finally managed to ask. "You should have arrested Sophia Marconi a long time ago. I told…"

"Quinn…Quinn," he spoke louder when I ignored him. "I've checked with Customs, there is no record of Sophia Marconi entering the country. According to them, she isn't here."

"Really." Sarcasm dripped from the single word. "I guess the person who was here last night and on many other occasions in the last year, is just a figment of my imagination. Maybe I'm the crazy one, not her. Why don't you lock me up? At least then I wouldn't have to put up with her visits."

"I didn't say I didn't believe you," he sighed. "I just said according to the feds, she isn't in the country."

"That does not mean she is not here," Sergio stated, his tone matter-of-fact. "If you know anything about La Cosa Nostra you know they are able to get passports under any name they want, for any country they want."

"And how would you know that? I thought you didn't have anything to do with the criminal element of your family." Again there was suspicion in the detective's eyes.

I gave a big sigh, but both men ignored me. "Just because I want nothing to do with that man, does not mean

I have no knowledge of what he is capable of. My life has depended on knowing exactly what he can do to me or anyone I care about. You must know that forgeries are possible, even United States passports are not foolproof."

Appearing to relax for the first time since arriving, the detective picked up the cup of coffee I'd poured for him. Taking a big swallow, he set it back down on the tray. He eyed the pastries hungrily, but didn't take one.

"I promise they aren't poisoned, Detective. Eating one won't compromise your integrity either." I didn't bother to disguise the disdain in my voice.

"No, but it will compromise my diet," he said, patting his slightly protruding stomach. "My wife keeps telling me to stop with all the goodies I enjoy so much." For the first time since he arrived, he sounded human, almost friendly. Ignoring his wife's voice in his head, he reached for a delicate cannoli on the plate in front of him. Closing his eyes, he savored the creamy treat, a moan escaping his lips. "You have to tell me where you get these. Even my wife would love them."

Wiping his hands on a napkin, he got back to business. "If she isn't officially in the country, can you give me anything that would help to locate her? The feds don't play nice with the locals, and aren't very forthcoming with information."

"Ask Barnard where she is," I suggested. "He was very chummy with her at Eunice's funeral." I'd told him this before, but maybe he hadn't followed up on it. "You'll have to hurry though. He retired from his company and is selling his house."

This piece of news seemed to surprise him. "Where's he going?"

I shrugged. "I have no idea. I can't find him to ask. I just know he's in a hurry to leave. Did the SEC ever recover the papers Daniel hid from Rick Frost? Do they even know how much money they stole from their clients?"

He sighed, "They aren't very forthcoming either. With

Daniel and Rick Frost both gone, I'm not sure what they hope to find, or how many others were involved with the scam. Frost took that information with him to the grave."

"Were you able to prove that he did not kill himself?" Sergio asked.

The detective looked at him; a frown drawing his dark brows into a straight line over his even darker eyes. "Why don't you think he killed himself?"

"Because he told Quinn he wanted a deal. He wanted protection. There was someone else behind this, not just him and Daniel. Whoever Daniel's girlfriend was, set up this entire scheme. I would say it was Sophia Marconi."

"Has the money Eunice got from blackmailing Frost ever been found?" When he shook his head, I continued. "I don't know if you'd be able to get any information out of the banks in the Caymans, but Eunice spent a great deal of time. I'd look there for the money she got from Frost."

"Why is it I'm just now learning this?" He turned his frown on me.

"I told you Frost said Daniel's girlfriend talked them into doing this. He said she came up with the plan. I'm also the one who told you Eunice was blackmailing Rick Frost. I'm not an investigator. Why didn't you ask Barnard where Eunice would have put the money?" Hadn't he listened to anything I'd said?

"I did," he admitted. "I believe the SEC also asked him. He denied having any knowledge of where she would have put the money."

"If you ask me, he knows where it is, and that's where he's heading. She had at least a half million dollars stashed somewhere. That would set him up very nicely."

For several minutes no one said anything, each of us lost in our own thoughts. Finally I broke the silence. "Not to change the subject, but what have you learned about Mr. Tucker's murder? Do you know who killed him?" It had been almost a month since his body had been found in the trunk of Sergio's car. "Since Sergio isn't under arrest, I assume he isn't a suspect?" Too many things had been happening for them not to be related. Was I the only one who could see that?

I got the usual answer from the detective. "I can't comment on an ongoing investigation."

"Of course you can't. Have you discovered what happened to Jenn Jones?" Even the media had moved on from those stories. It amazed me how quickly they lost interest when there was no salacious news to report. My thoughts and prayers went out to her family. If Sophia had done something to her, would she ever be found?

If the police could find Sophia, they could question her about all of these cases. It appeared that Detective Aguilar hadn't put much credence in my theory that she was behind all the crimes that had recently plagued our county.

I had to admit that Sophia's plan to get Sergio in so much trouble that he would need to ask her father for help sounded farfetched. If that had been her plan, it hadn't worked. Would she keep trying, or would she move on to something more heinous? I had no answers for any of my questions. Detective Aguilar didn't have the answers either.

"I can't question someone I can't find," he finally said as though reading my thoughts. "Do you know where your fa…Marconi is staying?" He amended when Sergio glared at him. "The feds won't even give me that information," he grumbled.

"I have not been looking for him. He seemed to find me easily enough though."

"Would his daughter stay with him, or would she have her own place?"

Sergio lifted his hands, palms up, in an 'I do not know,' gesture. "Before I left his house, she was his little darling even over his other daughters. She had him wrapped around her finger. I can only guess that nothing has changed. He will never do anything that will put her in jeopardy. Are the feds aware you are looking for her?"

The detective gave a humorless laugh. "They expect me

to give them all the information I have on anything they're interested in. They just won't share what they know." He laughed again, his sense of humor returning. "Just because they expect me to keep them informed, doesn't mean I do it." He paused for a moment, thinking over what I had just told him. "I have my own sources. I'll be doing some checking in the Caymans. Do you think she'd go after the money Frost gave Eunice?" He looked at Sergio.

"If she knew where it was, she would go after it." Sergio nodded in confirmation. "She would consider it hers if she was the one to come up with the plan to defraud their clients."

Detective Aguilar turned his dark eyes on me. "Why would Daniel go along with such a scheme? From all accounts he was making good money at the firm."

"And he was spending much more than we made. I have the bills to prove that. I don't know why he bothered marrying me when he wasn't faithful from the start. Maybe I gave him the cloak of decency he needed. It's something I'll never know. Sophia was just the last in a long line of girlfriends." Or maybe she was the first and only girlfriend. The thought came to me unbidden. These thoughts no longer hurt me. What Daniel had done no longer mattered. I just wanted to get out from under the mess he had left me, and move on.

When Detective Aguilar finally left, I leaned against Sergio. "What would you like to do today?" I kept my voice light. "Want to go dancing?"

He arched one eyebrow at me. "I can think of one dance I have been waiting to do with you for many years." He sighed heavily. "I am not sure I am up to that today though."

I could feel my face heating up. "Maybe soon," I whispered, placing my lips carefully on his, "maybe soon."

~~~

The new realtor was holding an open house the next day, meaning Sergio and I had to disappear. With his leg in the heavy brace and using crutches to get around, there were few options. His loft in Denver was the only place to go. I'd never been there, and was anxious to see where he lived.

The high-rise building overlooked downtown Denver. Floor to ceiling windows gave a bird's eye view of the city skyline and the mountains beyond that were breathtaking. The condo itself was like something out of a movie. A sweeping staircase led to the second floor where there were three bedrooms and a study. Each bedroom had its own bathroom. The bathrooms alone were larger than the bedroom I'd shared with my sister Ginger when we were growing up. The furnishings were elegant without being stuffy. Eunice could have taken some directions from his decorator.

The state-of-the-art kitchen with every appliance imaginable took my breath away. "Why such a big place for just one person?" I asked, rejoining Sergio in the living room after exploring on my own. Since he couldn't climb the stairs, he couldn't very well give me a tour.

He shrugged. "I purchased it after moving back to Colorado. When the real estate market crashed, this building was only partially finished. It was still empty two years ago. The development company had gone bankrupt, and the bank was looking to unload it on the first person or company to bid on it." He shrugged again. "I was the first."

He made it sound so simple, but I knew it probably hadn't been. The building was twenty stories high, with only two condos on each floor. The top two floors had been turned into a bi-level penthouse. "So you finished building it, and decided to live here?" I asked.

"Well, I didn't build it myself," he downplayed his involvement in the deal. "I could afford the asking price, and it was a good investment. I have made money on the deal, and I have a place to live. If I decide to sell it, I will make even more money."

We spent the day relaxing while I waited to hear from

the realtor. I kept praying that the house would sell quickly now that I had someone interested in actually selling it.

When my phone finally rang and the readout said it was the realtor, I crossed my fingers for good luck. It had only been three hours. Could I be so lucky to have an offer for the house this soon? "Hello, Barbara. How is the open house going so far?"

"I thought you said you and your husband didn't have any kids." She ignored my greeting and my question.

"That's right. We didn't have children." I wasn't sure what that had to do with selling the house.

"Then why do you have nanny cams in several of the rooms?" she snapped.

"Nanny cams?" I repeated dumbly.

"Yes, nanny cams," she was shouting now. "You know, so you can watch what is going on in your house when you aren't here? If you didn't trust me, why did you hire me?"

"I do trust you. I don't know what you're talking about. I don't have any nanny cams in the house." I wondered if she was in the wrong house.

"I'm looking right at it, so don't tell me you don't have any."

"Honestly, Barbara, I don't know what you're talking about. There aren't any cameras in my house. Um, are you sure you're in my house?"

"What kind of idiot do you take me for? Of course I'm in the right house." She repeated my address just to prove her point.

"I never installed any nanny cams," I insisted. "I had no reason to."

"Humph, well, they're here now. If you didn't put them in, who did?"

A very good question, I thought. My guess would be Sophia, but I kept that thought to myself. "Believe me; I wouldn't do something like that. They will be gone before you have another open house."

She humphed again, letting her ruffled feathers calm

down. "Well, there are at least two, so you might want to check for more." She drew a deep breath, letting it out slowly. "So far I've had three couples walk through," she finally got around to answering my original question. "They all liked the house, but thought it was a little overpriced. We can discuss this tomorrow. Another couple just walked in," she whispered. Without saying good-bye, she disconnected the phone.

I looked at Sergio. "Why would Sophia put nanny cams in my house? What could she hope to see?"

He had been pacing around on the crutches while listening to my side of the conversation. Running his fingers through his hair one more time, he looked at me. "It sounds like something she would do, but if she did it, the realtor would not have found them so easily. Unless the woman went looking through your things?" he lifted one eyebrow in question.

I shook my head. "If it was Jenn Jones, I would say that's a possibility, but Barbara is all business. She wouldn't jeopardize a listing to snoop."

Sinking down on the leather couch beside me, he laid his head back. "Will this ever end? Will the police be able to find out what is happening and who is behind it?" He sounded as discouraged as I felt.

The open house ended at four that afternoon. I wanted to be there before Barbara left. Giving ourselves plenty of time, we started up the mountain early. Each trip up and down that mountain caused my stomach to hurt. Would the big SUV come after us again? Would they succeed this time? I had never taken defensive driving lessons. I wouldn't be able to avoid going over the edge of the mountain the way Sergio had.

Until his leg healed enough for him to climb the stairs at his loft, he would be staying with me. The office Daniel kept at the house had a sleeper sofa, and Sergio could sleep there.

Barbara was just leaving when we pulled into the

garage. Her expression wasn't exactly welcoming. Maybe she was hoping to get away before I came home. Trying to be cordial, I smiled at her. "How was the last half of the open house?"

"I do have an offer. I was going to email it to you when I got back to the office." She heaved a sigh. "Since you're here, I'll give it to you now." When I handed Sergio the crutches from the back seat so he could get out of the car, she acknowledged his presence with a nod. She wasn't the most personable woman. If she was this unfriendly to the prospective buyers, I could only wonder how she made a living doing this. So far, she hadn't impressed this seller.

Back in the house, she handed me the written offer. "It's a good offer. Since you're in a hurry to get out from under these mortgages, I suggest you think long and hard before refusing it." She still sounded upset with me over the nanny cams.

The offer wasn't as good as I'd hoped, but I would be able to pay off both mortgages. There wouldn't be anything left over after Barbara took her commission though. That wasn't a big stumbling block for me. I wasn't looking to buy another house any time soon. I was curious about one thing though.

"Why would these people want so much of the furnishings?" I frowned at her. "Don't they want to pick out their own things?"

She shrugged. "I didn't ask. Unless you're particularly attached to these things, I suggest you accept the offer." That didn't explain why they wanted most of the furniture, but I didn't push it. It wasn't any of my business.

"I'll look this over tonight, and call you in the morning. Where did you find the cameras?" I was going to get rid of them before the night was over. If Sophia had put them in during one of her many clandestine visits, I didn't want to take the chance that she was watching everything I did.

Remembering Sergio in my robe after we were caught in the rain storm, I could feel my face heat up. Had Sophia witnessed that? If she was driving that SUV, is that why she tried to run him off the side of the mountain? Nothing made any sense.

Lost in these thoughts, I wasn't aware Barbara was speaking until Sergio gave me a nudge, bringing me back to the presence. "As I told you on the phone, three couples had gone through the house before I noticed the cameras. After each couple left, I walked through to make sure nothing had been moved.

"Every time I entered this room, a soft click and whirring sound started." She looked at me, expecting me to confirm hearing the noise as we walked into the room. When I shook my head, she sighed dramatically, pointing at the air conditioning vent. "I have very acute hearing," she announced haughtily. "I can hear even the slightest sound. Without anyone talking or the television on, I could easily hear the slight noise." We left the room waiting for several minutes before reentering the living room. Listening hard, there was the softest click and whirring noise coming from above us.

Sergio limped farther into the room, looking up at the vent. This was his specialty; he knew what he was looking for. Maybe Barbara also knew, since she had seen the tiny camera lens between two of the vent louvers.

I looked at Sergio for confirmation of what we were seeing. He nodded, "It is a miniature camera. A motion sensor must be attached so it only works when someone comes into the room. I would need to climb up to see what else is up there. With these," he patted the crutches, "that is impossible right now."

"Well, nothing is holding me back." I headed for the dining room for a chair to stand on. The ladder Daniel had kept in the garage was still wherever Eunice had stashed the things that had belonged to her son.

"Wait, *cara*," Sergio stopped me. "I will have someone come here to sweep the house to see how many others there are. We might be able to trace who bought them and when." Turning to Barbara, he asked, "You found more than one?"

She took us into my bedroom next, pointing again to the vent above the door. My stomach churned at the thought of someone watching while I dressed and undressed every day. Until these were removed, I would be doing all of my dressing in the bathroom or walk-in closet. Unless there were cameras there as well, I qualified.

"Thank you for finding these. As I promised, they will be removed before you hold another open house or before the new owners take possession." I held up the papers I was still holding. "I'll look this over tonight, and let you know in the morning."

She appeared satisfied that the cameras weren't my idea, and I hadn't been spying on her. I didn't need for her to back out of our contract just when there was hope of getting rid of this albatross hanging over my head.

CHAPTER TWENTY

"Who would put nanny cams in here?" I kept asking. "Why would they do that? What did they think they would see?" Sergio let me pace around the kitchen, working off my nervous energy.

When I finally flopped down on a bar stool next to him, he took my hand. Lifting it to his lips, he placed a kiss in my palm. "We will figure this out." He took the papers Barbara had left with the purchase offer. "It is unusual for people buying a house in this price range to request most of the furniture to be left behind as part of the deal. Do you have a problem leaving it?"

I didn't have to think very hard about it. I shook my head. "Most of the things here weren't my choice. Daniel had strong ideas about how a house should look. Probably something Eunice taught him," I gave a humorless chuckle. "Her house looked more like a model house than a home. If I objected to something he bought, he just said it gave the right impression to clients. I'm not sure who he was trying to impress, since we didn't entertain very often, and he never brought clients here."

Looking over the offer again, I made my decision. Picking up a pen from the breakfast bar, I signed my name. "At least I'll be out from under these mortgages." Already, I felt like a weight had been lifted from my shoulders.

We spent the remainder of the evening in the kitchen away from the spying eye of the camera in the living room. Instead of sleeping in my own room that night, I chose to sleep in the guest room. Even then, I tossed and turned most of the night. The thought that someone could be watching me while I slept made it nearly impossible to sleep.

First thing the next morning, Sergio had someone from his office come 'sweep' the house for more cameras. He would also be checking to see when they were purchased.

Maybe we would be lucky and get the name of the buyer. I still suspected Sophia had something to do with it. I couldn't imagine what her motive would be though.

"I think you've made a wise decision," Barbara told me when I called her. "How soon will you be able to vacate the house?"

Selling a house was a mystery to me, but I knew there were certain steps that needed to happen. The buyers were anxious to move in, and were willing to expedite the process. "I'll be out just as soon as both of my mortgages are paid in full." My nerves began to jangle. Suddenly I had a bad feeling about this deal. I couldn't put my finger on what though. Barbara's assurances only made me more nervous. The buyers were pushing a little too hard to get the deal done quickly. What was their hurry?

But what do I care, I silently asked? As long as I was no longer obligated to pay the mortgages, I didn't care why they were in a hurry.

While Sergio's technician worked his way through the house, I packed more of my things. Since most of the furniture was staying with the house, all I needed to pack was my personal belongings which simplified the process. Once the mortgage companies notified me that they had their money, I could just walk out.

By the end of the day, all the cameras were gone. In all there had been four, even one in the garage. What did the person who put them in hope to see in the garage? Maybe whoever had been watching had seen Tom's and Mr. Tucker's attempted attacks on me. Would that explain why they had been attacked in return? Would we ever figure this out? It would be several days before Sergio would know when they'd been purchased. The waiting game began anew.

Midmorning Detective Aguilar paid us a visit, again. This was becoming a habit, a bad one. "Good morning, Detective." I held the door for him to come in. "What can I get you this morning? I have coffee or iced tea."

"You know this isn't a social call, right?" A smile curled the corners of his lips into his mustache.

I shrugged. "I know, but a few social amenities don't hurt anyone, even in bad times."

He laughed out loud this time. "You're right. Coffee sounds pretty good right now. It's been a long day already." He waited while I poured a cup for each of us. If he'd had a bad day, I figured he was going to make ours just as bad. What would he think of the nanny cams we'd found? Unfortunately, they transmitted somewhere else, and didn't record anything onsite. We still had no idea why someone would be watching me.

Getting down to business, he looked at Sergio. "What happened to the SUV you tangled with?"

Sergio started to lift his shoulders in a shrug, but stopped when pain took a bite out of him. The broken breastbone was painful, and like broken ribs, there was nothing doctors could do for it. You just had to wait for it to heal. "I was too busy trying to keep my car from going over the edge. I didn't see where the SUV went. I remember nothing after crashing into the wall. What is this about?"

Ignoring Sergio's question, he asked one of his own. "You don't know if the other car crashed as well?"

"No, as I said, I was trying not to end up at the bottom of the mountain, the hard way. What happened to it, I cannot say." He didn't bother asking any more questions, knowing they would be ignored.

Detective Aguilar turned his dark eyes on me then. "How many vehicles did you and Daniel own?"

Daniel had been dead for almost a year. Why was he asking about vehicles now? "Two, my car, which is in the garage, and the one I assume Daniel was driving when he was killed. What's this about?" I asked the question this time with the same result.

"Did any of your friends own a SUV?"

Sighing in frustration, I tried to think of Daniel's

coworkers. They were the only ones we socialized with. "Cars aren't my thing, Detective. I don't recall anyone driving one, but that doesn't mean someone Daniel was acquainted with didn't own one."

"Do either of you know a Jeffery Goodwin?" He looked at Sergio, then me.

We both shook our heads. "Who is Jeffery Goodwin? And please do us the courtesy of not answering our questions with one of your own."

Sergio's mild reprimand had the desired effect when the detective finally answered a question. "He's the owner of the SUV that caused your accident." He kept his gaze on Sergio, watching for his reaction.

I gave a sigh of relief. They caught the guy. "What did he have to say?" I asked. "Why did he try to run Sergio off the road?"

"Well, that's the problem. We can't locate him. The only Jeffery Goodwin in Colorado is eighty-five years old and never owned a SUV. The address on the registration is an empty lot in downtown Denver."

"Why are you asking us about this person?" Sergio asked. "How do you know he owned the SUV if you can't find him?"

"For now, I'm just trying to get some answers. That SUV has been located at the bottom of the mountain not far from where you hit the wall."

"What about fingerprints?" Over the years, I've watched a lot of television cop shows. Fingerprints are the first thing the police look for in the vehicle of a suspect.

"See, that's the thing," Aguilar scratched his head. "The SUV was burned, much like your husband's car when he died. Only this time it was empty. Whoever pushed it over the edge of the cliff had planned on the gas tank exploding, burning up any evidence. It didn't exactly work out that way. With the recent storm, the vehicle was only partially burned. We managed to pull several prints, prints that belonged to two different people. From the size of one print, our guess is it belongs to a woman. Whoever she is, she doesn't have a criminal record anywhere. The other print belongs to your husband." He turned his hard gaze on me, watching my reaction this time.

My mouth dropped open. "How did his prints get in there?" My voice was a whisper, like I expected someone to be listening in. If Barbara hadn't noticed those cameras, maybe someone would have been.

Detective Aguilar had been sitting forward on the couch, closely watching us. Now he leaned back. His expression was hard to read. "His prints could have been there for a long time. They don't degrade over time. All I can say is that at one time, he'd been in that vehicle. Are you certain Daniel didn't know someone who owned a SUV?"

"He could have known a hundred people with one. That doesn't mean I would know them as well. Everything I've learned about my husband in the last few months proves that I didn't really know him at all." It was a statement of fact without any bitterness or hurt. That had all been replaced with relief that I was free from what he had become.

"Maybe this elusive girlfriend, Sophia Marconi?" he suggested. "Have you heard from her again, or her father?" He turned to Sergio. For once he didn't press the issue that Marconi was Sergio's father as well.

"I will be very happy if I never hear from either of them again." Sergio answered.

"If that's the case, we may never get to the bottom of this. If you have any ideas where either of them might be, try to contact them."

"I don't exactly have them on speed dial, Detective. I have spent my entire life trying to forget any connection to them."

With this latest news, I'd almost forgotten to ask if he had talked to Barnard. Detective Aguilar laughed at my question. "That man should be a politician. He's as slippery as an eel. He managed to spin every question I asked, giving half answers or non-answers to everything I asked him. He claims to know nothing about the money Eunice got from Frost."

"What's he say about moving? Why the sudden decision to retire?" I still hadn't seen him since the day I'd been to his house. It was like he was avoiding me. I just didn't know why.

"Oh, you'll get a laugh out of this one," he said, with a laugh of his own. "He said after losing his wife and his son, he wanted a change of scenery. There were too many painful memories here for him to stay."

"What a bunch of bunk!" I scoffed. "There was no love lost between him and Eunice. The entire time I knew them, they each went their separate way. He had very little interaction with Daniel either. I think he was most proud of his son's prowess in the bedroom. Did he say where he was going?"

"That's one of the questions he spun," he answered, shaking his head in disgust. "He's just going to travel for a while, find someplace that feels comfortable."

"Did you ask him about Sophia? What did he have to say about her?"

Aguilar shook his head again. "He's never heard of her, denies any connection to her."

I knew that was a lie. I'd seen her at Eunice's funeral with him. Barnard hadn't loved Eunice and what little love he had for Daniel had been misplaced. His first and only love was himself.

Maybe he wouldn't admit to the detective that he knew Sophia, but he couldn't deny knowing her to me. Did he know who she really was, who her father was? Until I could ask him, those questions would have to go unanswered. More waiting, I thought with a sigh.

As he stood up to leave, I remembered to tell him that I would also be moving soon. I didn't want him to think I had anything to hide. "Do you know where *you're* going from here?" he asked. The slight emphasis made me think he was comparing my move with Barnard's.

"If she will have me," Sergio answered before I could say anything, "she will marry me and live in Denver. We will not be going very far."

Seemingly satisfied with that answer, he nodded his head. "Well, keep me posted. Stay safe, both of you." His parting words were puzzling. Was he expecting more trouble?

Sergio was still sitting on the couch when I went back to the living room. Taking my hand, he positioned me so I was standing in front of him. His expression was serious, but his eyes danced mischievously. "With this thing," he tapped the brace, "I cannot get down on one knee, so this will have to do. Quinn Dunston Reed will you do me the honor of becoming my wife?" The previous times he had talked about marriage it had been in general terms. This was definitely a proposal.

He held up a small velvet box with a beautiful diamond ring nestled inside. Rainbows of colors shot out at me as a sunbeam from the window behind him struck the huge stone. "This is the ring Gino DeCosta, the man who was a real father to me, gave my mom when he asked her to marry him."

His tender words caught at my heart. This was what I had wanted for so long. Tears brimmed in my eyes and clogged my throat. "Yes, yes, yes," were the only words I could say as I sat down beside him. Wrapping my arms around his neck, I leaned in to him as his lips captured mine in a heart-stopping kiss. "How soon can we make it happen?" I whispered, before he could deepen the kiss.

"It would be today if I didn't have this thing." He tapped the leg brace again. "It would not make for much of a honeymoon." He slipped the ring on my finger, placing a kiss over the top of it to seal our engagement.

My stomach fluttered at the thought of finally making love with Sergio. This is what I had dreamed of since my freshman year of high school when I met this wonderful boy, now a man. It felt like I'd only been marking time, waiting to become his wife. How much of my life had been a waiting game, I wondered? For now, I would be happy to be his wife. The rest would come when the next part of this waiting game was over.

~~~

While I continued to pack, my mind replayed the conversation with Detective Aguilar. How had Daniel's fingerprints gotten in that SUV? Who was Jeffery Goodwin? Why had he used a fake address on the vehicle registration? What connection did he have to Daniel? Had he killed Daniel? Why had he tried to run Sergio off the road? The questions swirled around in my mind making me dizzy with the effort of trying to find the answers.

Another puzzle was the couple buying the house. Why did they want everything here? If they could afford the purchase price, couldn't they afford their own furniture? When selling a house, the appliances were usually left behind, but not everything else. It didn't make sense to me.

Finally giving up trying to puzzle that one out, I went in search of Sergio. He couldn't help me pack with his leg in the brace, and I wanted to make sure he was all right. With his legs propped up on the coffee table, a laptop on his legs, he was concentrating so hard on what he was working on he didn't hear me come in. His dark brows were drawn together in a frown. Whatever he was working on troubled him.

My future husband, I thought as I watched him, a goofy grin on my face. My heart was near to bursting with happiness. I twisted the ring on my finger which brought thoughts of other rings. I'd taken off the rings Daniel had given me shortly after he died. Had he known Sophia when he married me? Or did she come later? Had he turned to other women because I had held a part of my heart away from him? I couldn't let those thoughts ruin what I was going to have with Sergio. What Daniel did was on him, not me.

"Why the serious face, *cara*?" I gave a squeal of surprise as Sergio's words startled me. "Does the ring not fit? Would you prefer a different one?" He'd moved the laptop off his legs, and I sat down beside him.

"No, this ring is perfect, and I don't want a different one. I was just putting some troubling thoughts to rest. What were you working on?"

He studied my face for a moment before answering. "My technician talked to the company that made those nanny cams. A spy shop in Denver purchased them two years ago."

"Spy shop?" I frown, unsure what that was.

"Yes, one of those shops that sells all sorts of spyware, like nanny cams, to see what someone else is doing while you are not there."

"Did he find out who bought them from the spy shop?" I couldn't imagine anyone wanting to spy on me. Up to now, my life had been pretty dull.

Sergio's pause before answering my question said I wasn't going to like the answer. He was right. "It was Jeffery Goodwin," he said softly, "the man who doesn't exist."

My stomach churned. Once again that whirlwind took control of my life, twisting me every which way. Would this ever stop?

Sergio heaved a heartfelt sigh. "I called Detective Aguilar. He was not happy that we had failed to tell him about the cameras when he was here this morning, or that I had them removed without telling him." He sighed again. "I am afraid I am on his list again."

"What list is that?" I wasn't sure what he was talking about.

"His s… list," he said with a laugh. "That can stand for suspect or something else." I didn't know how he could joke about something this serious, but it was kind of funny. "He was on his way to get the cameras from my technician when he hung up. Maybe he can get fingerprints off them."

"What about your techs fingerprints? Wouldn't he have ruined anything this Jeffery Goodwin left behind?"

"Give my people a little more credit than that, *cara*. When they work on a job, they always wear gloves so they don't leave prints or smear those left behind by someone else."

"When did he buy them?" I wanted to know how long they'd been in my house, or did I?

Again, Sergio paused, and I braced myself for more discomforting news. "Four years ago, but that does not mean they have been here that long. Maybe he bought them for...something else," he finished lamely, lifting his hands palms up in an 'I don't know' gesture.

Leaving him to his computer, I went back upstairs. Until I started packing, I hadn't realized I had so much personal stuff. Clothes weren't the only things to pack. There were the small items that would mean nothing to anyone but me. This brought me to the safe. I still needed to clean that out. The only things left in there were the few pieces of jewelry Daniel had given me, and some pieces that had belonged to my mother.

Spinning the dial to open it, I sucked in my breath as I pulled on the heavy door. "Grrr, damn it!" I slammed the door without bothering to twist the combination to lock it. There was nothing there to keep safe any longer. Even my mother's jewelry and the rings Daniel had given me were gone.

"Detective Aguilar isn't going to be happy to hear from me again," I said as I came down the stairs. Before I made it to the bottom step, the doorbell chimed. Maybe I wouldn't have to call him after all. Maybe he'd come to me.

But the detective wasn't standing on my doorstep. I gave a heavy sigh. "What do you want now, Sophia?" I should have checked to see who was there before opening the door. Now I had to face the music, or rather face

Sophia.

"I want my brother. What are you doing with him? I need to know."

"Why, we're playing house of course. What did you think we were doing?" Taunting a psychopath might not be a wise idea, but I couldn't seem to stop myself.

Her face turned purple with rage. "You leave my brother alone. He is too good for you." Oh, brother. Wasn't it enough to be told that on a constant basis by my former mother-in-law? Now I had to deal with this delusional woman telling me the same thing.

Sergio hobbled up to the door. "Go away, Sophia. The police are looking for you. I don't think you want to deal with them any more than your father does. He is wise enough to know when to cut and run. The detective will be here soon. Would you like to spend some quality time with him in a small interrogation room?"

"You think I am afraid of the American police? They can do nothing to me. I have done nothing wrong." She chuckled. "At least nothing they can prove."

"Did you kill Daniel? Is that what they can't prove?"

"I did not kill Daniel," Sophia shouted at me, anger pouring off her in waves. "I would never do that. I love him!" She was losing touch with reality.

"Don't you mean you *loved* him? He's dead."

She stared at me for a long moment, insanity shining out of her clear blue eyes. Slowly, the insanity receded, and she laughed. "Of course, that is what I meant. But I will always love him. You know he never loved you. He loves me." Again her mind slipped away from reality.

Her words didn't have the power to hurt me like they would have a year ago. I no longer cared. "I suppose he did. Aren't you curious to know who killed him? I would think you'd want to know, if you loved him so much." If egging her on made her give up some information about all that's been happening I'd risk it.

She lifted one shoulder in a careless shrug. "If the

police are too incompetent to figure it out, I will not help them. Are you going to let me in?"

"No, I don't think I am. What did you do with my jewelry? How did you know where the safe was, and what the combination was?" I decided offense was called for in this situation.

Her serene smile had me wanting to claw her eyes out. "I know many things you would not like me to know." She gave an evil chuckle. The woman was enough to drive me to murder. "I want to speak to my brother alone. Go away." She turned away from me. If she pretended I wasn't there, maybe it would be true.

"I have nothing to say to you. Go away and leave Quinn and me alone. You can pass that message to your father as well." He stepped back from the door, pushing it shut. Her maniacal screech could be heard through the thick panel. Maybe my nearest neighbor could hear her as well.

"I need to call Detective Aguilar. If we can keep her ranting and raving long enough, maybe he can get here to arrest her." I pulled my cell phone from my pocket.

"I already called him." His words stilled my hands. "I don't know if he will get here in time to talk with her though. She seems to have a second sense telling her the police will be arriving soon."

"Shouldn't we have kept her talking then?" I reached for the door knob, but he took my hand.

"No, if we make it easy for her, she will know something is up. Let her stay out there screaming at us. I told him she was here. He will hurry."

"I think she stole all of my jewelry from the safe in my room. How did she know the combination?"

"Maybe she did not need it," he suggested. "Remember who she is and what her family represents. As a child, she enjoyed picking the locks on any door that was meant to keep her out or in." That was better than thinking Daniel had given her the combination.

Sophia's screaming voice was joined by a masculine

one, and I looked out the peep hole in the door. If we were lucky, Detective Aguilar was here to arrest her. Again I was wrong. A strange man was with her, trying to make her leave. A siren could be heard coming up the mountain road.

That quickly, Sophia turned off her screams, moving towards a car parked down the hill. She sent one final malicious glare back at the house before she left. Would the detective get here in time to stop her from leaving? Apparently not. The big car moved away as the unmarked police car rounded the last curve.

We stepped outside, pointing at the departing car. Detective Aguilar understood our message, making a quick turn in the road to follow the other car. His siren was still blaring as he disappeared from sight.

CHAPTER TWENTY-ONE

"Did you catch her?" I asked, before Detective Aguilar could even step out of his car only minutes later. If he caught up with the departing car, he hadn't arrested Sophia. She wasn't sitting in the back seat of his car.

"Catch who?" he growled at me. "The only person in that limo was the driver. He didn't know who I was talking about. He could barely speak English, or pretended he couldn't."

I sagged against the side of his car. How had she disappeared? "We saw her get in the back seat of that car," I insisted, looking up at Sergio for confirmation. "Maybe the driver stopped to let her out when he knew you were following him."

The detective shook his head. "I didn't lose sight of that car long enough for someone to get out and hide. The only time it stopped was when I pulled up behind him."

"Did you search the car?"

"Without a warrant?" he gave a harsh laugh. "I had no cause. The driver was courteous and cooperative. He opened all the doors and even the trunk without me asking him to. He was the only one in that car."

"But we saw her get in," I insisted. "How could she get away?"

"There's probably a compartment under one of the seats where she was hiding," Detective Aguilar said. "Without just cause, I couldn't go looking for it." He shook his head. "This is how the Mafia works. They don't give law enforcement a reason to search as long as what they don't want you to find is well hidden. When we come back with a search warrant, it's too late. The contraband is already gone."

"You might be able to get her fingerprints off the door handle to compare it with the ones you found on that SUV," Sergio suggested, pointing at the screen door. He was leaning against the house, steadying himself with the crutches without putting pressure on his broken leg.

While the detective dusted the handle on the screen door, I told him about my missing jewelry. "I don't care about the things Daniel gave me. I do care about the things that had belonged to my mother. Why would she take them? They meant nothing to her."

The detective shook his head. "You keep telling me she's a psychopath. You can't explain why someone like that does anything. You can't even prove she's the one who took them. How would she get the combination?"

"She was very good at picking locks when she was a child," Sergio explained. "Maybe she graduated to safes." There was no telling how many times she had been in the house without my knowledge. She could have opened the safe at any time. Even the realtor hadn't known about the safe or the combination. It had to be Sophia.

Within minutes, he had pulled several prints from the decorative handle before heading up to my room to dust the safe for prints as well. "I'll have the lab compare these prints with the ones found in the SUV. If we're lucky, they'll be a match." He took a report on the missing jewelry before getting back in his car. "If she's the one who took it, maybe she hasn't disposed of it yet, and we can recover it for you."

If he couldn't find her, how he would recover my jewelry? I had so many questions swirling in my mind with no answers in sight. Could he connect Sophia with the unknown Jeffery Goodwin? Was it a crime to push your own car over a cliff? I was being swept up in that whirlwind again. Would I ever be able to get out?

I was beyond caring what happened to Sophia, or who killed Daniel. I just wanted this mess to be over. So many things had happened in the last year, and it felt like it was all coming together. I just didn't know where it was going to lead me. Everything had to be connected, but what was the one unifying factor? I was missing something. The harder I tried to piece things together, the more elusive they became.

An hour later, Detective Aguilar was back. If he'd looked dejected when he left, he looked positively morose now. "What now?" I whispered.

Looking at Sergio, the detective shuffled his feet for a moment before finding his voice. "I know you claim no kinship to Sophia or her father, but she's still your blood. I'm sorry to tell you this." He drew a deep breath before proceeding. "That limo went over the cliff. It must have happened just minutes after I came back here."

I gasped, covering my mouth with my hand. Once again we were in my living room where Sergio was sitting on the couch, his leg propped up on the coffee table. The color drained from his face. "What happened?" I couldn't imagine what was going through his mind.

"The investigators are looking into the cause. I just know that somehow it went over. When I got to the spot where it broke through the guard rail, the first responders had just arrived. They were just now able to bring the car up. No one survived."

"Do you know for sure she was in the car? Maybe she had managed to get out before you caught up with it." I didn't know if I was hoping she was still alive to continue tormenting us, or if I wanted confirmation she was gone for good.

He shook his head. "According to the paramedics who went down to the car, the driver was still alive when they reached him. There were several bullet holes inside the car. One had gone through the seat, hitting him in the back. He kept pointing to the back seat, saying something they couldn't understand. But there was no one else in the car. He died still trying to make them understand. They searched the mountainside without finding anyone. When they got the car up on the road, blood was seeping out from underneath the back seat."

He drew a deep breath before continuing. "She had

been hiding in a compartment under the seat. She was holding a gun. As the car cartwheeled down the side of the mountain, she must have gripped it hard enough to squeeze the trigger, unloading the gun in the process. She was hit several times, probably by ricochets off the metal parts of the compartment. She also had a head wound from bouncing around in the compartment. The ME will have to confirm cause-of-death." He let out a heavy sigh. "Again, I'm sorry for your loss."

Sergio shook his head. "I cannot say I am sorry. She was an evil person. Why did the car go over the edge? If the driver thought he fooled you, why would he be driving recklessly?"

Detective Aguilar shrugged. "That's for the accident investigators to determine. It will be several days before they figure it out. Her father needs to be told." He sighed. "How do I get in touch with him?" He was asking the question of himself as much as he was asking us. He looked a little grey in the face at the thought of having to notify Antony Marconi of his daughter's death. What would a man like him do when hearing that kind of news?

"As I have said before, I have no way of contacting him. He just shows up. Maybe he will hear of the accident and contact…someone." He didn't want to be the one notifying that man either. I couldn't say I blamed either of them.

It didn't take long for the news to reach Antony Marconi that something had happened to Sophia, bringing him back to our door. The tentacles of his organization were far reaching.

"Where is my son?" Without any greeting, he snapped his question at me. When Sergio hobbled to the door, Marconi ignored me, pressing his demands on Sergio. "Where is Sophia? What happened to her?"

"I can only assume she is in the county morgue. I do not know where that is. I do not know what caused the accident. You will have to ask the county sheriff's department."

Marconi sniffed with disdain. "I want to see her. How did she die?" If his connections had told him she was dead, why hadn't they told him how she died?

"I do not have any answers for you. Go see the sheriff," Sergio said again.

Marconi turned his burning gaze on me. "Are you going to keep me outside while I try to find out what happened to my Sophia? Where are your manners?" He acted like I was an ill-bred hillbilly.

"No, we are not inviting you in," Sergio answered for me. "We have no answers for you," he reemphasized. "Go talk to the authorities. Only they can answer your questions."

The other man's face turned purple with rage. "You care nothing for your own sister? Someone killed her, you will avenge her murder." It was an order.

Now Sergio laughed. "That is your life style, not mine. I let the law handle criminals." He left the words *like you* hanging silently in the air. "The car went over the cliff; it was an accident, not anyone's fault."

"Carlo was an excellent driver; he would not let such a thing happen unless he was forced off the road."

"All the more reason you need to talk to the people investigating the accident. Maybe they will find evidence to prove what you are saying."

"They will not look for evidence," the older man said, scorn heavy in his voice. "They will just be glad one more of La Cosa Nostra is gone." His eyes had lost focus for a moment. Now he turned his hard glare on Sergio. "Someone needs to claim her body. That someone is you. It is your duty."

"Duty? No, I have no duty towards you or Sophia. Call one of your people if you are afraid to go to the police."

Marconi's face grew darker with the rage building in him at Sergio's insult. "I am not afraid of the police, but I will not place myself at their mercy. I want my daughter back," he growled. "It is for you to bring her to me. You owe your life to me."

"I owe you nothing." Sergio's growl matched the older man's. "You only supplied the genetic material to make a baby. The people who made me the man I am are my mother and Gino DeCosta. If you want Sophia, go get her. Leave me out of your little drama. I am through talking to you." He moved away from the door, leaning heavily on the crutch as he closed it in Marconi's face.

"Was that wise?" I whispered as though my voice would carry through the solid wood door. "What will he do now?" Before Sergio could answer, the powerful engine of the limousine that brought Marconi here started. With a roar, it sped off. Would he be the next one to go over the cliff? In the past year, more cars had gone off the mountain than in the four years that I had lived in Greenbrier.

He said something in Italian that I didn't understand, and probably didn't want to. Drawing a deep breath, he let it out slowly. "He will get one of his men to go to the morgue or send someone from a mortuary. He will not go to the police himself."

"Do you think he's right, that someone ran that car off the road?"

Sergio limped into the living room, sitting down with an exhausted sigh. The conversation had stretched out too long. He needed to sit down before he fell down. It had only been a few days since his accident, and he still had a lot of healing to do. With everything that had been going on, he hadn't been able to get much rest.

Laying his head against the back of the couch, he looked up at me. "Who is left that would want Sophia dead? Frost is dead; Daniel is dead. They were the ones involved in the scheme at Daniel's company. Or were there others involved? Is that what this is all about?"

Who else is there, indeed? My head was spinning with all the questions. I sat down beside him, and he wrapped me in his strong arms. Would we ever be able to figure this out? Would we ever be free of this mess?

"This will end," he whispered as though reading my thoughts. "Someday this will be over. It has to be. I don't want to wait until then to marry you. Will you go away with me? Marry me now. The honeymoon will have to wait until some broken bones have healed, but we can be married this week."

My heart jumped in my chest. "I've waited for this forever," I whispered against his lips. "As long as we're married, I can wait another month for the honeymoon."

We spent the rest of the afternoon, snuggled on the couch, making plans for our simple wedding. After a quick call to the pastor of the church I'd gone to since Daniel's death, it was all arranged. We would get married the following Saturday. Now if nothing more happened, I would finally be married to the man I had hoped to marry more than eight years ago.

~~~

"What did you tell the SEC?" Barnard snarled at me when I opened the door. "They've taken my money."

"I...I didn't tell them anything." I stammered in the face of his tirade. "What money did they take?" Why don't these people leave me alone? It felt like someone was conspiring against me. Just when I thought there was an end to all this, something more came up.

"All of it," he snarled again. "You're the only one who knew about it. It had to be you." His beefy fist hit the frame of the screen door. I was grateful I had insisted Daniel have a decorative security door installed. Without it, I would have taken the hits from all the people who have pounded on it in the last year.

"Knew about what? Barnard, you aren't making any sense. Why would the SEC take your money? You weren't involved with what Daniel and Rick Frost were doing, were you?"

He shook his head, but couldn't make his voice work. I kept pushing trying to find out how deep this conspiracy went. "You knew Sophia." It wasn't a question. "Did she talk you into defrauding your clients as well?" He shook his head again, but I wasn't through. I still wanted to know about Sophia and Daniel. Were you and Daniel both sleeping with her?" Without saying anything more, he turned, staggering back to his car.

Sergio had said this would all end someday. How long did I have to wait? How many more people had been involved?

CHAPTER TWENTY-TWO

Wandering around the house on my last day to live there was bittersweet. There had been good times here, but the bad far outweighed the good. I will just be glad to put it all behind me. Within a week, I would be Mrs. Sergio DeCosta. The thought made me smile as I did a little happy dance around the breakfast island in the kitchen.

I tried to recall some of the happy times with Daniel. I didn't want to always remember him with regret and anger. Our honeymoon in the Caymans had been one of the good times. Daniel had been so carefree then, no worries about work or money. It was before he had started running up a pile of bills we couldn't afford to pay. He even joked about all the people who hid money from the IRS or a soon-to-be former spouse there.

"Oh my gosh." My happy dance ended as I braced myself against the breakfast island. "That's where he put the money he stole from his clients. That's why Barnard had been so angry; he wanted that money." If he had been working with Daniel and Rick Frost in their scheme, they had all put their ill-gotten gains in a bank in the Caymans. I was willing to bet that's where Eunice had put her blackmail money as well. I needed to call someone, but whom? I had no idea how to contact the SEC. "Detective Aguilar," I announced to the empty room. "He'll know what to do."

Sergio had gone into his office that morning. He still couldn't drive, but someone from his company came to pick him up. I would be meeting him at his loft later this afternoon. Now I wished he was here.

Before I could pick up the phone, the doorbell chimed. Could I ignore it? The realtor was coming later to pick up the keys. That was the only thing left before I could walk away for a final time. Maybe she had come early.

But it wasn't the realtor. "Daniel?! You...you're dead." I

rubbed my eyes, blinking rapidly. My head spun as dark spots swam before my eyes. This had to be a hallucination. Or I'd been lied to, again. My back stiffened at the thought, as I glared at the man standing at my door.

"Yes, Quinn, Daniel is dead. I'm Jake Williams, an insurance salesman. Someone people try to avoid at all cost. No one wants to be pressured into buying something they don't want or need. I'm almost invisible to most people. That's the way I like it." He chuckled.

I stared at the man, confused. Why was he talking about himself in the third person? Was this Daniel or just someone who looks like him? Had his 'death' been a ruse to get him out of trouble with the SEC? He looked like Daniel while at the same time he was different. He was heavier than Daniel had been. His hair was longer and a lighter shade. His face and his lips were fuller, like he'd had plastic surgery. He also had a deep tan like he'd been spending a lot of time in the sun. Probably in the Caymans, I thought.

"May I come in?" He reached for the door handle.

"No!" I grabbed for the key in the lock making sure the deadbolt was in place. "I don't know you."

He chuckled. "What's wrong? Afraid I might try to sell you some insurance?" He taunted me, laughing like he'd just told a funny joke.

No, just afraid, I thought. If he was Daniel, someone else had died in his place. Had he tried to drive Sergio off the mountain? What about Mr. Tucker, and Jenn Jones? Did he have something to do with the accident that killed Sophia and her chauffeur? Would I ever escape this whirlwind that had taken over my life? "I don't invite salesmen into my house when I'm alone." It was the only excuse I could think of.

"It's no longer your house, Quinn. It belongs to me now."

My mouth opened and shut like a fish out of water, but no sound came out. "You bought the house?" I asked, finally finding my voice. "Why? Why did you fake your own death?"

"I don't know what you're talking about." He pretended ignorance. The smile on his face put the lie to his words. "I didn't fake anything. I would like to come in. I have that right now that your mortgages have been paid off." He gripped the handle, giving it a shake.

"Go talk to the realtor. She's coming to pick up the keys later today. Then I'll be gone, and you can come in with your wife."

He laughed again. "No, Jake Williams isn't married, but I'd like it if you'd stay. I think we'd get along very well."

"Ha! You had your chance. I'm getting married Saturday." But that couldn't happen if this was really Daniel. "Damn you," I whispered.

His face grew dark as anger overrode his humor. "You can't get married to that damned Italian."

"Why's that?" If I played along, maybe he'd say something to prove all the things he's done.

"Because you're already married." He smirked, like he'd caught me in a crime. But he'd just given himself away.

"No, my husband is dead, remember? You can't have it both ways. Either you're Daniel, and the authorities will arrest you, or you're someone else, and have no say in my life. Which is it?"

If looks could kill, I'd be dead. "That damned SOB should be dead," he growled

My stomach churned. He was the one who tried to run Sergio over the edge of the cliff! How many others had he killed? "Why did you come here? Why would you come out of hiding?"

"Because you need to know you're still my..." He stopped midsentence before he admitted too much. Drawing a calming breath, he was back in character. "We need to talk, Quinn. I think you'll see things my way."

"Not going to happen," I shook my head. "Go away."
Before I could close the door, an errant breeze stirred up,
sending in a whiff of something familiar: Daniel's
distinctive aftershave.

I gasped, staring at him. "You've been in here since
you…died," I finished lamely.

"What makes you say that?" He seemed nervous now.

"I've smelled your aftershave in here, several times."
He'd almost had me believing in ghosts. When I smelled it,
I couldn't come up with any other explanation. There was
nothing left in the house that had belonged to Daniel,
thanks to Eunice. How else would that particular scent have
gotten in here? "How did you get in?"

"I'm not admitting to anything, mind you, but you need
to remember to lock *all* the doors." His emphasis on all the
doors had me questioning which doors I forgot to lock.
"Did you ever think to change the code for the garage door
remote?" He asked smugly.

My stomach dropped. I hadn't thought to changing that.
Why would I? No one else had it but Daniel and me. "Did
you steal my jewelry?"

"I've taken nothing that wasn't mine," he growled still
not admitting he was Daniel.

"You took my mother's jewelry! I want it back. It
means nothing to you."

He lifted one shoulder. "We can discuss it later." With
another chuckle, he turned away. "See you, Quinn." There
was no car in the drive. Like Sophia, he must have stashed
his car out of sight so I couldn't tell the police what kind of
vehicle he was driving. I closed the door, leaning against
the solid panel. What next? I silently asked myself. Would
this ever end? Watching out the side window to make sure
he left, I ran for the phone as soon as I heard a car move
down the street.

"Daniel is alive!" I almost shouted when Sergio
answered his phone. My hands were shaking so hard I
could barely hold the phone to my ear.

"What? *Cara*, what did you say?" He sounded as confused as I felt. Even though the man had denied being Daniel, I had little doubt it was him.

Drawing a calming breath, I started over. "Daniel was just here. He's alive. This has all been a hoax."

"But why would he come back now? Why would he show himself?"

"Because he's an arrogant son of a gun," I answered. "He thinks by giving himself a new name and a new profession and changing his hair color, no one will recognize him."

"Why did he come to the house? What did he think you would do?"

"He bought the house." I wasn't making any sense, because this wasn't making any sense.

"You need to call Detective Aguilar. I will be there as soon as I can."

Keeping my fingers crossed, I dialed the detective's number. If he wasn't available, what would I do then? I whispered a prayer of thanks when he answered his phone after three rings. "I hate to keep asking you this, but can you come to my house?"

"What's wrong, Quinn? Has something else happened?"

"You might say that." A hysterical giggle bubbled up in my throat. He was never going to believe me. "Daniel was just here. Or I think it was Daniel. Does everyone have an identical twin somewhere on the planet?"

"What? Say again. You aren't coming through very clear, Quinn."

I tried to swallow my giggles so he would believe me. "Daniel was just here."

"Did he hurt you? Was Sergio there with you?"

"I wish. He had a driver pick him up so he could go in to work. I'm not hurt, just hysterical." One final giggle escaped before I finally got control of myself, and could explain what had just happened.

"I'm on my way. Keep your doors locked, and don't let anyone in until I get there." He hung up without waiting for me to agree.

It was thirty-five minutes before he finally pulled into my drive. I didn't wait for him to come to the front door. Instead I met him in the drive. "Did he touch anything?" he asked without preamble.

Like Sophia had, Daniel had tried to open the security door. After he had lifted Sophia's prints, I had cleaned the handle. No one had used that door since. Daniel's prints should be the only ones there now. It only took a couple of minutes for him to finish with that task.

"Okay, tell me what he had to say. Why did he come here?" Before I could answer, Sergio's driver pulled into the drive. As fast as his broken leg would allow, he had me in his arms, kissing the top of my head. His heart was beating as erratically as mine.

Daniel hadn't been there but a few minutes. It took me longer than that to retell what happened. "Has the guy gone completely off his rocker?" Detective Aguilar shook his head. "Did he think you wouldn't say anything?"

"I don't know. When you catch him, you can ask him. He'll be moving in here later today." In all the chaos, I almost forgot to tell the detective about the Caymans. "I'm willing to bet that's where all of their clients' money is. If he didn't put it under his own name, see if there is a Jake Williams with a large account. Or maybe Jeffery Goodwin. That will be Daniel." I couldn't guess what names Rick Frost or Sophia would use. That guessing game would have to wait until they finally got their hands on Daniel. He was the last of this gang of thieves left.

But Daniel was smart enough to know I'd call the authorities. He didn't bother picking up the key from the realtor. He'd disappeared again.

Instead of getting married as Sergio and I had planned, I started divorce proceedings. I wasn't sure how the courts would handle a divorce from someone who was supposed to be dead. As long as there was a chance Daniel would reappear sometime in the future, I wanted no more ties to him. I never wanted to see him again.

But that wasn't to be. A week later, Detective Aguilar came to Sergio's loft. His grim features were enough to tell me something new had happened. That whirlwind was still playing havoc with my life.

"We have Daniel in custody," he stated once we were seated. "He's asking for you."

I shook my head. "Too bad, I don't want to see him, ever again."

"I hate to put you through this, Quinn, but I'm asking anyway." He sighed. "He's in pretty bad shape. He says he'll confess all, but only to you."

Sergio took my hand, but didn't say anything. "What do you mean 'pretty bad shape'? What's wrong with him?"

"Someone worked him over, and left us to pick up the pieces. The docs say he isn't going to make it. I'm sorry, Quinn." Over the past year, Detective Aguilar had become more like a friend to us than a policeman. I knew it hurt him to have to ask me to do this. I couldn't muster up any sympathy for Daniel though. If even half of what I suspected of him was true, he was an evil man. He had brought this on himself.

"What do you want me to do? What does he expect of me?"

"He knows he's dying, and he wants a chance to explain." He shrugged. "It's up to you."

"If I don't go and he dies without admitting what he's done, what happens to all those cases? Will they just be laid at his doorstep, or will you have to keep looking for evidence?"

"We can't close those cases without evidence." It was that simple. Go, and maybe we would get the answers we needed. Don't go, and there would always be open cases. The police would go on looking for answers.

Finally I nodded my head, a sigh of resignation

escaping my lips. "Where is he? What do I need to do?"

Time was of the essence. He was stubbornly hanging on in the hope I would come see him. Detective Aguilar hadn't been overstating Daniel's condition. Entering the ICU cubicle, I couldn't stop the gasp from escaping my lips. If this was really Daniel, he was almost beyond recognition. There were tubes and monitors all over him.

"Quinn," he breathed softly, a wet rattle coming from his chest with each breath. "Thank you for coming."

"I didn't have much choice. I need closure as much as the families of those people you killed." My words were harsh, but I really didn't feel sorry for him. "Why did you do all this?"

"I didn't have much choice." I had to step close to the bed in order to hear his whispered voice. I just hoped it wasn't another act. "The feds were hot on our trail. If I didn't want to spend the rest of my life in prison, I needed to disappear."

"Who died that day? Who was in your car?"

He shrugged like it was no big deal. "Just a homeless man. No one even bothered to tell the police he's missing."

Was this really the man I'd married thinking he was a loving, honest person? But he hadn't been honest. I'd learned that much in the year since he died. Or I thought he died. He hadn't been a loving person either.

"How could you be so cold, so cruel? You killed a man, more than one," I corrected. "Did you kill Mr. Tucker? What happened to Jenn Jones, my realtor?"

He gave a wet cough, a trickle of blood running down the side of his mouth. He was dying for real this time.

"I didn't do anything to Jenn Jones. That one was all Sophia. Jones was becoming a liability."

"What do you mean a liability? What did she do?"

"She knew Sophia was getting into the house when you weren't home. She wanted money to keep quiet, or she'd tell you."

Greed again, I thought. Had the whole world turned

greedy without me noticing? "Do you know where her body is?" I wished I didn't have to ask him all these questions, but he wouldn't talk to anyone else. It was up to me to get the answers we needed.

"She's buried somewhere." He lifted one hand weakly. "I don't know where." It really didn't matter to him.

"But what about Mr. Tucker? He didn't have anything to do with any of this."

"He was going to hurt you! I couldn't let him do that."

"How do you know he was going to hurt me? Were you having me watched?"

He gave a little crooked grin. "I saw everything. After DeCosta ran him off, I thought for sure the cops would arrest him when Tucker's body was found in his trunk." He gave his head a small shake. "They couldn't do anything right. They didn't do anything when that teacher got beaten up by a big Italian either."

I gasped. "You had Tom beaten up? Why?"

"He was going to rape you; that's why. No one touches what's mine."

This was all surreal. "How did you know what Tom or Mr. Tucker did? How did you see it?"

"I've been monitoring what went on in that house since we moved in until your stupid realtor found the cameras."

My head swam, and I staggered against the bed. "You put the cameras in the house? Why?"

"I wanted to know if you cheated on me. And you would have if I hadn't sent Sophia to the house in the nick of time. You would have screwed him right there on my couch in my living room."

If he wasn't already on death's doorstep, I might have helped him along right then. "I never cheated on you while we were married! It was you who did all the cheating. Is that why you tried to run him off the mountain?" I had no doubt he had been behind the wheel the night Sergio managed to escape driving off the cliff.

"You've always been in love with him. He needed to

pay for taking you away from me." He tried to muster up some anger, but it required too much energy.

"What about all of your girlfriends? You were sleeping around right from the beginning of our marriage." He started to argue, but I held up my hand. "Don't try to blame me for that. I was faithful to you."

"You never loved me," he accused without any heat. He could no longer muster up the energy. "It was always him. I wanted to make you hurt the way I did. But you didn't really care."

"I loved you, Daniel. Maybe not the way I love Sergio, but I did love you at first. You killed that a long time ago. What about Sophia? What did she mean to you?"

He was quiet for a minute, and I didn't think he was going to answer. "She understood me," he finally said like that explained everything.

"What about your father? Did he sleep with her?"

He gave gurgling laugh. "That old man thought he was really something when she slept with him. She just wanted to get at his money. She got a big chunk of it, too, when she convinced him to invest with us." He gave another wet chuckle. "He deserves what he got. He knew she was mine, but he had to try and take her away from me. I'm surprised he never put the make on you." Even when he was dying, his only thoughts were of himself.

Daniel wanted Sophia, but he also wanted me. In the end, he lost both of us and everything else. Greed won out. But this wasn't what I came here to learn. "Did you kill her?"

His eyes closed, and he didn't say anything for a long minute. I thought maybe he had slipped away. Finally, he drew a shallow breath, looking out the window. "I'm sorry I had to do that, but she was going to go after you next. I couldn't let her do that. You're my wife."

"Why would she come after me? I didn't do anything to her."

"As long as her brother was with you, she knew he

would never return to the family. That was her life's mission, I guess you could say. Either bring him into the family, or kill him. She was crazy." He weakly waved his hand dismissing the subject.

"Sergio never would have joined the Mafia. He wanted nothing to do with them."

"Whatever, it's done now." He was growing weaker. I needed to ask the questions Detective Aguilar had given me.

"What about Rick Frost? How did he die? He didn't kill himself."

His lips quirked up slightly. "That was Sophia's doing. Her kind can reach just about anywhere. It gave her a thrill to know she could have him killed right there in the jail. She managed to bribe someone who works there. I don't know who."

"But why kill him?"

"Rick was trying to make a deal with the feds. We couldn't let that happen. He would have told them where the money was just to save his own neck."

"And how is that different from what you've done? How many people have died to cover up what you've done?"

"Rick killed my mother." A tear slipped down his face. That was the first real emotion he'd shown. "I couldn't let him get away with that."

"She was blackmailing him. She was as greedy as the three of you. The SEC found your money." This would be my parting shot at him.

"No! That was supposed to be ours, so we could start over again."

"You've got to be kidding! You really think I would stay married to you after all you've done?"

"You're my wife, Quinn. That damned Italian can't have you." He tried to grab my hand, but his grip was so weak I pulled away from him.

There was one more thing Detective Aguilar needed to

know. "Who did this to you?" But it was too late. He had unburdened himself. He turned his head away from me, closing his eyes. One final rattling breath and he was gone.

CHAPTER TWENTY-THREE

A nurse came into the cubicle, checked Daniel's vital signs, and turned off the beeping monitor. He was really gone this time.

"Are you all right, *cara?*" Sergio pulled me against him as I stepped out of the small room.

I breathed in his warm, masculine scent, laying my head on his shoulder. "I'm fine. He stopped having the ability to hurt me a long time ago. You heard what he said?" I turned to Doug Aguilar. "Do you think he was telling the truth?"

"We heard, and yes, I believe what he said. He knew he was dying. It's called a death bed confession. Only the most psychopathic person lies in that kind of situation." Doug Aguilar gave a sad smile. "I'm sorry I had to put you through all of that, Quinn. But I really do believe it was necessary to learn the truth."

I looked at Sergio. "I'm sorry he killed Sophia."

"It is okay, *cara*, she meant something to me when I was little, but not for a long time. She was willing to kill you. Daniel knew that. He couldn't let that happen. He loved her, but in his own twisted way, he loved you more."

"Where do we go next? He didn't say who did this to him." I turned to Doug Aguilar. "How did you even know what happened to him, where to find him?"

"An anonymous caller said there was a dead body in an abandoned building. He called me, not dispatch. Not the central number. He called me. The man had an Italian accent thick enough to cut with a knife. If you're asking for my opinion, it was Marconi."

"No," Sergio contradicted. "Marconi would never call the police himself. He would have one of his underlings do it, just as he would have someone else kill Daniel. He would be there to get answers though.. He wanted you to know where to find the man who killed his daughter." He released a long sigh. "If I must guess, he knew Daniel was not dead when the call was placed. He wanted Daniel found alive as part of his punishment."

"What about Barnard? Will he be charged with a crime?"

Doug shook his head. "That's up to the prosecutor. If he wasn't in on the scam and only wanted to get his money back, he's probably in the clear. I passed on your theory about what names to look for in the Caymans. They're working to bring the money back to the states. Their victims might be able to recover at least part of what they lost."

He drew a deep breath. "Officers searched the apartment Daniel had under his assumed name. He was living with a woman as man and wife, probably Sophia. They found the jewelry taken from the safe at your house. We'll return it to you."

I only wanted my mother's jewelry. What Daniel had given me no longer meant anything to me. That could be sorted out later.

"What about the poor man who took Daniel's place? What will happen to his body now?" Daniel had been evil to kill the man so he could get away with his crimes. It hadn't worked out very well for him though.

"His body will be exhumed and reburied in a pauper's grave." He shook his head. "So many lives ruined because of money and lust."

This wouldn't be over for me until Barnard had been told about his son's real death. I wasn't sure how he would take it, but I needed to be the one to tell him.

"Did you come here to gloat?" Barnard sneered at me when he opened the door. Did he already know about Daniel? I wondered. But there was no way he could know. The media hadn't been informed.

"I have nothing to gloat about, but I need to talk to you. May I come in?" He stepped back without a word, allowing me to enter. I gasped at what I saw. The house was no longer for sale, and it was a good thing. If a prospective buyer saw it this way, they wouldn't go any further than the front door.

"What happened, Barnard?" The living room looked like the whirlwind that had gripped my life for the past year had passed through. There were empty take-out food cartons and glasses on every flat surface. Whiskey bottles littered the floor, and were stacked in or on the dishes.

"The maid quit." He shoved aside some dirty dishes and flopped down on the food-stained couch. "She called me a pig."

I almost laughed at that. "Well, I can understand why. Why are you living like this?" I started stacking up the dirty dishes. There probably wasn't a clean dish left in the kitchen.

"Because I don't know how to do anything around here; the house was Eunice's department."

"But she just hired someone to clean. She didn't do anything herself. Why didn't Juanita keep things clean every day?" The woman had worked for Barnard and Eunice for longer than I'd been married to Daniel.

He gave me a sheepish look before tucking his head down like a little boy being scolded by his mother. "She tried, I guess, but every morning it was a mess again. She said she didn't need the money bad enough to put up with me. She walked out three weeks ago."

"And you haven't picked up anything for three weeks?" This isn't what I came here for, but I wasn't leaving until the house had been straightened up some. "Get up off your backside." He just looked up at me without moving. "Now, Barnard!" I barked out the order, and he finally stood up.

"What am I supposed to do?"

"Get a plastic trash bag and start putting these cartons in." For the next two hours, I help him clean house. I gave him the orders, and he obeyed. We'd only made a dent in the mess, but the garbage was taken out, and I'd run the dishwasher twice. It was a start.

"You didn't come here to make me clean house, Quinn. What's happened now?" He was resigned to hearing bad news, and I had the worst to tell him.

"Daniel's alive?" he interrupted, staring at me in confusion when I started to tell him about Daniel.

"No, but he didn't die a year ago. He just died a few hours ago." He listened silently while I explained everything Daniel had done. "I'm sorry, Barnard." I patted his hand when I finished.

He gave a heavy sigh. "I guess I wasn't a very good father to him. Somehow we always ended up in a competition. When that Sophia came on to me, I knew she was his girlfriend. I should have told her to get lost, but I couldn't resist." He shook his head. "She was one pretty little thing," A smile tilted his lips up, his eyes loosing focus for a moment. "She just wanted to pitch her scam to me though," he said on a sigh. "She just wanted to get some of my money, and I fell right into her hands."

"How much did you give her?"

"A half million." I gasped, and he shook his head again. "You can't be thinking anything I haven't already said to myself. There's no fool like an old fool. I thought I could get that back when I went looking for the money Eunice got from Frost. It was another fool's errand. The SEC confiscated that before I could even try to get it."

He gave a chuckle now. "Eunice wasn't the sharpest tool in the shed. She didn't try very hard to hide the money other than to move it offshore. She used her maiden name thinking that would fool everyone. Half the money in her account was money she had taken from me over the years. I'm still trying to get it back from that group of government thieves. What happens now? Am I in trouble with the law?"

It's what I had wanted to know. "Give Detective Aguilar a call. That's a question for him." So far, I thought he was in the clear though. If he was scared enough, maybe he'd think twice before doing anything even a little dicey in the future.

TRAPPED IN A WHIRLWIND

"Am I on the hook for a second funeral for Daniel? Who did I bury the first time?" The old Barnard was back. He still cared only for himself. He wasn't going to change his selfish ways in the space of a few hours. I gave him my suggestions regarding Daniel, and stood up to leave. "Call Juanita and beg her to come back. First you're going to have to promise her you won't be a pig anymore." I chuckled. Whether she believed him or not, wasn't up to me. I had done all I could for him and for Daniel. I was through.

~~~

The divorce proceedings were no longer necessary, and the small wedding Sergio and I had started to plan was back on. His mother was thrilled her son was finally getting married, and she would have grandchildren. My sister Ginger in Germany was also thrilled on hearing my news. I hadn't told her about Daniel's infidelity, and didn't see any sense telling her now. She knew I had been in love with Sergio for many years, and was happy for us. She even wanted to come for the wedding.

The small affair with just the two of us was turning into something a little larger. June Veracruz from school had been there for me at some of my worst times. She was there for me now at my happiest. She and Ginger would stand up for us. Doug Aguilar even agreed to be a groomsman for Sergio. After all we'd gone through with him by our side, he was now our friend.

"You're a beautiful bride, little sis." Ginger fluffed the veil covering my hair. I hadn't wanted all this hoopla. After all, this wasn't my first wedding, but everyone agreed we should do it up right. And this was right, they said.

Sergio's leg was healing without any complications. He was ready for the honeymoon, and so was I. I had waited for more than eight years to be his wife. My dream was finally coming true. As I walked down the aisle to my groom, I knew there was a smile as big as all outdoors on my face. What more could I ask for than a husband who

218

loved me, and just me. Until we have a baby, I silently amended. I could feel my face heating up with the thought of what was to come later tonight. It couldn't happen soon enough for me.

ACKNOWLEDGMENTS

I thank God for all the gifts He has given me. He has answered my prayers, allowing me to publish my books. I am so blessed by all He has given me. My thanks and gratitude also goes to Gerry Beamon, Cathy Slack, and Sandy Roedl for their suggestions, editing and encouragement. I am most appreciative for all the information retired Phoenix Police Detective Ken Shriner has given me. Thanks for your patience and for answering my many questions about law enforcement. I apologize to Ken for taking literary license with police procedure in an effort to move the story forward.

Dear Reader:

Thank you for reading my book. I hope you enjoyed reading it as much as I enjoyed writing it. If you enjoyed Trapped in a Whirlwind, I would appreciate it if you would tell your friends and relatives and/or write a review on Amazon. Check out my other books at:

Thank you,
Suzanne Floyd

P.S. I would love hearing from my readers. You can email me at: Suzanne.sfloyd@gmail.com.
Thanks again for reading my book.

ABOUT THE AUTHOR

Suzanne was born in Iowa but moved to Arizona with her family when she was nine years old. She still lives in Phoenix with her husband, Paul. They have two wonderful daughters, two great sons-in-law and five of the best grandchildren around. Of course, she just a little prejudiced.

Growing up and traveling with her parents, she entertained herself making up stories. As an adult she tried writing, but family came first. After retiring, she decided it was her time. She still delights in making up stories, and thanks to the internet she's able to put them online for others to enjoy.

When Suzanne isn't writing, she and her husband are traveling around on their 2010 Honda Goldwing trike. She's always looking for new places to write about. There's always a new mystery and a romance lurking out there to capture her attention.

Made in the USA
Middletown, DE
21 May 2022

66034878R00129